# The Romantic Agenda

# The Romantic Agenda

## CLAIRE KANN

JOVE

New York

A JOVE BOOK
Published by Berkley
An imprint of Penguin Random House LLC
penguinrandomhouse.com

Library of Congress Cataloging-in-Publication Data

Names: Kann, Claire, author.
Title: The romantic agenda / Claire Kann.
Description: First edition. | New York: Jove, 2022.
Identifiers: LCCN 2021049815 (print) | LCCN 2021049816 (ebook) |
ISBN 9780593336632 (trade paperback) | ISBN 9780593336649 (ebook)
Subjects: LCGFT: Romance fiction.
Classification: LCC PS3611.A549375 R66 2022 (print) |
LCC PS3611.A549375 (ebook) | DDC 813/.6—dc23/eng/20211220
LC record available at https://lccn.loc.gov/2021049815
LC ebook record available at https://lccn.loc.gov/2021049816

First Edition: April 2022

Printed in the United States of America
1st Printing

Book design by Daniel Brount

*For anyone and everyone who needs it*

# The
# Romantic
# Agenda

# One

**THURSDAY**

Dreams are such strange things to have and to hold.

They can be as big as wanting to be the next Naomi Campbell—the bougie-on-a-budget version. As outrageous as hoping to find true love in a seven-billion-person haystack. Or even as innocuous as hitting that fabled Inbox Zero before the end of the workday.

Forty-seven emails to go.

Joy doesn't know what happened. One second, she was wasting on-the-clock time by searching for and deleting junk email, and the next, she'd become intensely obsessed with seeing the number in the red notification bubble drop lower and lower and lower . . .

Her intercom beeps, breaking her concentration. "Joy?"

"This is, and you're bothering me," she answers playfully, holding the phone between her ear and shoulder to keep her hands free. Forty-three emails now.

"It's Meg. Do you think you could come to my office for a second?" Her voice sounds too high and strained.

Joy frowns, but says, "Be right there."

Down the hall and five seconds away, Megan sits at her desk, face crumpled in despair as she stares at a pile of papers. Her office is a mirror image of Joy's—from the slate gray pair of chairs for guests to the corny-as-hell inspirational wall art. Most employees at Red Warren added personal touches to make the space theirs. Megan brought in her adorable cross-stitch creations, displaying them everywhere.

Hanging on to the door jamb, Joy says, "You rang, my dear?"

"I did." She looks up—her hazel eyes dominate her light brown face, with her patchy freckles coming in a close second. As if she isn't already cute enough, loose brunette curls cascade over her shoulders like a Rapunzel in training. "Is that a new outfit?"

Joy twirls into the room, ending in a pose. "New-ish." She'd bought the chic olive green pantsuit—flared high-waisted slacks and sleek blazer, both tailored to perfection, and paired with a tasteful plaid crop top—a few months ago, but this is the first time she's wearing it to work.

"Special occasion?"

As far as Joy is concerned, fashion is life, but Megan clocked the situation correctly. Her hopes are sky-high for something about to go down, most likely in the next hour. It's why she abruptly decided to devote her immediate future to securing Inbox Zero.

Approximately sometime around two hours, thirty-seven minutes, and twenty-four seconds ago, her focus had shattered from anticipation after her boss, Malcolm, sent a short email.

He asked if she had plans for the holiday on Monday.

He hinted about clearing everything from her calendar for Friday *and* the following Tuesday.

He needed to talk to her about something important.

"Hopefully?" Joy answers. It's a miracle her heart hadn't spontaneously combusted after she finished reading the email because her brain moved at the speed of light, jumping to the only possible conclusion: her time has finally come.

A reluctant laugh bursts through Megan's stress. "Well, I'm rooting for you, whatever it is. Come look at this, please." She's holding a signed contract with some questionable language around distribution and follows it up with pictures of the product itself: a line of craft beers with an explicit NSFW label.

"Huh." Joy's eyebrows are nearly at her hairline. The image is so realistic, she can't tell if the model's 3–D or not. If she's real, despite her excellent, perky posture, she most certainly has back problems from having boobs that big and a waist that small. How she managed to hold a perfect spread-eagle side split would have been a small miracle on set.

The image slides straight past comical, bypassing artistic expression, and ends up a little too close to exploitation. Red Warren Nightclubs pushes the envelope here and there, but this kind of advertisement isn't in line with the brand.

"You approved this?" Joy asks.

"*No.*" All the color drains from Megan's horrified face. "I was there because I was filling in for Johnny. Remember when he got sick and was out for two weeks?"

"I do."

"I remember the product they showed us. I can literally see it in my head and it's *definitely* not this."

Joy nods, keeping her cool. "I've always wondered if people are born with a photographic memory or if they have to develop it."

"It's eidetic memory, not photo— *Oh, Joy*, oh no."

Joy grins, chuckling at her brilliant pun. She isn't above doing that. Everyone teases her for laughing at her own jokes, but it isn't her fault they don't appreciate her humor.

The most important thing is to calm Megan down. This mistake isn't the end of the world. Or her job. Situations like this happen all the time on the backend because Malcolm prefers working with a smaller team he knows he can trust. When one of them is out, they band together and fill in the blank even when they're not exactly sure what they're doing.

Red Warren Nightclubs have a somewhat infamous reputation in the local industry for being *the* places to be and work. They meet every code and regulation, have enough staff, supervisors, and managers, and pay them well enough to avoid burnout. Everyone who works for them is the best of the best: dancers, DJs, bartenders, and security.

Red Warren the Office, however, runs with a skeleton crew in a modern office building. Megan handles all things human resources, Allie watches their money like a hawk in accounting, Nikkiee networks like a cult leader in talent and communications, and Johnny uses his keen senses in development and acquisitions. Joy fills the role of manager to an unholy amalgamation of office, operations, and finance, and at times, doubles as an executive assistant. And Malcolm is the CEO—the dreamer, the face, and the heart of the company.

Megan says, "Johnny was reviewing everything and spotted the discrepancy."

"That must have gone well."

"He was so mad, oh my god. I thought steam was going to start whistling out of his ears."

Joy laughs, and Megan continues, "But it's not just me, though. Malcolm missed it too. He was *there*. He *reviewed* the contract before I signed off on it." Her gaze is practically a laser-beam of sincerity aimed right at Joy. "It seemed like he'd been doing better lately."

Malcolm hasn't really been the same since Caroline (the Cruel) called off their wedding a year ago. A Virgo through and through, Malcolm lives and dies by planning and micromanaging every detail he can get his hands on. He likes order and precision, needs structure and control.

Joy had seen Malcolm heartbroken before—he played fast and loose with his heart on a regular basis. He's in love with love, always searching for The One, but that breakup broke him. Completely and utterly. Afterwards, he missed important meetings, left work early on the days he even bothered to show up at all, overlooked major and minor details that caused everyone headaches later. Mistakes like this contract were a dime a dozen. Red Warren survived by staying in red alert mode.

But in the past couple of months, glimpses of the *real* Malcolm began to break through. His focus and dedication to Red Warren returned. Missteps became less frequent, nearly disappearing. He seemed better, lighter, and happier for some reason.

Joy fidgets at her side. "He's okay. He, um, I think he might be a little distracted right now."

Everyone knew Malcolm and Joy had originally met in college. A classic story of boy sees girl first, girl meets boy but then has an immediate revelation about her sexuality and completely ignores boy for two weeks before randomly popping back up into his life. They've been best friends, for better and for worse, in sickness but mostly in health, ever since. And she's deeply in love with him.

But no one at Red Warren needs to know a single shred of truth about her feelings for Malcolm. None. Nada. Over her dead and cold body. Hers is the kind of workplace secret you take to the unemployment line after promising to keep in touch even though you know that won't happen. Because you've had and left enough jobs to know better than to make false promises.

"I had a feeling." Megan nods. "Do you know what's up?"

"I don't," Joy lies. There are perks to moonlighting as an executive assistant. All signs point to Malcolm planning something big for the weekend. "Anyway"—she gestures to the contract—"this is fine. Everything is fine. Even if I have to go old school, pay them a *visit*, and remind them who they're dealing with. I'll take care of it."

"Knock, knock." Malcolm stands grinning in the doorway. Tall, dark, and ever handsome—in the literal sense. None of that thinly veiled colorist propaganda. Rich brown skin, black curly hair cut short, and deep chocolate eyes.

Joy unconsciously gives him a bright smile in return, just like she always does because she can't help it. Her brain recognizes him and there's an instant hit of dopamine to all the receptors that make her happiest.

He asks, "Joy, can I borrow you for a second?"

"Wow, I am *popular* this afternoon," Joy jokes to quiet her sudden nerves before looking at Megan. "Consider it handled, okay?"

Back down the hall in her office, Joy sits at her desk. Unlike Megan, she hasn't bothered with personal touches, preferring to keep her office sparse and clean. The cool grays and bursts of navy blue have a soothing effect on her. Something she relies on when she's forced to hop on one too many phone calls and her daily avalanche of emails start pissing her off.

All six feet and two inches of Malcolm collapse into the chair in front of her desk with a *thud*. The chair and his temperamental knees are probably swearing at him in a pitch only dogs can hear. "What are you doing this weekend?"

In case she was wrong about Malcolm's intentions, Joy had made a backup plan to visit her sister, a quick ninety-minute flight away. "My usual. A little of this, a little of that."

"No, you're not."

"I'm not?"

Malcolm's grin escalates to *devastating*. A true weapon of mass destruction, it has an impact radius of twenty paces and a ninety-seven-percent fatality rate. He's always wielded that perfect face of his like a formerly shy and gangly boy who just discovered the right side of puberty: completely earnest and unaware of how handsome he is.

Even after all this time, it still shocks Joy how much he can affect her. A quiet thrill ripples through her bloodstream, making her heart flutter. *It's happening, it's happening, it's happening.*

Two weeks ago, Malcolm scheduled himself out of the office on Friday *and* the Tuesday after the holiday—the exact same days he asked her to clear on her schedule today. After that, Joy spotted several browser tabs open on his laptop with telltale keywords such as "hot-air balloon" and "vineyard," and catering packages from her favorite restaurant. And most damning of all, Joy always helps him with his plans, for business and personal. This time, he hasn't even mentioned a single thing about it to her.

Malcolm King-of-Grand-Romantic-Gestures Evans is about

to make a comeback. And Joy has a sneaking suspicion it might *finally* be for her.

"Nope." He shakes his head. "Because you're going on a trip with me."

"Again?" Joy snort-laughs, playfully rolling her eyes. "Where are we going this time?"

Ever since Caroline-ageddon, Malcolm's been traveling nonstop, Joy being his companion of choice. They've driven to the Grand Canyon, watched the northern lights in Iceland, flown to remote beaches on private islands with sunsets to die for, visited museums and art shows, and attended fancy parties in skyscrapers that have no earthly business being so tall. A perpetual homebody, globetrotting has never been a dream of Joy's. But hey, if it's on someone else's wealthy dime with someone she loves, who is she to say no?

Besides, every time Malcolm asked, she was mostly shocked that he even wanted to spend time with her at all. Because according to Caroline, the main reason why she left him was . . . Joy.

"I know you figured out that I've been planning something. I can barely hide anything from you." Malcolm leans forward, locking her in his sights. No other human on the planet can make her feel like she's the center of their universe. No one has ever made Joy feel the way Malcolm does. "But I'm keeping everything close to my chest this time. I don't want anything to go wrong."

Joy frowns. "What do you mean?"

"I have this plan."

"A plan?"

"Yeah." He clears his throat. "I met someone. Summer."

A record scratch screeches in Joy's ears. "Summer?"

"We're friends. We've been hanging out for a couple of months now."

Everything suddenly feels blurry and detached, like she's watching a reflection of the moment instead of living in it. "Months?" When? How? She literally saw his calendar every day, they spent an ungodly amount of time together after work, and when they weren't together, they texted constantly. How in the hell did he squeeze a Summer into his life without her knowing?

"Two, to be exact." He laughs again. "I think there might be something there. I've been wanting to ask her out, and I'm positive she's into me, but it feels different this time."

"Different?"

"I don't want to just come out and ask. That's boring. I want to make her feel special, you know? So I thought: What if I planned a trip specifically for her? We'd do everything that she loves, a whole weekend in her honor, and then at the end, I'll stage a moment when it's just the two of us and I'll ask her."

This is how Malcolm, a hopeless romantic and serial monogamist, dates—he doesn't.

All his ex-partners came from their friend group. It always starts casual, hanging out and getting to know them, no pressure or pretense. Malcolm gets his patented "feeling," and one sincere heart-to-heart later they go straight from friends to being in a relationship. It's like a light switch flipping, friends to lovers so fast there should probably be a scientific formula to measure it.

Joy would know. She's witnessed the shift enough times. What's that saying? Always the bridesmaid, never the bride? That's her. By his side for ten years and he's never once made that record breaking shift with her. After the past year, after everything they've been through, she really thought—

"Joy? Are you listening to me?"

"Of course I'm not." She frowns for a second before forcing

herself to smile to keep him from reading her face, which he's an expert at. He's figured out how to guess her moods with ease, so she's learned how to trick him.

"Anyway, so Fox is coming too."

Joy discreetly reaches for the stress ball on her desk and holds it in her lap. Aiming for disinterested, she asks, "And who the hell is Fox?"

"I just told you. Were you really not listening?"

"I *said* I wasn't."

"I assumed that was a joke."

"You know what they say when you assume," she says. "You make an ass out of you, Malcolm Evans."

"Joy."

"*What?*" Joy snickers, giving the stress ball a mighty squeeze. Dad joke humor would get her through this hellacious situation one way or another. "Sorry. Please continue. You have the full remainder of my divided attention."

Malcolm levels a glare at her that doesn't last, softening in seconds. "When I invited Summer, I told her she could bring someone too because I thought she'd pick Fiona or anyone else besides Fox Yes-That's-My-Real-Name Monahan. But apparently it's his birthday." He rolls his eyes.

Not just Summer—there's also a Fox and a Fiona and an anyone else. It's like he suddenly has an entire second life he didn't tell her about. Why would he do that? She tries to not feel hurt. It's not like he isn't allowed to have friends, or he must introduce her to every person he meets. But it's just . . . that he usually does. He always has.

"And I take it you don't like this Fox person?"

"Let's just say we don't see eye to eye."

Joy stares at him. "What did you do?

"Nothing." He's lying. Malcolm's tell is always looking quickly to the left and then making direct eye contact. "But that's not the most important part. Summer wants to meet you. She asked me to ask you to come along."

Joy presses her lips together so her jaw doesn't fall open and slam into her keyboard. Her mouth barely moves as she asks, "You told her about me?"

He nods. "Of course. She can't wait to meet you."

"So. You're not inviting me? Summer is?" She unclenches her left hand and transfers the stress ball to her right, immediately putting it back into a death grip.

"No, no, it's not like that. Of course I want you there."

Joy's heart drops as she watches Malcolm look to the left and to her again. He continues, "It's just . . . I don't know if you'd have a good time. That's all. But. If you do come, I was hoping you could do me a favor? Fox is . . . a lot. Maybe you could keep him company."

"Oh, I've always wanted to try being an escort." She hates how breathless, almost winded from shock, she sounds. "Will I be getting paid?"

"Joy, that's not funny."

"What? I think I'd be good at it. I happen to be an excellent companion."

"I'm aware." And there it is—the smile that never fails to light up her whole world. Even when she's been plunged into suffocating darkness, he's there to lift her back up with hardly any effort. "I'd like to spend as much time with Summer as possible, but I know her. She's going to spend all her time making sure Fox doesn't feel like a third wheel because she knows we don't really get along."

"And if I'm there, it'll be four-wheel drive."

Malcolm gives her a rare laugh. Puns and wordplay aren't exactly his favorite thing about her. "We could just sort of naturally pair up for some of the activities I have planned."

"Natural. Organic. Not at all from concentrate or staged."

"Joy."

"What?"

"Will you please come and spend time with Fox?"

Malcolm waits for her to say something. She doesn't. Her voice feels shaky, so it'll probably sound worse. How could she have been so wrong about everything? The secret trip isn't for her, he isn't planning to ask her to be with him because there's a Summer, and he wants to pawn Joy off on a Fox.

This is hell. Hell truly is other people.

Joy trains her gaze on the ceiling, exhaling into a horrible-sounding sigh. She closes her eyes and focuses on her breathing before turning back to him. He looks concerned but patient. "Why haven't you told me about Summer before now?"

"I don't know." Malcolm shrugs like it's nothing. "We met on this forum called Jilted Hearts. It's full of people with failed engagement stories. She planned a local meetup for a bunch of us, but we were the only two who showed up."

Malcolm doesn't even glance at Joy while he tells the rest of his story. His eyes are unfocused and lost in a memory. She takes in his wistful, effortless smile. His relaxed posture. The awestruck cadence of his words as he talks about Summer and the past two months he's spent getting to know her.

Joy has never heard him talk about *her* like that. Never seen him go soft when people ask how they met, how they managed to stay friends for so long. Joy always faithfully by his side because that's *her* spot, pathetically hoping that someday he'll see she's *right there*.

And then, it's like Malcolm suddenly remembers she *is* there, locking her in his sights again. "I just wanted to find someone to talk to who would understand what I've been through, and there she was. I'm convinced we could be more. I think that's why I've been waiting for the perfect moment to introduce you. This weekend is it."

# Two

Joy storms through her front door and throws her purse on the counter, but carefully hangs up her keys on their hook because misplacing them would truly break her. With no choice left but to die alone, she flings herself facedown onto her sofa—and screams into the couch cushions as long and as loud as she can.

A heavy loaf with four paws lands in the middle of her back and immediately begins to make biscuits. Rolling over carefully, Joy scoops up her cat, Pepper, into her arms. "Not on Mommy's suit jacket. It was expensive." She hasn't quite lost the will to live, and to care about fashion, just yet.

While Pepper heads to purr-town, happy to have her human home, Joy stares at the ceiling. At times, falling, and then staying, in love with Malcolm felt like the biggest mistake of her life. Awareness is supposed to be the key to healing and getting over him. But no, her feelings stalk her like some unspeakable deep-sea horror. Every time she thinks she's free, its lovesick tentacles wrap around her, dragging her back into the depths of the Struggling Sea. Every time she thinks that maybe, just maybe, Malcolm has fallen in love with her too, he chooses someone else.

A cheery chorus of bells sounds from her phone. Right on time. Her sister Grace video calls every night to check in.

Joy holds Pepper up close to her face. "Say hi to Auntie Grace."

"Hi, Pepper," Grace says, sweetly before sharpening her tone. "What are you doing?"

"Nothing." Joy walks to her kitchen.

Unlike her office, every inch of her apartment is meticulously designed—even down to the smallest plastic succulent. With white as a primary color, each room's accents have a different overlapping color scheme, blending to create a near perfect transition. She chose brilliant blue and buttercream for the living room, which is parallel to the buttercream and soft marigold in the kitchen.

Her parents had gifted her a massive TV for Christmas. She set in on top of the glass entertainment center full of consoles and devices courtesy of Malcolm. The couch cost an arm and a leg (paid in installments), but she can never resist velvet, and she inherited the small round table and matching set of chairs stationed in her postage-stamp-sized dining room from a neighbor who moved across the country. It took an entire weekend to sand it down and repaint it flash copper with a satin finish.

Grace says, "Something's wrong. I can feel it."

They're fraternal twins, but Grace swears they still got the psychic gift—and she might not be wrong about it. Joy's been spiraling since Malcolm asked for help. Just free-falling into an underwater trench with no bottom and a bit too much momentum. Everything feels cold and numb. Her feelings are there but it's like she can't reach them. All she can do is . . . scream into her pillows. That's it. That's all there is.

"I'm fine," she lies, and places her phone in its usual holder while Grace keeps talking, rattling off her best guesses at what she thinks is going on.

Opening the cabinet, Joy pulls out a can of wet cat food. Pepper has the cutest squeaky meows, but she never begs for *anything*. Regal as ever, she waits patiently by her empty food bowl. She's yet another present from Malcolm, gifted to her about a week after Grace flew their communal coop for a job seven hours away. Joy pretends that Pepper didn't come from a breeder. That Malcolm got lucky and happened to find a Ragdoll kitten at a shelter.

"Fine. I give up. For now." Grace huffs in defeat. "How was work?"

"Same as always."

"Ooh, I *love* how passionate you sounded about that."

Joy snorts. A job is a job, and at least at Red Warren, she gets to support her best friend.

In college, Grace did the practical thing, studying industrial organizational psychology. She decided no one and nothing would stop her as she bulldozed her way through grad school, a rotational program, and secured a job as a consultant in the private sector.

Meanwhile, Joy studied to be an oceanographer, but both her bank account and academia had something nasty to say about her post-bachelor's-degree dreams. Years ago, the owner of the bar she and Malcolm both worked at decided to take Malcolm under his wing. When the time came for Malcolm to open his own club, he offered Joy a job.

He said, "I need you with me on this. I can't do this without you."

It wasn't like she was doing anything else. Out of college, oppressive loans smothering her, barely scraping by working at a call center by day and go-go dancing her heart out every night. She didn't know a thing about finance or business. But Malcolm had believed in her, that she could learn and help him and that they were meant to do it together.

When he looks at her, really looks at her, it's in a way that no one else in her entire life ever has. He knows her—all her faults, all her good parts. Everything she thinks she can hide with flawless mastery after years and years of practice, he sees. There are no walls with Malcolm. Hell, they barely have boundaries.

Joy says, "It's not like we can all live our dreams. It'll upset the balance of the universe. Some of us are destined to be unhappy and suffer so the rest of you can prosper."

"You're so dramatic. And for what?" Grace shakes her head. "When's your flight coming in?"

"Uh, about that."

"You're not coming? Why?"

"Malcolm invited me to some trip he planned."

"Oh good, so you told him no because you already have plans to see your sister for the first time in three months. Right?" Grace dislikes Malcolm by circumstance. She and their mom are convinced he's the roadblock stopping Joy from getting on with her life. And by life, they mean marriage and babies.

Joy says, "I didn't because it's a group trip. I'm still thinking about it."

"Who else is going?"

"Someone named Summer, and someone named Fox."

"Who the hell are they?"

"No idea. Never heard about them before today, but apparently he's been hanging out with some new people."

"Without *you*?" Grace narrows her eyes and turns her head slightly to the side. "Like, he was keeping them a secret or . . . ?"

Joy sighs. "This is why I like talking to you, because in my mind, I think I'm being irrational and paranoid, but then *you* just come out and *say it*."

"Hold on, let me get a drink. I'm gonna need a drink for this."

"And I'm gonna start cooking my dinner."

Joy's dinners all came from a meal kit service. She justifies the purchases by viewing them as cooking lessons. Eventually, she figures, if she follows enough recipes with fresh ingredients, she'll turn into a badass home cook through practice and osmosis.

Her dad is the cook in their family, and Malcolm is the cook in her life now. She does love baking and is surprisingly good at it. However, she learned the hard way that eating nothing but cake all day isn't exactly the best idea after turning twenty-five.

The chicken is roasted, the vegetables are grilled, and both are ready to be wrapped in lettuce leaves by the time Joy finishes telling her sister about the curious circumstances of Malcolm's invitation.

Grace drains her second glass of wine and says, "Welp. That's Malcolm What's-the-Point-of-Having-Money-if-You-Can't-Use-It Evans for you."

Joy laughs. As much as Grace claims to hate him, there's no denying that they've all rubbed off on each other. They all met in college during sophomore year when their roommate, the fabulous Dorothy I'm-Too-Pretty-to-Struggle Stewart, dragged them to an LGBT Alliance mixer. Joy remembers almost everything about it—how hot it was that day, drifting around the room, talking to everyone at each booth, trying to learn as much as she could because she knew she wasn't straight. She wasn't gay either. She didn't think she was anything.

While most of the booths were manned by a few people, Malcolm stood alone at his and was such an adorably serious nerd about it. He made cute three-fold pamphlets and put "So You Might Be Asexual?" with a picture of a piece of cake on the front of them. Even now, thinking about him in his button-up shirt and bow tie makes Joy laugh. That was the moment that changed her life.

Malcolm is the reason Joy found where she belonged.

When no one else understood her, Grace included, he did. From the moment they became friends, he's always been there for her, looking out for her, making sure she's happy, calling, texting, making sure she never feels alone. When they snuck into bars with fake IDs and went to random house parties, he kept her safe. She could drink and dance and have *fun* in peace without having to worry about someone pushing themselves on her. He protected her. Never judged her. Never expected more.

When everyone else left them, they always had each other.

It didn't take much more for her to fall in love with him.

Grace continues, "He such a *dick*. Do you want me to call him? I can get him sorted out right quick."

"No."

"Are you gonna set him straight, then?"

"No."

"So you're just gonna go on this little trip and act like everything's fine? Like you're not in love with him and he's not making secret friends for some secret reason?" Grace's voice hits a louder, angrier pitch. "It's really fucking suspect that he's told them about you, but not the opposite. What is it going to take for you to snap out of this?"

Joy tries to keep her voice even to help bring Grace back down from hellfire on high. "Nothing. I'm going to stay in the dumpster like the trash that I am."

"You are not trash. You're only in the dumpster for Malcolm! Climb the fuck back out!" Grace says. "Stop letting him treat you like his kept woman. He's your sugar daddy minus the sexual favors, but you caught feelings and he didn't."

Joy glares at her. "Thanks. So helpful."

"I'm not here to be helpful. I'm here to tell you the truth," she says. "Joy, my light, my love. It's time to listen to the devil on your shoulder named Grace whispering in your ear. I know what I'm talking about. After everything that happened with the C-word? I don't think it's in the cards, babycakes."

Caroline disappeared, but she hadn't left quietly. She sent both Malcolm and Joy an email detailing *exactly* how she felt. Joy tries to not think about it, but after reading the carefully constructed sentence "manipulative, man-stealing bitch who is so pathetic and co-dependent you barely have your own life," it's hard to forget. Caroline felt that Malcolm put Joy before their relationship and she was always an afterthought.

Truth be told, it's always been like that between Malcolm, his partners, and Joy. It starts out fine, but before long, they hate her for no other reason than Malcolm loves her more than they think she deserves.

Joy isn't his family. She isn't some ex he's never gotten over. She's just a friend.

Just.

A just who shouldn't be important.

A just who should be discarded.

A just who should disappear.

Joy fought for Malcolm, refusing to drift away, standing by him, until he realized she would always be there. Until he believed it. And so far, she had succeeded where they all failed. The greatest love of his life was, as they put it, *just* a friend.

It had never reached such an extreme breaking point before, like it did with Caroline. Malcolm swears he doesn't blame Joy for his relationship ending but she doesn't believe him.

Summer being kept a secret is proof he does.

"Do you think that's why he didn't tell me about Summer? He's worried I'll ruin it again?"

"You didn't ruin anything *before*. It's not just you. You played a hand, but it wasn't *your* game, you know?" Grace shakes her head. "I really think it's time you started trying to move on. It's time to let him go."

"I can't. Meeting Malcolm that day was my one-in-a-million lucky shot. I'll never find anyone else like him."

"Then you at least need a break from him. Maybe this trip is a good idea. He wants you to spend time with Fox, so do it. See what it's like to not devote almost every single second of your life to Malcolm."

"It's not every second. More like every third second."

"Joy. You'll never know what and who else is out there if you don't try to find it. How much more of your life are you going to give up waiting around for him?"

Is she waiting? And is it truly so bad if she is?

Joy tries seeing the situation from Grace's point of view. She wants her to try. Try what? Dating? How could replacing Malcolm with someone else possibly be the answer?

It's not like she has a plethora of alternatives available to her. Even *thinking* about trying to find someone else feels impossible. Her mom is notorious for trying to set her up with her friends' sons, most of whom make it obvious sex is their first priority. If she's good enough, then *maybe* they'll want to get to know her after. Some dating apps don't even have the option to choose asexual as an orientation. Not to mention that she's thirty—a good percentage of single people her age have kids, and no offense . . . but no. Finding someone else seems highly unlikely to happen at this point. It's too late. She waited too long. But she can't tell Grace that.

"I don't know. I honestly don't know," Joy says. "It really doesn't matter, anyway. It's not like I'm hurting anyone."

"Except yourself," Grace says.

I n college, Joy was known as *the* party girl in her dorm. Years and years ago, back when her knees didn't hate her and her world didn't revolve around a bullet journal.

Getting older isn't bad—it's insidious.

Slowly, she stopped drinking every kind of alcohol except for wine at dinner. No more going out every weekend. Her friends settled down. Spontaneous adventures turned into scheduled nights out. Before she knew it, she was thirty with a strict schedule that's practically sacred and a nine-to-five job. Trading up from go-go dancer to corporate manager wasn't a half-bad change to make, but Joy couldn't even remember the last time she saw the inside of the nightclub during operating business hours. The only two-a.m. club she belongs to these days is run by anxiety-induced insomnia.

Being an adult went from creeping up on her to knocking her upside the head with little warning. One night, she realized that watching Netflix and going to bed at ten p.m. (no exceptions!) had become her life. And it was perfectly okay.

After a long peach-scented bubble bath, Joy selects a silk pajama short set in a deep burgundy color for bed. Her full-body skin care routine takes exactly seventeen minutes and she uses a satin headband around her edges to keep her hairline neat. Her braids are only a week old—she's hoping they'll last a full three before they need to be redone.

Usually by now, Malcolm has called to bother her or sent several good night texts in a row before giving up and calling her anyway. She keeps checking her phone, but there's nothing. He's waiting for her answer. She knows he is.

The added weight of his expectations sends her hurtling even faster into her internal depths. At times, she used to think he was rubbing it in her face—that he knew how she felt and kept trying to tell her without telling her it was never going to happen. Joy would never be one of the friends he wanted to jump then fall into *more* with. Friends like Summer are different from *her*, like there's a boundary she's never going to see the other side of.

But that's not Malcolm. In her heart, she knows he would never do something like that to her. They're a perfect match on paper. It's reality that keeps crumpling it and doing a trick shot straight into the garbage can.

Joy crawls into bed with Pepper, scrolling aimlessly through a streaming catalog until Julia Roberts's exquisite smile catches her eye. *My Best Friend's Wedding.* She remembers enough of the movie to know she's never really seen it. She can't recall the ending—if Julia's character is successful in the end.

"This is going to bum us out," she says to Pepper, who has already begun to snore. "Lightweight."

The movie captures Joy's attention immediately. Wide awake, she watches in rapt fascination as Julia's character, Jules, executes every underhanded trick in the book to win her best friend so he'll marry her instead.

"*Michael's chasing Kimmy. You're chasing Michael. Who's chasing you? Nobody. Get it?*"

Joy instantly disintegrates into a puddle of sobs. God, that line lampooned her straight through the heart and yanked her back to the surface with deadly force.

Body racked with sobs, she covers her face with a pillow to muffle her misery. She hits the volume button, turning the movie up in hopes that her neighbors won't hear her instead. "*I knew watching this was a bad idea,*" she says in a high-pitched whine. She's so *hurt*. She'll cry forever, or until her dehydrated body crumbles into dust. Whichever comes first.

Because that's her life on the screen. The cool and flirty girl with impeccable fashion sense who's in love with her best friend. She had almost been his best person at his wedding, standing by his side in a hideous purple dress because it was the right thing to do.

Because that's what unconditional love meant.

Joy didn't *settle* for friendship with Malcolm. She welcomed it, making a choice, and stood by it and him for ten years.

After Caroline left, she filled his days, because that's what friends did. When he called her in the middle of the night, she answered, never missing a single call. She navigated the afterburn of romantic devastation with him, encouraged him as he crawled out of his depressed shell, helped him remember how to breathe, how to find and hold on to happiness. Every whim, every idea, every emotion he had, she had been there. And it still hadn't been enough.

*I just wanted to find someone to talk to who would understand what I've been through, and there she was.*

There's a line between being a good friend and expecting a reward for being a good friend. Joy never expected Malcolm to fall for her—but maybe. Just maybe . . . maybe she hoped he'd at least consider it. Does that make her a bad person? A bad friend, terrible and selfish?

It takes three hours for Joy's tears to slow from a river to a creek to a trickle, but the pain hasn't gone anywhere. It lives in her like a collapsed lung—it only hurts when she breathes or moves.

Malcolm has always been the only one for her. There was something almost magical about the moments when she went from being fine with the way things were to tensing at his touch, reading too deeply into every conversation, relishing every thrill of eye contact, and experiencing the surreal confusion of discovering there was a more to even want.

Slowly, carefully, she unplugs her phone from the charger with as little movement as possible. She blinks until her eyes adjust to the sudden burst of light.

No messages. Her fingers hover above the keypad as she thinks of what to say.

**JOY:** Wardrobe recommendations?

Malcolm replies in ten seconds flat with a short list. It's almost three a.m. Not only is he still awake, but he's also been waiting.

He probably knew exactly what she'd ask and had the answer ready.

> **JOY:** Have you slept at all?

> **MALCOLM:** Not yet. I didn't want to miss your text.

Fuck, she was right.

Joy smiles, vaguely aware of how demented she must look in the pitch black of her room. Eyes red and swollen, face wet and reflective because of the phone's screen shining on her. Screw couples who could complete each other sentences—they predicted each other's every move.

> **MALCOLM:** Cutting it kind of close there . . .

> **JOY:** Sorry not sorry. It takes me ten minutes to figure out what kind of cereal to buy at the store. This was a way bigger decision than that.

> **MALCOLM:** Why?

> **MALCOLM:** What do you mean?

Grace wants her to try.

Joy knew she felt . . . different than Grace and almost all their friends early on—at fifteen, sixteen, maybe? While they all had crushes and started dating, she couldn't even be bothered to pretend at liking someone so her friends would think she was "normal." There'd just never been anyone worth pursuing. Not a single soul worth the risk of heartbreak to make them hers.

Until Malcolm.

Waiting for him hasn't worked out for her, and Malcolm doesn't wait around, period. His heart lives permanently on his sleeve—battered and bruised but still beating and always searching. It wasn't Caroline, and if it's not Summer, it'll be someone else, because he's never had a problem trying.

Grace was right—it is Joy's turn to try. Just not in the way her sister hoped. Before she can think herself into changing her mind, she replies:

**JOY:** What time are we leaving?

**MALCOLM:** Seven.

Quickly, Joy hops out of bed and stands in front of her closet, hands on her hips, contemplating her choices. Most of the daytime clothes could be mixed and matched but she'd still need sufficient options to make it work. She also needed nightwear—a few dresses suitable for formal dinners.

She packs a second suitcase for jewelry, loungewear, her pajama sets, bathing suits, lingerie, toiletries, and all her skin care products and lotions. Thank god she decided to get her hair braided. She only needs to pack rosewater spray and hair oil to keep her scalp moisturized.

Selecting the right shoes nearly takes Joy out. It pains her to narrow down her choice to two pairs of tennis shoes, one pair of boots, and three pairs of heels, all in neutral colors. Her clothes can do the heavy lifting with daring colors and bold cuts of fabric.

Throwing together a sophisticated yet functional vacation wardrobe in under two hours takes a sharp eye and nerves of steel. Ever since she was a little girl, nothing was more important than dressing up, finding new and daring ways to express herself. She even looked forward to church on Sundays because she always got to wear her best dresses—frilly with puff sleeves, nylons, and shiny patent leather shoes. Her mom would press her hair and let her wear tinted lip gloss.

Now, having nice clothes is imperative to both of her jobs, making most of her wardrobe tax deductible. Red Warren has a dress code, but she also does online modeling by posting on an app called Rule of Thirds, whose acronym is unironically pronounced *rot*. It started off as a hobby until a brand reached out, asking if they could license some of her photos. Things escalated fairly quickly after that. Her hobby became her side hustle, enabling her to drop literal thousand-dollar payments on the principal balance for her student loans.

Joy packs up Pepper's overnight bag as well. Four days is too long to leave her alone.

The sun is starting to rise when she knocks on her neighbor's door forty-five minutes before she's supposed to be at Malcolm's house.

Mrs. Norman, an early riser, squints at Joy through a crack in the door. "Joy, baby? Is that you?"

"Yeah," she says. Pepper meows inside her carrier. "And Pepper."

She opens the door, adjusting her robe soon after. Mrs. Norman is old enough to be Joy's grandma and kind of looks like her too. Her hair is in pink spongy rollers secured by a black net and white scarf. Full of kindness, her eyes twinkle with the mischief of a life well lived, and she has a knowing patience that only comes from having seen it all. Joy absolutely adores her to the moon and back.

"Everything okay?"

"I know this is last minute, but do you think you could watch Pepper for a few days?"

"Oh, of course, come on in, baby, come in. Let me make you some tea," she says, ushering them inside. "Was that you I heard making all that fuss late last night?"

"Yeah." Joy laughs awkwardly. "That was me."

"Crying and hollering like the world was ending—I swear on my sweet John, God rest his soul, I almost came right on over to check on you, yes I did. Had me over here worried out my mind."

Joy leans against the small bar as she watches Mrs. Norman flit around the kitchen, spry as ever. "Sorry about that. I'm feeling better now."

Mrs. Norman gives her a knowing side-eye, waiting for the rest of the story.

"You're as bad as Grace." Joy exhales into a reluctant laugh. "It's about Malcolm."

"I *knew* it." She shakes her head as she retrieves two mugs from the cabinet. "You know, I have a grandson about your age."

"Not you too. Please. My mom has the whole *let's set Joy up with a bunch of strangers* thing covered."

"Now, now, hear me out. He's smart with a good job, handsome. You should let me introduce you. Let me get you his number."

"That's okay," Joy says quickly. "Thank you, but no. I'm really not interested in dating right now."

Because she's only interested in Malcolm. He doesn't know this, but he's inadvertently broken Joy's heart exactly four times since they met. Each time after, he pieced it back together again as if it never happened. Not a single crack or seam left uncared for.

This time, though, she'll hand her heart directly to him. For better or for worse.

There's never going to be anyone else for Joy. It *has* to be Malcolm.

# Three

FRIDAY

Not a single red light or stop sign slowed Joy down on the way to Malcolm's house. Clearly a surefire sign she's on the right path because everyone knows when you're desperate to get somewhere you hit every roadblock imaginable.

But as she's sitting in her parked car near his driveway, Joy's hands tighten around the steering wheel. "Get out of the car," she says to herself. "Get. Out. Of. The. Car." If this *is* her right path, then why does she suddenly feel like the most intense hangover of her life has slammed into her like a freight train? Head throbbing, stomach churning, balance gone, ready and willing to get up close and personal with a toilet bowl—she didn't drink *that* much wine last night.

"This is a bad idea. A terrible idea. The worst," she whispers. Trying to steal her best friend when he's clearly interested in someone else feels like a supremely shitty thing to do—no denying that. There's also the tiny problem that she's never tried to seriously pursue anyone in her life.

Starting a romance always seems easy enough in movies. There's the adorkable approach. The fake dating disaster. The good girl gone bad ploy. Her primary inspiration—the conniving best friend caper—had a happy ending, but certainly not the one Joy wanted for her life.

Just the thought of all that lying and sabotage . . . dear god, her *nerves*. She isn't going to make it. As soon as she gets out of the car (she's never getting out of the car), she'll walk up to Malcolm's door, go inside, and promptly puke everywhere as soon as they make eye contact.

The problem is that Malcolm knows her too well. The second she starts, well, *acting*, he'll suspect something is up and immediately ask her about it. He'll be concerned and she'll be speechless while being boiled alive by shame.

Joy takes a deep breath, willing herself to find her happy place. The memory of the first time she realized she fell in love with him. All of him. There are so many kinds of love out there and the way she felt about Malcolm in that moment didn't have a name. It felt like forever moving in slow motion. An unconditional bond cemented by infinity. They would *always* be together. No matter what.

The romantic feelings came later, ushered in by thoughts of the future and family and growing old together. Intensifying when her eldest sister got engaged and had a lavish destination wedding. When her friends started moving in with their partners, buying furniture, adopting furbabies, and having *actual* babies. When she began living in her apartment alone.

Even if Malcolm doesn't love her back romantically, he'll never leave her. But that doesn't mean the fall won't leave her crushed and heartbroken in the end. That's the risk she's taking. And he's worth it.

Joy takes another deep breath and steps out of the car.

One terrifying step at a time, she marches up the walkway to Malcolm's front door. Unlike the rest of their friends, he's the only one who made enough money to buy a home. Everyone else, Joy included, is still renting small apartments and condos, filling them with wistful dreams of someday having a backyard. He's painted the outside of his house a soothing deep tan trimmed with cream and transformed the front yard into a wild garden of tall grass, flowering bushes, and a vegetable garden for the neighborhood rodents.

His human neighbors really hate him for the last part. Malcolm doesn't care. He always does exactly what he wants, the way he wants, and he wants to feed animals to keep them out of the garbage because they deserve better. Thoughtful acts like that are Malcolm at his best. And make Joy love him even more.

Joy uses her key to let herself in. She closes the door, slipping off her shoes as she pauses in the entryway next to the coat closet.

An extremely feminine-sounding someone giggles in the kitchen.

*Summer*, her brain hisses. Joy turns right and walks softly, body pressed close to the wall like a wannabe spy in a Lifetime movie. Not wanting to be seen yet, she carefully peeks around the corner.

She instantly loses interest in the voice when she sees Malcolm.

Flannel shirt. Old, comfortable jeans. Hiking boots. A baseball hat.

The only time he dresses like a damn amateur lumberjack is to go camping.

Malcolm planned a romantic *camping* getaway—Joy feels the

truth of it weighing down her anti-outdoor bones. He *knows* how much she hates it.

Nothing about camping appeals to Joy. *Nothing.* There'll be an endless stream of insects determined to suck her blood (ticks and mosquitos) or kill her for the fun of it (yellow jackets), wild animals that will eat their food and their livers, no sanitized place to use the bathroom, and worst of all, shitty cell phone reception that'll magically stop working when she needs it most.

Joy grips the door frame as she tries to tamp down on her rage.

If they accidentally wander into a slasher horror movie, Joy knows she'll be the first to die. Those are the rules. Black? Check. Female? Check. Virgin? That might save her, but racism almost always trumps "purity," so she's still shit out of luck.

Malcolm shifts slightly to the left, revealing the giggler. She's white, shorter than him with blonde hair and wide-set chocolate brown eyes, and is slender to the point of waif levels. Her back has that definitive hunch of someone who spends hours at a desk, but her calves scream *I can run in high heels.*

Summer has Final Girl written all over her. Great. Perfect. Even her name fits Joy's horror movie of death fantasy.

"When will she get here? I thought we were leaving at seven," she says in an angelic-sounding voice.

Joy's grip tightens. How is it possible for her to sound like *that*? High-pitched and melodic without being tinny or annoying.

"Soon. She's never late for anything." Malcolm checks his phone. "You're going to love her. She's the sweetest person in the world."

"I've heard so much about her, how can I not?" She tops off her proclamation with an arm caress paired with an adoring *See? I'm totally not threatened by your female best friend* gaze.

Joy rolls her eyes. She can recognize that look from space because she's spent almost ten years maneuvering around it. Dating may be a rarity for her but being asexual hardly put a dent in Malcolm's relationship game. The aftermath of Caroline the Cruel has been the longest stretch of time she's ever seen him single.

"Eavesdropping is rude."

Surprise sprints up Joy's spine, making her eyes widen. The speaker is behind her, and she's clearly been caught in the invasive act. But she manages to turn around slowly, calmly flipping her braids over her shoulder.

"If they didn't want to be heard, they shouldn't have decided to talk in the middle of an open kitchen." Joy stands her ground, looking directly into his dark eyes—smoldering with haughty intensity, openly judging her. "And who, exactly, are you?"

"Fox." His voice, a deep soothing rumble, surprises her again. She takes her time, assessing him from head to toe, wanting him to see her judge him right back.

Fox. The hateful thorn in Malcolm's side. His brown hair, shot through with a shocking amount of gray for a face that looks so young, is mostly slicked back. A few curly locks have gone rogue, spiraling in front of his ears and near his temples. There's nothing exceptional about his face, but she recognizes broody-pretty when she sees it. Conventionally attractive white man du jour who lands movie roles because he looks like the actor they actually wanted and couldn't afford.

Since Fox allegedly hates Malcolm, she isn't too keen on playing nice with him. Her next words to him could set the tone for the entire trip. He's already on the defensive. What would surprise him the most?

The answer comes to her almost immediately.

Joy lifts her chin and says sweetly, "Happy Birthday." Without waiting for his response or reaction, she turns around and strides into the kitchen.

"Oh!" Summer taps Malcolm's arm with one hand and points with the other. "She's here! Hi!"

Before Joy knows what's happening, she's trapped in a bear hug, and *wow*, Summer is strong. Uncomfortable, Joy pats her on the back with stiff hands. She smells like oranges—a balanced mixture of sweet fruit and bitter rind.

Summer releases her and steps back, all smiles. They're the same height, eye to eye. "Sorry." She glances at Malcolm, then back to Joy. "Sorry, I'm a hugger."

"You don't say."

"I *love* your outfit."

Joy chose to wear a black velvet pinafore pocket dress with copper buttons running down the front. She paired it with a white blouse with flowy sleeves, a wide brim black sun hat, and black heeled boots. Not exactly camping attire.

Summer continues, "I've heard so much about you. I can't believe we finally get to meet."

"I wish I could say the same," Joy says, while staring at Malcolm. Her upbringing won't allow her to be rude to Summer right off the bat—not without her starting it first. Grilling Malcolm, however, is fair game.

Backing up a step, he holds his hands up in resignation. "Oh, Joy"—he points past her—"this is Summer's friend Fox."

"We've met. He seems lovely," Joy deadpans.

Summer laughs beatifically. "Sounds about right."

"Since we're all here now, we should get going." Malcolm checks his watch and mutters, "Six minutes behind schedule."

Fox sighs loudly, rolling his eyes. He leaves the kitchen first with Summer on his heels. She tosses a bright smile at Joy as she goes, bouncing on the balls of her feet with each step.

"She's certainly excited," Joy remarks dryly.

Malcolm kisses her cheek. "You're going to love her."

Joy decides to take this excellent moment of closeness to grab the back of his shirt and say, "I should rip out your kidneys with my bare hands and then feed your liver to a bear, because I know we're going camping, you inconsiderate asshole. You know how much I hate that."

"Violence? Wow." Malcolm snickers as he pulls her into a hug. "Thank you for coming."

Joy stares up at him, into the eyes she's known and loved for ten whole years. "Don't thank me yet," she says honestly.

Outside, Fox is bent over and waist-deep into the trunk of Malcolm's silver Jeep Wrangler Rubicon.

"My bags are still in my car," Joy says.

Malcolm volunteers to get them and when she pops the trunk of her faithful Honda Civic, he says, "*Three* suitcases? Joy."

"What? This is pretty good for *me*, all things considered," she says. "It's not like I knew we were *camping* or anything."

Malcolm effortlessly pulls each one out and sets them on the sidewalk. "I meant it when I said I didn't think you'd have a good time." He wheels the two larger suitcases, leaving the smaller one for her.

"And yet you invited me anyway. Because Summer asked." Joy nods toward her, already inside the Jeep, having claimed the front for herself. "She's in my seat."

Malcolm doesn't even seem bothered by her thinly veiled accusation, shrugging it off as if her feelings don't matter. "Summer made a playlist. She's really excited to help navigate once the GPS drops out for part of the drive."

Joy stares at him as he plays Tetris with her suitcases to make them fit into the already packed trunk. She gets it—he's nervous and wants the trip to go well—but it's hard not to take this personally. Suddenly he's like a neon sign in the dead of night, so bright it burns her eyes. Joy reads him loud and clear: Summer comes first right now. Chewing on her lip, eyes downcast, she says, "Fine."

Is it truly too much for him to make space for her feelings too? She won't get an answer even if she asks, so she doesn't. When she looks up again, her heart skips a tiny, shocked beat. Fox is there leaning against the side of the car. Watching her.

Joy forces herself to smile, covering the conflicting emotions she knows are written all over her face and locking them away. "Problem?"

Fox shakes his head.

"Good." Joy moves past him and opens the door to the back seat. "Because if I remember correctly, eavesdropping is rude, right?" She winks at him before climbing in.

Moments later, Fox opens the opposite door and sits next to her. He puts on his seatbelt, slides on a pair of sunglasses, crosses his arms, and slumps down in his seat.

Summer turns around. "You could at least wait until we've been driving for a while before you fall asleep." She looks to Joy. "He always does this."

"What? Pretend to sleep so he can spy on people in peace? Because that's absolutely what he's doing."

A small noise sounds on Joy's right. Fox hasn't moved—face still unexpressive, arms still crossed—but she swears he made a quiet snort-laugh.

"No, he's not." Summer laughs, shaking her head. "You like indie music, right?"

"I don't dislike it."

"I made a playlist for us. I even put in some gospel songs for Malcolm."

Summer's playlist isn't awful but that doesn't mean it's *good*. Too much indie, too many male singers with raw, grating voices that pop culture had begrudgingly branded as "unique" instead of untrained. Not that it matters, because Summer and Malcolm start talking the second he gets in the car. On the freeway, over the bridge, through the toll booths, past the winding hills and dirt-paved roads—the whole time, as if they're the only two people in the car.

Not once does Malcolm look up into the rearview mirror to invite Joy to join their conversation. She might as well not even be there.

*Which is the obvious point*, Joy thinks sadly. Being forgotten hurts worse than being ignored, like an accidental kick in the teeth. If she points it out, they'll make an effort, but they don't want to. She knows they don't. Instead, Joy busies herself on her phone by texting Grace, checking her hundreds of backlogged mentions, and replying to comments until her cell service drops out.

# Four

S till en route to Malcolm's Cabin of Dreams, Joy rolls down the window, angling her phone toward the sky. "Don't leave me, civilization. I need you." The last bar of service disappears, and a giant red *X* takes its place.

"You'll be fine." Malcolm glances at her through the rearview mirror.

"Oh?" Joy pretends to be surprised. "Are you talking to me now? I was sure you forgot about me and Fox Van Winkle back here."

"His last name is Monahan," Summer says.

"That was a joke." Malcolm smiles at her. "You know, like Rip Van Winkle."

"Who's that?"

Joy mutters, "Oh lord," at the same time Malcolm explains the short story. Nothing kills a good pun faster than it having to be explained.

"Oooh." Summer begins typing on her phone. "I should tell that story to my kids."

"*Kids?*" Joy's voice cracks.

"My students," Summer clarifies. "I'm an elementary school teacher. Currently third grade."

*Oh lord.* For a super-hot second, Joy's brain flashes to imagining Summer with kids, *plural*, and their new stepdad Malcolm. His new family moving into his empty house. Him asking Joy to give her key back because it makes Summer uncomfortable . . .

"Teacher." Joy has to clear her throat before she can continue. "I can see that."

"I've always wanted to be one. It's super rewarding but it's harder than I thought it'd be. It's also good practice for later." Summer and Malcolm exchange the kind of grin born from sharing secrets. She breaks eye contact with him to look at Joy. "I want to homeschool my kids. My actual kids. When I have them, I mean."

Joy's stomach flips with unease. This is bad. *Really* bad. She balls her hands into fists at her side to ground herself. That wasn't a coincidental, *by the way* aside. Summer *wanted* Joy to know that.

Malcolm has always been open about wanting kids. Family is one of the most important things to him. His parents, who are the epitome of delightful eccentrics and utterly devoted to him, planned to have only one child and that's precisely what they did. Everything they do has to be on schedule. Joy spent Thanksgiving with Malcolm's family the year they graduated college, and when she mentioned feeling a little lost and aimless in life, his mom laid out the *entirety* of her own life plan, complete with pictures. Finish undergrad at twenty-two, grad school at twenty-five, marriage at twenty-six, buy her first home at thirty, and become a mom at thirty-two. She ended up being off by one year—she had Malcolm at thirty-three.

It's no wonder Malcolm is the way he is.

Starting his own family has been at the top of his to-do list for a few years now.

Up until that second, Joy felt like she stood a chance. Malcolm loves her and she has a lot to offer a partner—she's funny, supportive, responsible, thoughtful—all excellent qualities. Not to mention, she knows how to present herself. Beauty isn't solely based on facial symmetry, tiny noses, huge eyes, and impossible bone structures. For Joy, it's a total package: confidence, presence, style, and execution. Plus, Malcolm thinks she's beautiful. Not pretty. Not cute. *Beautiful.* Sometimes she'll catch him staring at her and when she asks why, he says, "Because you're beautiful," with a completely straight face like it's a fact.

But kids? *Kids?* Not only have they discussed Joy's one true adult kryptonite, but they're also on the same page.

The last time Malcolm had talked to Joy about wanting kids, he asked her if she did, and she answered honestly: she didn't know. She's thought about that moment ever since. Because maybe that had been The Moment—the second he decided Joy wasn't The One. Not being sure about kids was a deal breaker for him.

Dark, bleak feelings begin clawing at Joy's edges again. Ready to pull her under, ready to make her shut down and stop feeling. Her brain does it to protect her, but it never stops feeling like a betrayal. She needs to think, she needs to plan, she has to find a way to make this work—

"Are we there yet?" Fox grumbles.

Joy nearly smiles at the sight of him. He's taken his sunglasses off and is pouting like a grumpy old man.

Malcolm mutters, "Does it look like we are?"

"Nearly." Summer holds up the map. The path to the cabin has been highlighted in yellow and she points to a red tick mark not too far from a giant green circle near a lake. "We just passed the last marker. We're two exits away from getting off the freeway."

"Thanks, Summer."

She beams at Fox—it's literally like the sun is shining straight out of her pores. The power that she has, dear god.

Fox angles his head toward Joy. He keeps his gaze down, toward the seat, and waits for Summer to turn her attention back to the front before whispering, "You're welcome."

Joy blinks at him, raising one eyebrow like a question mark. Her whisper is warmer than his but just as imperceptible to anyone else. "For?"

"Changing the subject." He slides his sunglasses back on and resumes his sleepy ruse.

Did he really think he had just helped her?

More important, how had he known she needed it? And why did he care?

Not one to look a grumpy gift horse in the mouth, Joy takes the reprieve, letting the conversation go in favor of looking out the window.

Several narrow tree-lined roads, a few worrisome cliffs, and some mountains later, Malcolm drives them into a valley with a shimmering lake at its center. He turns onto a street of charming rustic houses—a lakefront community comprised of sizeable two-story wooden cabins.

Joy inhales the clean mountain air, cheesing within an inch of her life as Malcolm parks in the gravel driveway. An array of colorful flowers borders the walkway leading up to the front door and the spacious cabin porch even has a bench swing. On the second floor, there's a large window nestled under a triangular arch. If that perfect east-facing window is in a bedroom, she'll fight *all* of them for it. No holds barred, cage-match style.

Malcolm leans against his door, craning his head toward the back seat, catching Joy's attention. "It's like you said: I know you hate camping." The proud twinkle in his eye almost sends her over the edge.

Joy's smile falters, nearly falling away completely. Why did he have to say something and spoil it? Her almost good mood begins to unspool like a runaway bobbin rolling across the floor, because none of this is for *her*.

Malcolm rented that beautiful cabin for Summer.

An annoying funny feeling begins whirling in her chest, winding her up again and instantly stressing her out. How long will it take to come back down from this panic? It hasn't lasted this long in years. Every time she thinks she's fine, she's back in control, something happens to remind her *no, bitch, you're still anxious as fuck*.

Joy opens her door and jumps out of the Jeep, leaving her phone, purse, and everything else behind. She skips around back, tramping through the grass, rocks, and fallen leaves, ready to explore instead of helping with carrying the suitcases inside. Tall trees encircle the sides of the house, and in the backyard there's a fire pit, a covered jacuzzi, and a hammock. Farther down, there's a dock and a small boathouse.

She makes a beeline straight for them, running down a slight hill until she reaches the glistening lake. The dock bobs gently under her feet with each step as she walks to the end. Sunny morning rays scatter across the calm water. Warm, calm wind flutters the hem of her dress, and somewhere nearby a chorus of ducks quack as loudly as they want. There are more houses on the other side of the lake too—all evenly spaced with clusters of trees between them.

Joy sits down, taking off her boots and socks. Her feet don't quite reach the cool water. Somehow, she's landed herself in a picturesque nightmare. Her horror movie prediction might not have been too far off.

Discussing kids (and their future lesson plans because Summer is probably gunning to be a stay-at-home parent) is a massive step in a serious direction. *I'm positive she's into me* doesn't even come close to suggesting *we've talked about having kids.* Not by a long shot.

Being honest, Joy still isn't ready for kids. She isn't sure she'll *ever* be ready. Her eldest sister, Natasha, let her be in the room when her nephew was born. Caleb, in all his terrible twos glory, brought her an outrageous amount of happiness. But making the leap from World's Best Aunt to World's Okayest Mom scares the life out of her. There's also the impending body horror, the medical racism, and the mortality rate for Black women specifically to think about. If she even survived pregnancy and delivery, she'd then have to deal with the costs of healthcare and childcare, the ramifications of raising a Black kid in a world that would never treat them fairly, never value their life.

There's just so much, too much, to consider.

Malcolm, of course, would understand. She knows he would. But he might want easier. He might not want to have a million repetitive conversations to soothe her relentless anxiety.

It isn't fair to let her fears hold him back from having the life he wants. Wanting to be with Malcolm meant accepting that future as inevitable.

Was she *really* prepared to do that *for* him?

Someone is coming—their heavy footsteps are making the dock move. Joy doesn't turn because she knows it's Malcolm. He always finds her.

"Here you are," Summer chirps.

Joy reacts slowly, moving like she has a crick in her neck. *You've got to be kidding me.*

Summer invites herself to sit down, as smiley as ever. "Did Malcolm tell you it's Fox's birthday?"

Can't she tell this is an introspective pity party for one? Joy would rather jump into the lake, fully clothed, than continue to sit there with Summer. She answers anyway. "He did."

"Perfect! I want to get him a cake. Will you come with me?"

"With you where?" By the grace of sweet baby Jesus, she manages to keep her tone even.

"To the store." Summer pulls out her phone and shares the downloaded map on her screen. "There's a bakery not too far from here. If I tell Malcolm, he'll say something ridiculously helpful, like 'I'll order one and have it delivered.'" She laughs. Her impression of Malcolm was spot on. Not good enough to make Joy laugh too, though.

Summer continues, "I want to pick it out myself, but I need a driver because that car is gigantic and I *will* wreck it."

"He won't take you?" Joy forces herself to stop leaning toward the water by holding the wooden dock with both hands.

"I didn't ask," she admits. "I was hoping we could have some girl time. You know, just me and you."

Joy takes a deep breath . . . and launches herself into the water.

For some silly reason, she didn't expect the water to be so cold. She stays under, floating and relishing the feeling of pins and needles pricking her skin. This is good. This is calm.

Joy hadn't felt that impulsive in *years*. The longer Summer talked the more wound up she felt, and she just needed to find a way to release the suffocating pressure building inside of her. Immediately. This was not a drill. Abandon ship. *Some girl time* really took her there and so she . . . jumped.

Her lungs begin to tighten, demanding air. Guess that means she still isn't part mermaid.

Something large crashes into the water next to her, assaulting her peaceful escape with a barrage of bubbles. Joy kicks her legs, breaking the surface—only to find Summer maniacally laughing next to her. "Oh my gosh! I can't believe we did that!"

Joy stares at her, treading water. "Me neither." The wonderous quick rush of relief she experienced begins to give way to numbness. She swims back to the dock and hauls herself onto it. After grabbing her shoes, she power walks back to the cabin with the sound of Summer's wet, slapping footsteps trailing close behind her.

The sliding glass door is unlocked. Joy pulls it to the side and enters. It's a good thing this place has hardwood floors because she's still dripping water everywhere.

Malcolm stops putting the extra road trip snacks in the kitchen pantry. His expression shifts rapidly from curious to confused to concerned and back to confused. "Why are you all wet?"

"I felt like going swimming." Joy nods to Summer. "I don't know what her excuse is."

"In your clothes?" Malcolm asks.

"The water, she calls to me," Joy says, feeling partially dead inside. "My life, my love, and my lady."

"That's the sea. Not a lake." Fox is sitting in the living room directly in front of the kitchen area. The couch and love seat fill most of the space, which has a perfect view of the abnormally large TV and the backyard.

Joy stares at him for a beat. Usually, people don't catch her references that fast. Mildly impressive. "I'm sorry. I don't remember asking you, or your bushy yet wonderous eyebrows, for your opinion."

Fox opens his mouth and closes it again.

Joy turns back to Malcolm. "Which room is mine? I obviously need to change."

"Upstairs. End of the hall." His tone is oozing suspicion—she can even see it in his eyes. But he doesn't ask.

"Are my—"

"By the closet."

"And the—"

"Straight and to your left."

"Great," Joy says. "Really love it when you answer my questions before I'm finished asking, by the way. Ten out of ten." As she's leaving, she catches Fox touching one of his eyebrows. When he realizes she's watching, she grins at him and he drops his hand, quickly turning away.

Upstairs, her room has a queen-size bed, a private bathroom, and as promised by Malcolm's psychic interruptions, her purse and suitcases are there, arranged in a row from largest to smallest, in front of the closet. Joy strips off her clothes, hopping into the shower to rinse her braids and get the lake water off her skin.

Showers are the perfect place to think. The water pressure is divine and perfectly lukewarm, complementing the hot summer air outside. Joy inhales and sighs as the smell of lavender and mint fills the bathroom as she lathers the soap on her loofa.

What in the hell is she going to do?

The accusations in Caroline's goodbye letter slammed into Joy's ego like a runaway freight train because she wasn't completely wrong. Even now, thinking about it made her stomach roil with guilt. Malcolm *did* put Joy first. Not always, but enough to be noticeable. Like the time he nursed her back to health when she got the flu on the same night Caroline threw a party to celebrate her promotion at work. Or the time Joy's Christmas flight home got canceled and he volunteered to drive with her across the state instead of spending his first couple's holiday with Caroline. Tricky situations like that happened often. Sometimes, Joy asked. Other times, Malcolm offered. In the end, it was always at Caroline's expense. Their intentions weren't malicious or deceitful, even if they looked that way. Malcolm wouldn't choose between them, so Caroline chose for him.

If Caroline was right about that, Joy thought that maybe, perhaps she was also not wrong about Joy being the spawn of Satan, sent directly from hell to ruin Caroline's life.

Joy gasps, freezing in place, mouth hanging open while the water continues to run down her body. All at once she realizes that's the root of her irrepressible anxiety—isn't she *purposefully* plotting to do the same thing now? Or attempting to? As much as Joy inherently dislikes Summer by circumstance, she doesn't deserve to have her life potentially ruined, especially not by Joy's doing.

But giving up without trying isn't an option either.

Joy shuts off the water and steps out of the shower. After drying off, she lugs one of her suitcases to the center of the room to find something to wear. She decides to go with a pair of high-waisted black jeans and a blue sweater crop top with short sleeves. Her makeup somehow survived both the lake and the shower, but she removes it and goes for a more natural look—just concealer, powder, mascara—with black lipstick because she just can't help herself. She takes a few pictures, saving them to edit so she can post her outfit of the day later.

Switching apps, she calls Grace, who answers on the second ring.

"Finally, *Jesus.*" Grace glares at her through the screen. "What are you doing?"

Joy laughs. If Grace had a catchphrase, that'd be it. It's never *hi, I love you, so glad you made it there safely.* It's always *what are you doing?* Straight to the point and ready to jump right in.

"I just got out of the shower." Joy explains the car ride and her brief swimming session.

"If you don't go get a damn therapist—what were you thinking?"

"I wasn't." Joy begins to pace the room. "That's why I'm calling you. I'm way more stressed out than I thought I'd be."

"Of course you are," Grace says kindly before sighing. "They seem nice, though. Are they?"

Joy shrugs. "So far?" She thinks of Fox in the car, changing the subject because he correctly guessed she needed it. That was definitely nice. And strangely observant.

"Summer seems a little weird but she's probably fine. Malcolm has the oddest taste in women, I swear." She rolls her eyes. "That's why he's not into you. You're too perfect."

Joy scoffs and plops down on the bed. "No one delivers a backhanded compliment quite like you."

"I know, right? But I do mean it—you're perfect to me. If you're serious about wanting to date now, it won't take long for someone else to see it too."

"I never said I wanted to date in general. And I don't want someone else to see it—"

"I *know*, you want Malcolm. Gross. I just can't respect that choice so don't ask me to. I won't do it."

"I'm not saying I'm doing this, but"—she pauses, focusing on making sure her tone sounds hypothetical and not confessional—"do you think I'd be a bad person if I told Malcolm how I feel even though Summer is here?"

Grace doesn't answer immediately, face folding into a contemplative frown. "No. But that's because you're not a bad person, period. You've always cared about other people's feelings too much for that. A bad person wouldn't even have bothered to ask."

Joy refuses to be the person Caroline thinks she is.

For one thing, her nerves and stomach can't handle that kind of stress.

Deep down Joy always thought she never got along with Caroline because they never gave each other a chance. It doesn't have to be that way with Summer.

If Malcolm did choose Joy, that didn't mean Summer would disappear from his life. Malcolm's friends always turn into her friends and vice versa anyway. Taking the time to get to know Summer, same as how she would with anyone else, wouldn't hurt anything.

Grace continues, "That said, I really don't think that's something you should do or even be focusing on. Stop making your life revolve around him. You're on vacation in a beautiful cabin with a beautiful room and lake. Act like it. Try to have a good time, okay?"

"Okay."

"And send me lots of pictures. I want to see what Fox looks like."

"Of course you do." Joy laughs.

"I'll tell you if he's fine or if you should keep it moving."

"I can tell if someone is attractive," Joy says dryly.

"I didn't say attractive. I said *fine*." Grace raises an eyebrow and says in a singsong voice, "Meaning he's our type."

"*Our*." Joy laughs again. Grace thinks she's the blueprint for if Joy weren't ace. If Grace is attracted to someone, that means Joy, in theory, would be too—probably once she got to know them. It's a silly, harmless idea that always cracks Joy up because it completely disregards the fact that they're almost total opposites personality-wise.

"If he is, I'll get his number for you." Joy scrunches her nose. "I wish you were here."

"Well. That would take Malcolm inviting me and we both know how he feels about yours truly."

"He loves you."

"No, he loves you. I'm just your bio-doppelgänger who refuses to be ignored."

# Five

Back downstairs, Malcolm is still in the kitchen. Summer is sitting opposite him at the island countertop, in dry clothes with her wet hair pulled up into a bun. Her smile grows impossibly bigger when Joy walks in.

"Oh, Malcolm," Summer says, leaning forward. "Can I borrow your car keys?"

"Why?" He leans on the counter too, matching her stance and playful smile.

"I want to go to the store. Joy's going to drive me."

*Driving Miss Summer*, coming to a theater near you . . . It literally pains Joy to hold that joke in. Summer must have interpreted Joy jumping into the lake to avoid answering her as an enthusiastic *Yes!*

Malcolm's smile holds as his gaze slides to Joy for confirmation, but the expression in his eyes is clear. *This is not a part of my plan. Fix it.*

Joy looks past them toward the door. Fox is there, glowering and watching, baseball hat still pulled down low on his forehead. His arms are crossed as he casually leans against the doorjamb. When his gaze locks with hers, he raises one of his now infamous bushy eyebrows. There's an easiness to him, an *I don't care* vibe, but he's not fooling her.

He's waiting for her response too.

Per usual, Malcolm is completely oblivious to how the politics of dating works. He leads with his heart and excessive planning. Strategy beyond that has always been beyond him.

Summer's birthday cake idea could be nothing more than a search-and-destroy tactic Joy's seen executed dozens of times because she's always on the receiving end of it. Malcolm's partners want to get in good with her to make him happy. Show him, *Look, I'm not threatened by her at all. We're friends.*

In this instance, though, there's a bonus factor.

Malcolm has to be the one to say no to Summer, because if Joy does it? It gives Summer the perfect opportunity to twist it around. She gets to play the innocent white damsel and paint Joy as the angry Black woman who's *mean* to her.

A face and stature like Summer's screams *helpless*—whether it's true or not doesn't matter when everyone in the room is socialized to believe it. And when white people actively use it to their advantage, it could mean automatic game over.

Maybe Summer will. Maybe Summer won't.

Joy hates having to be aware of ploys like that all the time, constantly speculating about the worst in people to protect herself. That doesn't make it any less necessary.

All three of them are still watching her, still waiting. She doesn't feel like being charming but she pushes that aside.

Joy digs deep for this one, inhaling and exhaling with a casual hair flip—and her braids slap her back because they're still wet, *DAMN IT.* She rolls her grimace of pain into a convincingly smug smile. "Malcolm." She keeps her voice low and playful while walking to his side of the counter. "Give me your keys." A subtle nod toward Summer. A wink. *Let me talk to her,* she says with her eyes. *We need to get to know each other.* She holds out her hand, fully expecting him to do as she says.

Malcolm gets the message, and he doesn't like it. But trust overrides the worry in his eyes—he straightens up and reaches into his pocket. "One hour." He places the keys onto her palm.

"I have executive dysfunction. Time means nothing to me."

"Joy."

"I love you. Very much." Joy gazes up at him, smile set to stun. "If I die, remember those were my last words."

"We're not going to die." Summer giggles. Joy is beginning to think that's her natural response to everything. "Why would you say that?"

"I literally jumped into a lake an hour ago. Being dramatic and giving Malcolm gray hair is my lifeblood." Joy gestures toward Fox, who hasn't moved. "I see you must have worked the same magic on him already."

"Oh no, he's been gray since high school." At that, Fox walks out in a frustrated huff and the room is blessed with more Summer giggles. "He's very sensitive about it."

In the car, Summer jumps into the passenger seat, immediately queuing up her playlist again.

"Actually, let's not." Joy adjusts the mirrors. "I need to concentrate on the directions."

"Oh sure." Summer enters the address into the Jeep's built-in navigation system and puts her seatbelt on.

Joy backs out of the driveway smooth as butter. Once they're on the road, Joy glances at Summer out of the corner of her eye. She's looking straight ahead, hands in her lap with a pleased look on her pleasant face.

Agreeing to one-on-one time with Summer wasn't the worst idea. Caroline aside, Joy always tried to give his partners a fair shot. A blank slate to get to know them. If they weren't important to Malcolm, he wouldn't have chosen them, so she'd hoped they'd be important to her too. Eventually.

More than a few of Malcolm's exes, of which there are *many*, were two-faced as hell. That second face never appeared while he was around. Some snapped faster than others. Some hissed the truth at her the moment Malcolm turned away. Some fooled her for an entire year. She'd truly seen it all.

It didn't help that Joy was petty. She wouldn't know how to be the bigger person if she took an immersive course on it. The second they acted out of pocket, the moral high ground ceased to exist. Michelle Obama she was not—if they went low, Joy went to hell. Jesus could walk out the pearly gates and down that stairway to heaven and she'd look him dead in the eye and say, "*They started it! I'll stop if you ask me to, but you saw what they did!*"

*Now or never*, she thinks to herself. "So, Malcolm says you met at a failed meetup?"

Summer nods enthusiastically. "I like planning get-togethers and stuff. It's kind of my thing. I like hanging out, getting to know people. I had a good feeling, so I invited him to my weekly game night. He's *amazing* at trivia."

"He does like to know things."

"And before I knew it, we were friends," Summer says. "I don't think I've ever met anyone like him. You know how it is with guys—they're nice to you until they get what they want and then they leave. And if you're lucky enough to find someone decent you're constantly paranoid someone is going to try to steal him away or that he'll cheat."

Joy's hands twitch, but she keeps her eyes on the road. Summer didn't pull that paranoid line out of nowhere.

"Dating is so stressful. I hate it. I'd rather just be in a relationship because most guys don't want to be friends if there aren't any benefits, and then have the nerve to get all possessive anyway." Summer turns to her with a conspiratorial expression on her face, as if they're in on a secret together.

That's . . . a lot to unpack.

They see things differently, that's for sure. Joy has no problems making friends with men but she also mostly runs in queer circles, which tend to be a bit more open—and less patriarchal.

Maybe being white, blonde, and small has something to do with it too. It isn't Summer's fault that she represents the gold standard or whatever, but the grass obviously isn't greener. Men must see her and get hit with the atavism stick. SEX! WIFE! BABIES! BAREFOOT IN THE KITCHEN!

Summer continues, words bubbling out of her like a fountain. "Malcolm isn't like that, you know? He feels so genuine. What you see is exactly how he is. No pretense, no lying, just a genuinely nice person who cares *so* much. We can talk for hours. Hours! I've never done that with a guy before. He honestly cares about what I have to say and how I feel. He really knows how to make me feel special. Like I'm the only person in the whole world who matters to him. I'm probably preaching to the choir. You already know that."

She's looking at Joy with the energy of a bird perched and

ready to take flight—with more to say but waiting for Joy to jump in. That's . . . considerate. Joy had assumed she was the kind of person who steamrolled conversations, not caring if the other person joined in or not.

"Malcolm definitely feels like he's perfect. He isn't. Even I can admit that. But I get what you're saying."

"Fox is the same. He's not as, umm, emotionally open, I guess, but he's still amazing. He does things without you having to ask and always tries to make people feel better if they're having a hard time. I'm lucky to have him. Do you know about love languages? I think his is acts of service. I think Malcolm's is a mix of gift giving and words of affirmation."

A nagging voice whispers to Joy that Summer really cares about them. She isn't pretending or trying to endear herself to Joy. It's honest. Her feelings for them are the real thing.

But then another voice yells, *Do not let your guard down! The enemy will try anything!*

Enemy.

*Is* Summer her enemy?

Does she even have to be?

Summer interrupts her thoughts. "Do you know yours?"

"No." Joy glances at her. "I know what they are, but I've never taken the test."

Wrong answer. Joy basically just handed Summer a loaded gun. They spend the rest of the drive taking the test—Summer reading the questions and Joy answering. When she finds a parking spot near the front of the store, Summer exclaims, "You're a split between words of affirmation and quality time! I *knew* it!"

Summer continues chattering on next to Joy as they enter the store, completely oblivious. Nothing out of the ordinary for her.

This isn't the first time Joy's been with non-Black people who didn't go into immediate high alert when in new places.

It's a sick game she's forced to play where she counts all the Black people she sees. And if that fails, she moves on to non-Black POCs. It doesn't mean she'll be safe. It just helps ease some of her anxiety.

Immediately, she spots two workers at the register and one behind the deli counter whom she's pretty sure are Black. She sees people of other races and ethnicities shopping. It's a good mix. The tension automatically releases from her shoulders and neck as she exhales. Malcolm planned this trip—but even knowing that he'd never take them somewhere dangerous can't stop her from fretting.

In the bakery section, Summer carefully scans the display, systematically inspecting the cakes from right to left, face screwed up in concentration. She's giving each cake a once over with the seriousness of someone disarming a bomb. The fate of the world rests on her finding the perfect dessert.

"None of these look good." Summer's gaze flicks up toward the bakers behind the counter, probably hoping they didn't hear her.

Joy asks, "Why don't you just make one, then?"

"He would see us making it. It would spoil the surprise."

*Us.* Who the hell is *us*? Oh, she's good—already laying another trap for Joy. She could picture it: Summer desperate for approval and complaining to Malcolm about how unfriendly Joy is when all she wants is to be friends. The plaintive *but she doesn't like me* combined with a pout molded from sheer manipulative precision.

Summer's feelings about Fox and Malcolm might be real, but that doesn't mean she's in the clear for Joy.

"Cakes are hardly a surprise on a birthday. If it were Malcolm, he'd expect one from me."

"I'm not good at baking, but you are, right? Malcolm said you were."

Joy frowns. Exactly how *much* had Malcolm told Summer about her? "Maybe."

Summer transitions from dejected to hopeful in a split second, and she takes off practically running to the baking aisle. Joy sighs, following her deeper into the store. When she catches up, Summer is holding two different boxes of cake mix.

Joy asks, "What are you doing?"

"Picking out a cake."

*"From a box?"*

Summer doesn't exactly giggle, but it's close. "How do you make your cakes?"

"From scratch. Put those down."

Joy pulls out her phone, thanking the reception gods for blessing her. She opens the recipe book she's been making—a written collection of all her dad's best dishes. He cooks everything from memory, never measuring a single spice. Her dupes aren't an exact match and have lost some of that daddy magic, but Joy wants a record for her family to share and have always. She even started adding a few of her own baking recipes, mostly cakes and pastries, that she had perfected. Her sisters followed suit too, adding their favorites whenever they remembered. "What kind of cake does Fox like?"

"Angel food?"

"Absolutely not."

"Chocolate? With some fruit maybe? He loves berries."

"Any allergies?"

"Nope."

Malcolm isn't a fan of berries. He loves her family's special yellow cake but wouldn't be opposed to chocolate with the right recipe. "How does he feel about Funfetti?"

"I thought box cake was a no-go?"

"It is. Funfetti is just white cake with melted sprinkles." Joy keeps scrolling.

"This is so nice of you." Summer tries to look over her shoulder—Joy moves, hiding the screen, but throws a playful glare to cover up her rudeness. It works. Summer takes a step back, her smile unbothered. "Thank you for doing this. Fox is gonna love it."

"I'm not doing it for him or you," Joy says, careful to keep her tone playful. "I happen to enjoy having my cake and eating it too."

Giggles, giggles, giggles everywhere. "You're so funny."

That wasn't a joke, but Joy lets it stand like one. Maybe Summer is one of those people who only sees the good in everyone. *Jesus.* Not being able to figure her out immediately is giving Joy whiplash. Is she a two-faced demon or a sweet fairy angel? People contain multitudes, sure, but not *that* many.

"How about marble cake with buttercream frosting? I can also make raspberry ganache."

Summer's eyes widen. "That sounds fancy."

"It's mid-tier for me. Two layers? Three?"

Summer scrunches her nose. "Would three be too much?"

"No, as long as I remember to rotate the pans so the cakes can cook evenly it'll be fine. Malcolm would never go on an extended trip with a kitchen that didn't have a stand mixer."

"So you can bake stuff?"

"No, so *he* can. Cooking makes him happy." Joy wonders why Summer doesn't know that but doesn't linger on the thought. "This cake is for a special occasion. One-time-only exception. Vacation means *vacation* to me. Clear?"

Summer bounces on the tips of her toes, excitement overtaking her. "Since you're making it, I'll buy whatever you need."

More whiplash.

Joy narrows her eyes. Now where in the hell did *us* go?

They traverse the store together, collecting all the ingredients and grabbing some candles. After breezing through the self-checkout line and loading up the trunk, they head back to the cabin.

"Can I ask you a question?" Joy tried for nonchalance, but her voice sounded higher than she'd like. Her nerves lose approximately *all* of their chill when she's stressed or anxious. Malcolm always teases her about how many tells she has, saying she'd be a horrible poker player. He's not wrong. Hopefully, Summer doesn't know that—even though she seems to think she knows quite a bit.

Summer shifts in her seat so she's partially facing Joy. "Shoot."

"Don't you think it's a little weird that Malcolm's never mentioned you to me?" Joy glances at Summer to catch her reaction—there isn't one. "I mean, he tells me *everything*, but not a single peep about you."

"Um, maybe you should talk to him about that."

"Oh, I will. But right now, I'm talking to you."

"I see. Well. I don't think it's weird." Summer shrugs. "Considering what happened with you and Caroline."

"What's that supposed to mean?"

"Nothing." She answers quickly, eyes wide and innocent as she could probably make them. "Malcolm told me what happened. I put two and two together and figured he wanted to be sure before he brought anyone else around you."

Wait. What? "Me?"

"Yeah." Summer nods. "You're like his family. He wants to be sure new people won't hurt you like she did."

*Family.* The word hits her like a shot to the heart. If anyone else called her Malcolm's family, she'd roll with it because it might as well be true. But coming from Summer, that word in her mouth feels like a backhanded compliment so good Grace would be proud. *You're like a sister to him, Joy.*

One thing's for sure: Joy isn't his damn sister.

If that's how Summer wants to play it, Joy can dish it right back. Summer called Malcolm a "friend." Someone so indoctrinated in traditional dating values would claim Malcolm if he were hers. She's definitely the kind of person to correct someone the second she got engaged. *He's my* fiancé *now. We're getting married.* While using a voice that's equal parts snotty and sweet.

"For his partners, sure. Not his friends. I mean, that's what you said, right? You two are friends."

"We are." Despite Joy's panic, there's no tension between them. No animosity filling up the car. Summer seems fine, relaxed even. "But that's how it always starts with him, isn't it? Caroline was his friend first too."

Joy turns back to the road, hands gripping on the wheel. *She knows.*

# Six

Summer carries most of their haul into the house, multiple bags looped around her arms like a pro. "One trip."

Joy snickers, amused despite her inner turmoil. "Impressive. My delicate hands are happy to leave you to it."

Malcolm's face lights up when he sees them. Joy isn't sure if it's for Summer or her, but for now the best she can hope for is both. "Get what you need?"

Summer quickly scans the room. No sign of Fox. "We're making a cake for tonight."

"You are?" Malcolm asks Joy, who reclines against the counter after setting his keys down.

"We."

"A cake? Together? Really?"

"I said *oui*." It takes several heartbeats for her joke to register— and the resulting look in Malcolm's eyes as his soul tries to leave his body sends Joy cackling into oblivion.

"What's so funny?" Summer, dedicated to secrecy, begins stashing the ingredients as far back in the cabinets and fridge as she can push them.

"Nothing," Malcolm says. "That's the problem."

Joy snorts. "But you recognized it, though. Ten out of ten for effectiveness."

"Anyway." A reluctant laugh escapes him. "I have a small aquatic surprise planned. So if you want to go put on your swimsuits . . ."

"Is it a boat? Are we going boating? Wait, don't tell me. I want to be surprised." Summer plants a kiss on his cheek before dashing out of the room, presumably to go change.

Malcolm didn't react to that kiss at all. A very good sign.

Joy squints at him, making her best Marge Simpson–type groan.

"Don't start. You *love* the water." Malcolm moves to stand next to her and begins to rub her back. She turns her body toward him, head hovering dangerously near his shoulder. It'd be so easy to just wrap her arms around him and rest there.

Malcolm asks, "Are you feeling better?"

Joy frowns up at him. "Better?"

He nods. "You two ran off before I could ask."

"Why would you think I was upset?"

"Well, one second you're in the car and the next you're in the lake. You know what? You're right. That's perfectly normal Joy behavior."

Joy laughs lightly, grinning at him. "Fine. I'm tired."

Giving in, she places her forehead on his shoulder, and he meets her the rest of the way, wrapping her up in a hug. Malcolm is affectionate by nature, both giving and receiving. The only time he draws a hard line with Joy is when he's in a relationship with someone, out of respect for his partner's feelings.

His breath whispers across her ear, voice soft and concerned. "That's all?"

*No.* "Yeah."

"Promise."

"Absolutely not."

"Come on." Gently, he tugs her toward the stairs. "I want to get your opinion on something while you decide which of the thirty swimsuits you brought you're gonna wear."

"Excuse you. I only brought *two*, thank you very much."

Upstairs, Joy plops down in the middle of her room while unzipping her suitcases.

Malcolm sits on the bed. "I'd like to keep the surprise shopping trips to a minimum so we can stay on schedule."

"Hey, that's on her."

"You could've said no. Next time, you should."

Joy bites back her retort, deciding to cut her eyes at him instead. Malcolm has . . . control issues. Everything always has to go according to plan, and she hates that for him. Truly. Most times, she can work around it, but once he starts telling her what to do? Telling instead of *asking*? Things fly off the rails with the quickness.

Several calming breaths later, Joy busies her hands sorting through her clothes and putting some of the items on hangers. "I figured it was a good opportunity for some reconnaissance, since she knows oh so much about me and I don't even know her last name."

"And? What do you think about her?"

"Too early to say. She cares about you, I think." Being honest with him will only help her in the long run. This isn't her first potential girlfriend rodeo—just the first time she's planning to use what she finds out for herself. If all goes well, he won't be able to tell anything is amiss.

"Good." Malcolm tugs at the hem of his shirt. "Earlier, I didn't mean that I don't want you two to spend time together. I do. Obviously." His short, nervous laugh implies otherwise. "But I think it might be better if you focused on Fox like we agreed."

For an apology, it's one of his weaker ones. He knows he was rude, but he said what he said. And he meant it.

"I know how to multitask. Let me work, damn. You're cramping my style."

"All right." Malcolm grins at her, shaking his head. "I sent you the weekend agenda while you were gone."

Joy finds the swimsuit she wants—a navy blue bikini with gold chains for straps—and lays it flat on top of her other clothes. She quickly reads the weekend agenda email and suddenly her vacation feels like work. Like they're prepping for a new pitch or executing a new contract. He's given her the details and it's up to her to help him see it through, because he's the dreamer with the big ideas and tireless work ethic and she's his touch of realism keeping him grounded with the finer details.

Malcolm approaches romance almost identically to the way he approaches business. If an exact formula for romantic interludes existed, he'd find it, patent it, and make even more money off it. The email contains an hourly schedule of events, extensive notes, conversation topics to avoid, and a list of Summer's favorite things—even more proof that this trip had truly been custom-made specifically for her. Camping, boating, animals—

"Hiking!" Joy glares at him. "I don't have—"

"*Aht*, hold on." He gets up and retrieves a shoebox from the closet, sitting it down next to her.

"And I didn't bring—"

Back to the closet he goes, returning with a bag from her favorite clothing boutique. "Already washed."

Summer hit the gift-giving nail on the love-language head. Malcolm gives everyone presents all the time. Little things to let them know he appreciates them or that they're on his mind. He's so generous that it's hard not to read more into the presents than what really existed on his end.

So no one, not even Grace, was surprised when Joy fell for Malcolm all those years ago. All their friends had thought he was *so* into her too because he didn't pay attention to anyone else the way he did to Joy. For her, they weren't just little gifts from him—they were earnest proclamations of his feelings. She built it up in her heart on her own, but her friends built it up in her head first.

"*He's not into me like that.*"

"*Girl, yes he is!*"

The more they speculated, the realer it felt.

Joy glances at the bag and box, heart swelling uncomfortably in her chest. He'd gone out of his way to specifically pick these items out for her, washed them, hid them in the closet so he could surprise her because he knew she would complain about not having hiking gear. Malcolm doesn't do that for everyone. He only gives this level of attention to Joy and Joy alone.

*Now.* Joy should tell him now while they're alone and her feelings are bubbling up so close to the surface.

But what would she say? How would she say it? In all her frantic panic of the morning, she never once considered the words she'd use to confess. She hasn't had time to find the right combination of sentences or how to make it sound heartfelt.

Joy decides to start slow. "When did you buy this? You invited me yesterday, so you couldn't have gone this morning."

Malcolm shrugs. "All that matters is you're comfortable. I really do appreciate you being here."

*Now! Now! Do it now!*

"Malcolm." Joy hiccups a breath. She can't look at him, *she can't*, but she can say it. "Malcolm. I love you."

"I love you too." He says it quickly and without thought. Of course he does.

"No, really." She risks a glance up at him. *Oh lord, please don't let me throw up.* "I mean it."

"So do I." Malcolm leans over and kisses her on the top of her forehead. "I'll go so you can get changed."

Frozen in place, all she can manage is, "But—"

"Ten minutes," he says, as he walks out of her room.

Summer's yellow polka-dot bikini, where the dots are hearts, suits her. "Oh my god, I love your swimsuit!"

"As do I," Joy says without a hint of humbleness. Immediately she notices Fox noticing her with a bit too much interest. The easiest way to stop someone from staring is to subtly point it out to them. It isn't a bad stare on his part. He's looking respectfully, just a little too long for her liking. His shorts are the exact same shade of blue as her bikini. "We match. Imagine that."

"We do."

Joy tilts her head. "Do you ever say more than a few words at a time?"

"Why?"

Suddenly feeling mischievous, she says, "Because it's usually the quiet ones I have to watch out for."

"What?"

"You're not fooling me."

"I don't— What are you talking about?"

Joy leans closer to him, whispers, "Seven words that time. New record," and quickly walks away. She tosses a casual glance over her shoulder—his eyebrow is still arched in response. *Got him.* She pauses at the entrance to the boathouse before heading down the short set of stairs.

Malcolm is near the back, winding a thick rope around his arm. When he finishes, he pokes her in the side as he passes her to head for the rented boat. After he left her room, she may or may not have gone on a mini crying jag that thankfully no one was there to witness.

Using words Malcolm has heard before, and often, won't help her get her point across. Lesson learned. She has to find a way to shock him somehow. Force him to listen to what she has to say without him prematurely assuming he knows what she means.

"Are you going to take pictures for RoT?" Summer suddenly appears by Joy's side. "I could help. I take *great* pictures."

Joy practically flees closer to the boat to put some distance between them. Summer keeps popping up like a jump scare in a horror movie—the risk of being startled by one is low, but never zero. "RoT?"

"Yeah! Oh, I follow you. I almost had a heart attack when Malcolm said he knew you, and then I did have one when he said you've been best friends for years."

"You're an influencer?" Fox's rumbly voice snuck up on Joy like a thief in the night. And that was still only three words.

"No." Joy inches toward the boat. She knows jack all about them, but this one seems nice enough. Sleek and pointy with a white racing stripe cleanly cutting through green paint. "I wouldn't call myself that."

Fox is silent for a beat too long, clearly thinking. "Would other people call you that?"

Six. Joy smiles, suddenly feeling ridiculously pleased by this development. Petty speaks to petty—she has a feeling he counted his words first.

"I like to dress up in nice clothes, do my makeup, take pretty pictures of myself, and post them on the internet. I can't help it if other people like them as well."

"Thousands," Malcolm adds unhelpfully while offering a hand to assist her on the boat. "Hundreds of thousands of other people."

Joy sits down on the blue cushioned seat. "What are numbers, really?" *This thing doesn't have seat belts, what the hell?*

Summer giggles at something on her phone and holds it up for Fox to see as they board together. "Holy shit."

Joy sighs deeply, assuming she showed him her Rule of Thirds account. "Thanks, Summer." Typically, she likes to ease people into the reveal that she has the equivalent to the population of a small country following her online life.

"Sorry." Summer scrunches her delicate nose. "I think that's incredible, personally. I couldn't ever imagine being that popular."

"My sister would disagree with you. Every time someone mistakes her for me, she literally sends me a bill for pain and suffering."

"There are two of you?" Fox asks abruptly.

Joy narrows her eyes in response. "That had a tone," she says, and then gives him a teasing smile.

"They're not identical," Malcolm says. "Grace is the evil twin."

"No, she's not. Anyways, we're like the Olsen twins. You know them, right? Fraternal—but we look similar enough to be identical." Joy holds a hand under her chin. "Grace swears her face is like five percent more symmetrical than mine or whatever"—she rolls her eyes—"and she has a mole above her left eyebrow."

Malcolm adds, "You can also tell them apart because Grace is a little bit taller and they sound different. Joy's voice is higher."

"So." Fox continues only focusing on Joy. "There are two of you."

"Does that bother you?"

He doesn't get a chance to answer because Summer decides to give him another patch of gray hair when she asks, "Can I drive!?" and positions herself behind the wheel.

"No," Fox says sternly.

Malcolm glares at him before answering, "Once we're out on the lake in open water, sure." He gently maneuvers her to the side.

Summer begins asking him rapid-fire questions like when he got his license, has he ever been on a sailboat, and if he would ever get one, because *she* loves sailboats. Malcolm answers each question patiently, always with a smile, as he drives them farther away from the dock.

Joy isn't exactly upset that Summer has become Malcolm's radiant center of attention. Seeing him happy really does make her happy. When Summer looks at him, it's warm and precious. It brings out his wide grin and crinkling eye-smile. He teaches her how to drive the boat by being attentive and not overbearing. Some of his best traits on full display for everyone to see—

everything she sees in him all the time. The things she never loses sight of, that are there even when they fight, even when he's being impossible. All the things she loves about him so much it makes her cry sometimes because she can't understand *why?*

Joy has always struggled with expressing the feeling of wanting something someone else has. The only concept she's ever heard of that comes close is jealousy or envy. If someone is on the brink of having something you want, of course it's jealousy, right?

But it isn't. The feeling doesn't eat her alive or try to consume her or twist her insides until they turn green. It can't be.

If Summer is who Malcolm wants, then good for him. Good for them. When she confesses, if that's his answer, then she'll quietly step aside. But until that moment, she's stuck, unable to understand why not her? What's wrong with her? It hurts, this unrelenting longing wrapped in unconditional love. Tender and excruciating all at once.

Joy forces herself to tear her gaze away from them—and meets Fox's eyes. Startled, she says, "Hi," because that's the first thing that pops into her brain.

"Hi."

Has he been watching her? If he feels guilty about being caught again, he doesn't show it, continuing to maintain eye contact from the other side of the boat. He's also wearing a bright orange life jacket now.

"Lovely weather we're having."

"Sure."

Joy's never met a person she couldn't initially dazzle. She's too quick, too flirty, too aware—most people never stand a chance. Fox might drive her into overtime, though. His stoic grumpiness isn't exactly Mount Everest since he's shown enough interest to play off, but it won't take her much further if she can't find the right angle.

Her online popularity clearly spooked him, and he also had a weird reaction to her being a twin, so she needs to hook him with something he would consider normal—relatable yet intriguing. He wants to know more. She can feel it.

Whatever preconceptions Malcolm unintentionally planted about her must have been shaken once he met her. The same thing was true for her, wasn't it? All she knew was that Malcolm claimed Fox hated him, but she hasn't been able to figure out *why*. She hasn't even seen anything that could lead to an explanation for it. He seems grumpy by nature, and it's pointed in all general directions, not specifically at Malcolm.

"You're into all this outdoorsy stuff too, I'm assuming."

"No."

Joy crosses her leg at the knee and leans toward him, resting her arms on her thighs. She watches him carefully as she asks, "Do you hate Malcolm?"

The right side of his mouth *twitches*. "No."

One-word answers. He's testing her.

"I see you," she says in a singsong voice.

When he lifts that eyebrow again, she knows she's right.

"That's so *petty*." Joy winks at him. "I approve." She straightens up, turning her back on him in favor of watching the rippling waves as the boat cruises across the water.

That exchange needed a hard stop. If she pressed, the fun would wear off and become annoying. Dealing with Malcolm and Summer stressed her out to the high heavens. Having Fox around could be a blessing in disguise. Someone to spar and have fun with to balance out her constantly fluctuating moods and keep her grounded.

Fox's voice cuts through everything—the boat's engine, the water, the birds, Joy's thoughts. "For the record, I see you too."

It takes everything Joy has to not turn back around. She grips the railing of the boat, lips pressed together to stop her smile from overtaking her face.

Seven words again. Damn, he's good.

# Seven

Malcolm gave Summer free rein with the music in the car, but the boat's playlist is all Joy. She pairs her phone with the stereo system and selects her ~vacation vibes~ playlist. The first song kicks in with a hypnotic baseline layered with sweet soprano vocalists and a simple drumbeat.

"Can I drive by myself now?" Summer holds her hands together in the prayer position.

"In a second. I promise." Malcolm heads toward the back of the boat, where two blue coolers and a small table have been set up. He sets out the food he brought—sliced summer fruits, fancy meats and cheese with toothpicks, an assortment of chips and dips, and drinks—into a neat display.

Joy watches him, patiently waiting for a moment to slide in. If Malcolm wanted help, he would have asked. His attention to detail can occasionally be lethal. He's been known to slap someone's hand away if they invade his creative space. He's almost finished when Joy sidles up beside him. She reaches under his arm, swiping a bottle of champagne from the ice bucket.

"Would you like a glass?" He laughs as he asks.

Joy takes a swig from the bottle as an answer. The cool, fizzing bubbles tickle the inside of her mouth.

"Heathen."

"All the best people are." Joy blows a playful kiss at him.

He pretends to catch and toss it back at her, smiling the entire time.

"You wound me, sir. My champagne and I don't have to take that." Grinning, she saunters back to her seat and on the way she accidentally makes eye contact with Summer. Her usual ray of sunshine expression is a bit cloudier than normal, but she recovers quickly, perking up and bounding off to stand next to Malcolm.

While Summer drives, Joy distracts herself by dancing around the boat. Resisting a good song isn't in her DNA. Everything fades into the non-rhythmic background—no Summer, no Malcolm (gazing at Summer), and no Fox. It's just her, the music, and her drink. And her phone. She takes funny pictures, like up-close shots of her forehead, lips tucked in with her cheeks puffed out. More of her pretending to cry at the water so the non-existent dolphins will come back. They're the assholes of the sea, but hey, at least they like humans.

Malcolm truly spared no expense because the boat's Wi-Fi must have been set to Speed Racer status. Instead of posting the pictures to her main grid, she adds them to her powershots— uploads that disappear after forty-eight hours—tagging everything ~vacation vibes~ for consistency since she shares her playlist with her followers too.

The champagne goes straight to her head, leaving her feeling light, airy, and loose. All vibes and no strife. She's been nothing but a giant ball of functional frustration, flipping between despair and scheming so fast, it was beginning to wear her down. Being able to dance, worry-free and almost happy, to her favorite music on a beautiful boat in the middle of a magnificent lake almost made up for it. Grace was right. Trying to have a good time feels *so much* better.

She's in the middle of a rather sensual move involving quite a bit of balance and divine intervention supporting her knees when the music suddenly stops. A boat similar in size to Malcolm's approaches them from the left.

"Hey, neighbor," someone from the intruding boat calls.

Both Malcolm and Summer opt for being friendly because of course they do. Joy slinks away to the back of the boat alone. Champagne bottle empty, she grabs some water to give her body a break. Her drinking rules are absolute: cut all the alcohol with water or alternate between the two. She's mid-drink when inspiration for another picture strikes.

Standing close to the edge, Joy poses with a dead look in her eyes, the invading boat in clear view behind her. Perfect. She's lightly editing when Fox quietly joins her. He leans in close but not too close. Sensing what he wants, she shows him her screen.

He snort-laughs, just as subtly as before in the car. "Nice."

"Thank you." Pleased, Joy uploads the photo, and then tugs on one of the straps of Fox's life vest. "Are you really getting in the water?"

Joy's had an ongoing love affair with the ocean since she was five, but lakes are a different story. There isn't much that can convince her to swim in one this far away from the shore without proper diving gear.

Fox frowns. "Hopefully not."

"Then why the jacket?"

"I don't really know how to swim."

Joy resists the urge to laugh. Admitting that clearly made him uncomfortable. "But Summer said you two were going to boogie board behind the boat?"

"Hmm."

Fox's non-committal grunt suits him so well, Joy almost teases him about it, but decides to save that for later. "I'm not trying to tell you how to live your life, but if you can't really swim that's probably not the best idea."

"She shouldn't go by herself." He says it like it's an obvious fact, glancing Summer's way. She's standing like a captain, with one leg on the gunwale, the other on the bench seat, and her hands on her hips as they continue talking to the strangers.

"Well, that's certainly an admirable reason to risk your life, I guess." Joy shrugs. "Lucky for you, I happen to be an excellent swimmer. In the event you do foolishly decide to get in the water, and something goes wrong, I suppose I'll have no choice but to save you."

A grimace flits across Fox's face so quickly Joy almost misses it. She's about to take back her offer—hey, if he doesn't want her help, let them eat cake and all that—when he asks, "Why are you here?"

"Physically or existentially?"

"Why did Malcolm ask you to come?"

"Why did Summer ask you to come?"

"I'm being serious." Fox keeps his gaze trained on the distance. "I think they're trying to set us up."

Joy's field of vision instantly flares white hot with realization, like a superpowered lightbulb clicked on behind her eyes. She has to sit down. Now. Gripping the rail on the boat, she lowers herself onto the seat.

Are they . . . are they being set up? Did Summer ask Fox to come here for Joy the same way Malcolm asked her to be here for Fox?

Would putting her head between her knees make it too obvious that she's three deep breaths away from full-blown panic? She prides herself on almost never letting the absolute chaos destroying her insides ever, ever show on her face. But this might be the thing to break her.

It doesn't make sense.

Malcolm claims to have a huge problem with Fox. He would *never* set her up with someone he truly dislikes. Actually, he would never try to set her up with someone, period.

Joy doesn't date. Everyone knows that. She's made sure of it.

The tingling in her limbs begins to disappear in time to her slowing heart rate. She laughs at herself, shaking her head.

"You all right?"

Fox hasn't moved. He's still standing in the same spot with the cooler between them, but he's angled toward her now, concern drawing his glorious eyebrows together. From the outside, she must have looked ridiculous. Fine one second, close to hyperventilating the next.

Joy isn't ashamed of many things, including her anxiety. "Does your brain ever just let your thoughts run away from you? Like they're gunning for first in a one-hundred-meter dash and dead set on leaving common sense in the dust?"

"That's quite an image."

"I know. I've spent a lot of time coming up with different ways to describe what happens." Joy takes a deep breath, filling up her lungs, letting the air sit before exhaling. "Anyway, sometimes my brain overreacts, and it takes me a second to find myself again."

"So you have anxiety?"

"I do, but I feel like just saying *I have anxiety* doesn't really capture what I'm personally going through because everyone has their own interpretation of what anxiety means. I prefer to just explain how it *feels* for me outright."

Fox nods. "Do you need anything? Water? Food?"

"I'm okay." Joy smiles like she means it. "Thank you for asking. Not many people do."

"Hmm."

"And no, I don't think they're trying to set us up. Malcolm wouldn't do something like that."

Fox sits down next to her, hands clasped between his knees. "Summer might. If she thinks she's helping—" He pauses. "Let's just say her good intentions aren't always that well thought out."

"You know what they say about hell and good intentions." Joy tries to make sense of what he said, but it feels off. "Why would she think setting us up is helping anyone? Helping what? Who?"

"You." Fox exhales into a sigh. "I'm not sure which of them came up with the idea, but I think they're both in on it. Sorry. I see the way you look at him."

Joy's enduring cool slips for a split second, surprise flitting across her face. Are her feelings that obvious? And if they are . . . why can't Malcolm . . . She exhales through her nose. *Does he know and just . . . not care?*

Deciding to lean into distraction, Joy scoffs and says, "I look at everyone exactly the same. Except for racists, rapists, and child molesters. I'm sure they can see the flames behind my eyes as I imagine them spontaneously combusting."

"Wow." Fox shakes his head, laughing quickly. His mood returns to solemn before she blinks again. How long has he been thinking about this setup situation? It's clearly weighing him down—she sees it in his posture and furrowed brow. She's sure he really believes what he's saying, that he's right. It's kind of sweet how concerned he is.

"How come you two didn't come say hi?" Summer appears with Malcolm in tow. "They invited us to a party."

Joy stares at Malcolm with a clear *that's not on the agenda* look. He gets the message, saying, "It's the night before we leave. It'll be fine."

"I bet," Joy says dryly. She didn't believe Fox over Malcolm— he's done nothing to earn her trust and Malcolm has done everything to earn her benefit of the doubt.

All she knows is someone is lying to her.

Big mistake.

Summer picks up the bright pink board resting on the ground. "I think I'm ready to go in. Fox?"

Fox obliges, grabbing the orange board that matches his vest. Once they're in the water, Joy volunteers to be lookout and direct Malcolm. She projects her voice, making sure Fox can hear her. "Remember, the key to staying alive is to stay calm. My swimsuit is for show and not swimming, but don't worry. I'll still save you even if I have to do it naked."

"Joy," Malcolm snaps from behind the wheel.

"What? I'm trying to make sure he stays calm."

"By saying you'll rescue him naked?"

"In matters of life and death, nudity is irrelevant." Joy gives Fox two thumbs up and a big smile. "Don't panic! I'll come get you! Summer, you're on your own!"

"*Joy.*"

"*What?*" She turns to Malcolm exasperated. "I can't rescue two people at once. I already promised him."

"You're doing too much."

"I'm only doing what you asked me to." Joy looks him up and down once, twice, and a third time, gaze brimming with suspicion and hard as flint. "You told me to focus on Fox, did you not?"

To his credit, Malcolm holds her gaze but can't quite match her attitude. He begins navigating the boat forward slowly at first, looking back to make sure they're holding on before accelerating to a slightly faster speed.

They don't return to the cabin until late in the afternoon. After unloading the boat and taking everything back inside, Summer says, "I'm going to put on some shorts, and then we'll go?"

Malcolm nods in agreement. The next item on the agenda is a leisurely walk around some of the trails and roads surrounding the lake.

"Fox?" Summer asks hopefully.

He doesn't answer, turning to Joy instead. "Me? Are you asking me? Is that what that look means?" she teases, expertly hiding her surprise. "Unfortunately, no. I'm only allowed one outdoorsy thing per day and walking through bear country is a bridge too far."

Besides, the only slot in the agenda where she can make the cake is now. Dinner is scheduled to arrive at the exact time their little excursion is set to end. Malcolm will need the kitchen.

Fox says, "I think I'd rather lie down for a little bit," directly to Summer.

"Okay."

Joy doesn't bother changing out of her swimsuit. There's a rack

of aprons in the pantry—she selects a black one covered in strawberries and ruffles—and gets to work rummaging around the
kitchen for everything she'll need. As expected, she also finds a
teal stand mixer waiting for her. She's arranging her ingredients
around the counter when Malcolm and Summer descend the steps
together.

Every ounce of her concentrates on not glaring at them. Her
thoughts haven't stopped whirling around the fact that it's possible
the two of them decided to play Cupid with her life.

Summer's crestfallen face does nothing to affect Joy's mood.
"Oh, you're baking now."

"You wanted it for tonight, didn't you?"

"Yeah. He's asleep so now *is* the perfect time. I just thought we
would make it together." Summer glances at Malcolm. "Well,
Joy would make it and I'd keep her company."

Not wanting to have another eye battle with Malcolm, Joy
sighs theatrically. "Go. Do your outdoorsy thing. Betty Crocker
worked alone and so do I."

Betty Crocker isn't even a real person. Not that they know
that.

"Now I really can't leave." Summer pouts.

"You really can." Joy queues up her baking playlist. "Now.
Get out."

Malcolm walks around the counter and kisses Joy's temple before he goes. "Come on, Summer." He wraps an arm around her
shoulder.

The key to making a good cake is to sing to it. Just like plants,
cakes appreciate positive encouragement. It's not long before Joy
loses herself again—just her, the music, and the cake batter.
Nearly forty minutes pass before she finishes weighing the last

pan, making sure it has the perfect amount of batter, so each layer comes out even. She slides the cakes into the preheated oven, making sure again they're the perfect distance apart. She closes the door, turns around, and almost jumps out of her skin.

"*Fox!*" she shouts. "Don't do that! You can't just sneak up on people in a kitchen full of knives. Make a noise or something!"

He's standing near the island and turns her music down before saying, "You were going to stab me?"

"I was going to defend myself," she says. "I've never been here before. There could be serial killers running around for all I know. That's how it happens. That's how they get you. Take the strangers out and no one will notice they're missing until it's too late."

"You watch a lot of horror movies?"

*Yes.* "Maybe. You think that boat showed up today out of the kindness of their nosy hearts? They're planning something, and I don't think it's some innocent party."

"Hmm." He sits on one of the gray stools in front of her. "We need to talk."

"Maybe." Joy creates a pile of her dirty dishes and walks them to the sink. "I'm still deciding if I believe you or not."

"Because I don't have proof?" Fox scoffs. "What would I gain from lying to you?"

"You tell me. You're the potential lying liar."

"Can you at least admit that it's strange we're both here? I had no idea you were coming. Malcolm asked Summer, then she asked me, and I couldn't figure out why until I saw you today. She even said, 'Maybe you can spend time with her while I'm with Malcolm.'"

A wildfire begins to rage in the back of Joy's brain. *Stay cool. Stay calm. It's not his fault.* She turns on the tap and quickly washes everything, setting the clean dishes onto the drying rack. After wiping her hands, she leans against the sink, watching Fox from across the room. *Stay cool. Stay calm. It's not his fault.* "Malcolm said she invited you because it's your birthday and you two had plans."

"We did, but she could have canceled them."

Joy nods, biting her lip. "He asked me to keep you company so he could spend time alone with Summer without you getting in the way. I didn't think anything of it. I don't think he did either."

"I guess we can agree to disagree on that. Doesn't change that something *is* happening around us. And that something is trying to push us together."

"What's your story, then? No fair you've got my number and you haven't given me yours."

"I don't have a number."

"Lying liar."

"Only that time." Fox's amused half-grin barely lasts two seconds and it stuns the shit out of Joy. She flinches from the force of it, eyebrows leaping without her consent. It's undoubtedly sexist to ask someone to smile, but *oof.* Finding out what kind of jokes he likes magically shoots to the top of her to-do list. "Summer and I used to date. We decided we'd be better off as friends."

"'We'? Or she?" Joy asks, knowing she won't get an answer. And she doesn't. "I get it."

"You do?"

"Two strangers, both alike in dignity, and in love with our best friends who are interested in each other." Joy takes the seat on his left. There's no harm in being honest with him. "Not to bare my soul a smooth four hours after meeting you, but this is old hat for me. His partners come and I'm still here when they go."

"Here waiting?"

"Not exactly. Things . . . changed for me this past year. I don't think there's anything wrong with being friends with someone you may or may not be in love with as long as you don't expect anything in return. My love for Malcolm isn't conditional. I just haven't figured out a way to be honest with him about things yet."

"About said changes?"

"You're a smart one," Joy teases. "This whole best friend setup is really blowing my mind, though. Why would she bother doing all of this?"

"Aren't you supposed to be obsessed with bad puns?" Fox's friendly assessing squint nearly makes her laugh. "I'm surprised you didn't say 'The Ex-Trap.' You know, like *The Parent Trap*."

Joy laughs. "Okay, one, I am, and that was *excellent*. Unfortunately, two, it doesn't exactly fit because I'm not Malcolm's ex."

"What?" Fox looks genuinely confused. "I just assumed that—"

"Nope. Never."

No dates. No flings. No drunken one-night stands. But there was one kiss.

Years ago, during college, she and Malcolm were at a bar with their friends. Somewhere in between sober and sloppy drunk, they had found themselves alone in a hallway. He stood so close to her she almost forgot how to breathe. When he leaned down, nose brushing against hers, she'd been sure her heart would stop before what was happening could happen. It hadn't.

That one kiss with Malcolm changed the course of her life story for the second time.

It took five years for her to realize it'd barely been a footnote in his.

Fox says, "That changes things."

"How so?"

He's silent long enough for Joy to get bored while waiting for him to explain. She gets up and gathers the cold ingredients to start the raspberry ganache while he continues to take his sweet time thinking. To keep the pressure on him, she throws well-timed eager glances in his direction while cooking, but the most he does is bite his lip. It takes nearly ten minutes for him to finish his thought.

"They're trying to pair us up, so what if we did? Let's give them exactly what they want and see what happens."

# Eight

Joy blinks at him once, twice, and a third time. She waits for the punch line, not at all picking up what Fox dropped.

"Stay with me," Fox says slowly. "Malcolm is obsessed with you."

"It's not just him." Joy fidgets from a modicum of self-aware discomfort. "We know that we're . . . how do you say, preoccupied with each other?"

"Joy, I knew you before I even saw your face because all he does is talk about you. I don't even think he realizes that everything he says somehow circles back to you. *My friend Joy saw that movie and she loved it, I took my friend Joy there, my friend Joy this,* and *my friend Joy* that—he always has something to say about you. About how wonderful you are."

She winces knowing she's just as guilty of doing the same. "We're working on it. Sort of."

"So you can admit there's more to it, but he can't? I think that's because he hasn't realized it yet. Making him jealous might do the trick."

"Nope. Not gonna work."

"Have you tried it before?"

"Also nope."

"Then how do you know it won't work?" Fox asks earnestly. "Let's put it to the test. We pretend like we've hooked up and go overboard with PDA in front of him to see if something sticks."

"You trying to ram your tongue down my throat and dry hump me will look super fake. Or things will really go sideways, and he'll try to fight you for making me uncomfortable. I'm asexual." Joy can't stop herself from laughing at his suddenly bewildered expression. "And so is Malcolm."

"Seriously?"

"I'm a card-carrying member. Ran for club president twice." She winks at him.

"Are you winking because you're joking or . . . ?"

"You know how bisexuals get cool jackets and finger guns? Aces get winks."

"Really?"

Joy snorts. "No. Now I'm messing with you. I just like winking." She pushes her pretend glasses up her nose. "Every ace is different. Some are like Malcolm, who experience zero sexual attraction but still enjoy sex more than any human I know. Some are like me, who also don't experience sexual attraction, but haven't quite figured out the rest of it. And some are elsewhere. Everything in between, beyond it, and beside it." She makes a show of creating a semicircle with her hands, like the rainbow meme. "It's a spectrum. The more you know."

Joy gives him time to process. People usually need it. Some can be super rude and start bombarding her with questions, expecting her to quickly spit out answers like an internet search engine. She can only speak for herself and has vowed to always be upfront about how she felt.

"But your pictures? And your clothes? And on the boat? The dances you did . . . I'm confused." Fox rests his elbow on the island and his chin in his hand. "And I'm sorry in advance because I'm somewhat sure I just fucked up somewhere. I'm not trying to be offensive."

This is the other reason why Joy likes to wean people into telling them about her side hustle. She models clothes of all kinds including lingerie—whatever *she* feels like wearing, she puts it on. The day Savage X Fenty sent her an email she damn near fainted.

Bodies are just meat suits and she happens to love hers. The way it looks in clothes *and* the way it looks naked. She loves feeling her version of feminine and loves that she's asexual. All parts of her respected and treated with equal care.

Being confident in clothing doesn't *have* to equal sexy. The way her legs look in a good pair of thigh-highs makes her giggle with delight. She routinely walks around in a flowing satin robe with feathered cuffs because it makes her feel chic. The perfect dress, the perfect pair of shorts, the perfect sweetheart neckline, the perfect pair of flannel pajamas—everything she puts on her body has to feel exactly right. Every photo she posts has to make her feel that same loving energy.

Joy isn't ever *trying* to be sexy, but she knows that's a projection and misconception she'll always have to contend with.

"I don't know if I like you yet," Joy says. But she appreciates Fox being aware enough to know that he had toed the bigoted line and apologized. "I'm going to go out on a limb and help you anyway."

He nods, giving her his full attention.

"I know that what I consider confidence is mistaken by most for me wanting to be sexy. Being ace doesn't mean I'm a prude or modest or celibate. It means I don't experience sexual attraction. Point-blank, period. It has nothing to do with how *I* feel about my body. Nothing to do with how *I* choose to express myself. Nothing to do with me trying to attract a man or 'trick' people. Get past it or don't. It's not my problem. I'm not responsible for someone else's arousal when everything *I* do is for myself."

Fox sits back in his seat, processing.

She continues, "And I dance because I love it. As far as I'm concerned, shaking my ass is a competitive sport. It takes time and practice to learn how to do that, okay?"

"Okay, yeah. That makes sense. I think I get it."

"I won't dim my shine for *anyone*."

"Not even Malcolm?"

"No. He would *never* ask me to."

"Just one more question," he says. "Has he ever seen you with anyone else?"

"No," she says, taking the conversation shift in stride.

"Have you ever dated anyone since you met him?"

"No. What are you getting at?"

"You love him *and* you're in love with him. He must know that because you're overbearingly honest, so I'm assuming you just came out and told him."

"Was that an insult?" She narrows her eyes. "And a pun?"

"I think he knows how you feel, and I think that's his excuse for never following through. What if he's just used to having you all to himself? He's assuming you'll always be there because you always have been."

"Hmmmm, but I *am* always going to be there for him."

"Yes, I get it, you're honorably devoted. The point is, he *thinks* he doesn't have to do anything else because he already has you." Fox huffs in frustration. "He's told Summer all about his past, and she's unfortunately told me against my will, so I *know* he gets around."

Joy snorts with laughter.

"Meanwhile, he's never had to share you with anyone else. I'm proposing that maybe it's time for him to see how that feels."

"Proposing," she says, thoughtfully. "Does that mean I get a ring if I say yes?"

"Are you saying yes? I don't want him with Summer, and you want to be with him instead. I think this'll force him to face the truth."

Fox's proposal seems so counterintuitive, though—Malcolm *asked* her to spend time with him. He's expecting her to do it. But . . . what *would* happen if she fell for someone else while he's watching? Even if it isn't real, what happens if he believes it is? Joy can predict almost everything about Malcolm. Strangely, she doesn't have an immediate answer for that.

"I'm not saying you're right or I agree. But some points may have been made." Joy tries to play it coy, looking over her shoulder at him. "What about Summer? What brilliant realization is she supposed to reach?"

"That Malcolm is in love with you."

"He's not, though. I'll give you obsessed because that's admittedly mutual, but he does like her. He's not faking it, if that's what you think."

"I know," he says. "But that doesn't change the fact that they want us together, which is the topic at hand."

"Summer. Not 'they.'" As far as Joy can tell, Summer is the only one who stands to gain anything at the end of the charade. It adds up nicely: Malcolm told her about Caroline, which means he probably told her about the email. If she's heard so much about Joy, she could have orchestrated a plan to meet in a controlled environment . . . with a distraction thrown Joy's way so she could keep Malcolm to herself.

Or prove Caroline right. Joy is the problem. Joy is the one holding Malcolm back, sabotaging any chance he has being happy with someone else.

Shit.

Joy upgrades from chewing on her lip to gnawing at her cuticles. Summer truly has her stressed. "It doesn't bother you that she's doing this?"

"Things could be worse." He meets her gaze. "Pretending to like you wouldn't make the top ten worst things to ever happen to me."

"What a nice, diplomatic way of saying I'm number eleven. Thanks."

Fox tries not to laugh, but he's struggling. He seems determined not to smile or show any expression other than harassed and grumpy ennui.

Joy crosses her arms in triumph, mirroring his posture. "Hypothetically, how would this work? Between us, I mean."

His whole face brightens, but he still doesn't smile. "Well, you said no kissing. No dry humping. Anything else off-limits?"

"A lot, probably."

"Like what? I'm just trying to make sure you won't slap me if I hold your hand. If we're not comfortable with each other, he'll never believe us."

"I think I'll reserve the slapping for when you do something with a bit more *umph*," she says. "And I never said no kissing. Trying to lick my lungs and kissing are two completely different species of PDA. But don't kiss me, though. I don't like surprise kisses."

"Is all kissing off-limits?" he asks. "There's more than one kind of kiss."

Affection can be tricky. It honestly depends on the person and her mood. Romantically speaking, she loves it when Malcolm touches her. There's never been a time when she shied or shimmied away from his good morning hugs, drunken cheek kisses, or cuddles on his couch.

The thought of Fox touching her doesn't make her stomach flip in excitement or turn into a black hole of anxiety. Thinking about him feels okay. Neutral. That could be promising.

"May I?" Joy holds her hands out to him, smirking. "Touch me, please."

Fox looks at them, at her face, and then places his left hand on top of hers. She lets it rest there for a moment, waiting for something to happen. When it doesn't, she takes his hand in both of hers.

"You're so warm." His skin is surprisingly soft, but his palms are rough and calloused from overuse. What could he possibly do for work to make his hands feel this way? Joy continues exploring, tracing the blue-tinted veins down his wrist.

"That tickles," he murmurs.

"You have nice hands." But what would it take to let her give him a manicure? Because his palms and cuticles are hollering for help.

"Hmm." Fox pauses and adds, "Thanks."

Joy lifts her gaze to his face so she can see his reaction when she smiles at him. He looks tired—gray half-moons have set up shop under his brown eyes—and tense. The movement is so slight, if she wasn't looking for it, she would've missed it. Her smile affected him like he had to brace himself for impact in a good way. He knows the crash is coming and he's ready for it.

It's what convinces her to say yes.

"Okay, I'm in. I've tried everything else. Might as well go for the Hail Mary too." Joy lets him go. "Don't kiss me on the lips or anywhere near my mouth without permission. If I say stop, you have to give me space immediately."

Fox places his hand on the counter, but only for a moment. He curls his fingers into a fist and moves it to his lap. "Maybe we should come up with a code word. *Stop* is firm but also alarming. I don't want them to worry because we're figuring out boundaries."

In their earlier game where she counted his words, he had limited himself to single-word responses. Quick, playful, and petty. "How are you at word association? If I say a flower, you have to say one back that starts with either the first or last letter. That way if they ask why I randomly keep saying flower names, we can say we made a bet and are trying to stump each other."

Fox gives her an appreciative look. "I like that. All right. Flowers." He stays with her in the kitchen while she moves on to making the frosting. By the time the front door opens, excitement is buzzing in Joy's veins. She gasps, exhilaration getting the best of her.

"Relax," Fox whispers.

Joy's never done anything like this in her life before. Will they really be able to pull this off? "I don't know if I can. Does this feel really exciting to you too?"

"I wouldn't say 'exciting.'" He glances at the entryway. "Shh, here they come. I'll start it. Follow my lead."

"Okay. Yeah. Okay. I can do that."

He holds her gaze, skeptical but amused. "You sure?"

"Yeah, I got it. I can be cool. I fake date people all the time."

Summer appears first, surprise written across her face. "Oh," she says, gaze darting to the cakes set out on the cooling racks. "Have you been up long?

That poor sweet Summer child. Still clinging to hope that a birthday cake could be a surprise on someone's birthday. Fox didn't even ask about it.

"Unfortunately. Still having a hard time sleeping, but Joy's been great company."

"It's true. I *am* great."

"That you are." Malcolm's eyes are on his phone. He probably doesn't even realize he spoke out loud. "Delivery should be here soon. Do you need help cleaning up?"

"I got it." Fox stands up. He walks around the counter, picking up the remaining dishes that Joy hadn't taken to the sink yet. "Tell me more about your twin."

"You *do* have a weird thing with twins. I knew it."

"It's not weird."

"But it's a thing." Joy joins him and asks, "I wash, you dry?"

"No. And yes." He pauses then adds, "You're very . . . intense. Two of you would be too powerful."

Joy considers this, trying to keep a straight face and not laugh. "Intense how?"

"Just intense."

"I need more than that. I'm trying to decide if I want to be offended or not." She turns on the tap, letting the water run until it warms up. "You think you're slick, but I see you. I'm Annie Oakley and I got you in my sights."

"You did not just quote *Kill Bill*?"

Joy gasps.

"And don't think I didn't catch that *The Strangers* reference earlier."

Joy gasps again.

Fox playfully side-eyes her. "You're not slick either."

She gets an idea, ready to drive this dry-run performance home. She's all in, cards on the table. "Are you flirting with me? Because if you are, I'm totally into it. Movie flirting is the best kind."

This seems to be too much—a *what the heck?* expression breaks through Fox's cocky demeanor. Overbearingly honest is her brand, he said it himself. That's exactly what she would say even if they weren't trying to make it seem real.

Joy winks at him, as if to say *trust me*, then pretends to do a double take over her shoulder.

Summer and Malcolm are side by side with mirroring blank expressions on their faces. They're both just *standing* there, staring at them.

"What?" Joy asks. "Is something wrong?"

"No," Summer says quickly. Malcolm doesn't answer.

Joy shrugs, turning back around. She grabs the soap, squeezing it onto the sponge. "Why be cool when you can dazzle?" she says to Fox. "Good luck figuring that one out."

"Oh, I will," he says and then *winks* back at her.

# Nine

The food delivery arrives right on time. Malcolm wastes no time shooing Joy and Fox out of the kitchen, but Summer stays behind. He's going to teach her how to make . . . something. The dinner menu isn't listed on the agenda.

Fox says, "Joke's on him. Summer can't cook. At all."

"Malcolm's a good teacher. There's also recipe cards."

"At. All."

Joy laughs as they sit on the couch together. "What should we do, then? Sitting here is nice. It's an extremely comfortable couch."

"It is. But sitting might be too passive."

Joy glances toward the kitchen. Malcolm and Summer aren't worried about them in the slightest. All their focus is devoted to each other and the food.

Fox continues, "We need to come up with something they can see us doing while they're cooking." His arms are loose at his sides, but he taps his right thumb against his knee as he thinks. He's wearing a gold band—there's an engraving on it but the words are hard to make out.

"Like what? I don't really know what couples are supposed to *do*."

"The most important thing is we spend time together." Fox scratches the side of his face. "I have an idea, but I'll have to touch you."

Joy eyes him, trying to keep her suspicions at a non-antagonistic level. "Touch me where?"

"Wherever you want. I'll be right back."

Fox rises from the couch and heads for the kitchen. He asks Summer something, she nods with a grin, and then he leaves, taking the stairs two at a time.

As much as Joy doesn't want to admit it, the fish out of water vibes are thriving at the moment. Relying on him when his idea starts with *I'll have to touch you* is mildly terrifying because it's way too open-ended. She's never dated, but she isn't *inexperienced*.

Dating suggested eventual permanence. An agreement to join forces and be something together to see where it leads. She's never done anything of the sort. The furthest she's gone is connecting—that's what she likes to call it. Malcolm has always been the only one for Joy, but she's kissed people before.

Joy actually likes kissing. Quite a bit. At parties with friends of friends of friends, after spending time together, talking all night, and maybe drinking a little too much. She doesn't suddenly get filled with a raging passionate fire and the only thing that can put it out is sex. Kissing someone, being close enough to share body heat, to caress their skin and revel in the texture, to touch and memorize their face and feel their breath, the rise and fall of their chest—that's an experience all its own. A connection.

But it always stops there. No calls. No messages. No exchanging contact info. One night, a couple of hours, and a handful of kisses doesn't mean she isn't thinking about Malcolm or that she doesn't want to be with him anymore. It's a nice distraction from the pain, until her heart pipes up: *No one will ever accept you the way Malcolm has. No one will ever understand you the way Malcolm does. No one will ever love you the way Malcolm could.*

No matter how hard she tries, she can't think her way out of that logic because deep down she believes it.

When Fox returns, he hands her a package. She reads the label. "Temporary body markers. Why do you have these?"

"They're not mine." He sits beside her again. "Summer loves tattoos but is too scared to get one, so she uses these all the time instead."

"Your plan is to give me a temporary tattoo? Well, okay. Rome and all that. Can you draw?"

"I'm decent. Where do you want it?"

"Right here, please." Joy places her arm on the back of the couch, palm up. "Just under the crease."

"I'm going to touch you now." It's a statement but the question is in his eyes. Not quite worried. Not confident either.

Joy nods to give her consent. Fox takes his time, moving at a measured, even pace. His rough hands glide gently along her skin, repositioning her arm to give him clear access. She gets the distinct feeling he's treating her with kid gloves, like she's a scared cat who'll lash out at him if he moves too fast. Slowly, because she doesn't want to startle him either, she slides toward him to make it easier for him to work. There's a clear swath of space between their torsos, but their heads are bent together, their knees touching.

Joy doesn't mean to whisper, but it feels right to do it while sitting so close. "What are you going to draw?"

He whispers back. "Let me surprise you."

"Okay." Her smile grows shyer with anticipation. "It better be good, or else. This is my first temporary tattoo after all. No ragrets."

"You're in good hands." He lifts his gaze from her arm to her face, expression soft. Still no smile, though. "Keep talking to me like this. It's good."

"What do you mean?"

The first stroke of the pen tickles her skin. "They're too far away to hear us. They have to go by what they see, and right now, I'm sure we look very cozy together."

"I do feel cozy, yeah." For a moment she watches him work, creating large, curved lines and loops, gracefully arcing across the length of her forearm. "What should we talk about?"

"Whatever you want."

"What does your ring say?"

Fox inhales sharply. His frown is quick and doesn't last. "It's a reminder."

"You don't have to tell me. Forget I asked."

"It's fine. My best friend died a few years ago. My ring reminds me of a promise I made to him before he was buried."

Oh. *Excellent work, Joy. Simply fantastic.* Now that she's opened the door, it'd be rude not to honor his honesty with sincerity. "Do you miss him?"

"Every day. But he'd be mad at me for being sad that he's not here anymore, so I don't let myself be."

Joy considers him carefully, gaze searching his side profile. His answer was unexpected to say the least. It's not that she doesn't believe him, but is it possible to have such a command over something as wildly unpredictable as mourning? He spoke with such assuredness, she almost believes it is. "I didn't know grief worked like that."

"It's mine," he answers, glancing at her quickly. "I can do whatever I want with it."

"That you can." Quiet settles between them. Joy laughs, gently and embarrassed, to ease the awkwardness. "I'm sorry, I don't know what to say now."

"You can say whatever you want. By the way, don't look. Malcolm's watching."

Joy reflexively tenses up. Saying "don't look" makes her want to do the exact opposite. "Maybe I should laugh and say 'ahahaha, Fox, you're so funny' or something?"

Fox gives her a curious look, shaking his head. "Definitely not. Just be natural. You're doing fine."

"Natural, yeah. Okay."

"The trick is to let their brains do the work for us. Nothing you'd say would ever be better than what he makes up for you."

His gaze flicks upward to the kitchen and back down to her arm in the span of a second. "They're both watching now. It's working. All we have to do is keep up appearances."

Keep up appearances because this shared moment isn't real.

Joy drags her teeth across her bottom lip before pulling it into her mouth. Are constant reminders that they're only pretending supposed to be an integral part of fake dating? Striving to "keep up appearances" sounds no better than going through the motions—dry and repetitive.

She isn't sure she wants to do that. How *boring*. Performance or not, there's no reason why they can't have a good time. They should be taking this time to properly get acquainted. Eyes on the prize *and* each other.

Unless Fox doesn't want to. Maybe this is all business to him.

"Finished." He's drawn a butterfly with oversized antennae wearing a three-pointed crown. "It's called a Lange's metalmark."

"I love it. Thank you."

"You're welcome."

Joy would never confess to having a romantic bucket list under oath, in a court of law. Its alleged existence may or may have not included a list of fifteen items she may or may not have wanted to experience someday. Hopefully with Malcolm, but seeing as how the alleged list began when she was in high school, she hadn't had him in mind when writing it. His name filled in the alleged blanks much, much later.

If she had known she'd love sitting on a couch while a cute guy drew a temporary tattoo on her arm, she would have added it. Allegedly.

There's also something on that alleged list she could do that night. "I kind of want to dress for dinner. I'm going to head upstairs and get ready."

Fox doesn't hide his surprise, replying, "Oh. Okay. I'll see you later, then."

Joy takes the time to properly unpack, hanging up her clothes so the wrinkles will fall out. She isn't sure what she wants to wear yet. A poll on Rule of Thirds could help her decide, but she doesn't feel like logging in. She must have posted close to twenty powershots of her on the boat. No need to punish her click-through rate any further.

According to the agenda, after the dinner they would watch a movie and then follow Summer's lead for the rest of the night. She needs to be comfortable for that, but she isn't quite ready for a pajama set. Her hand stills over one of the fancier dresses she brought. Because she has a date.

They're "together" now. Joy has a "boyfriend." Imagine that.

Besides being unsure about wanting kids, one more obstacle nagged at Joy: whether she'll be a good *romantic* partner for Malcolm or not. She has being a supportive best friend mastered and down pat. They're already affectionate. They have ten years of history behind them. They barely have any secrets. But something must change when the shift from friend to girlfriend occurs. There has to be some additional element she's never experienced before.

What else will Malcolm expect from her? Will she be able to handle it?

Spending time with Fox can be her chance to find out if she's even capable of going beyond connecting with someone. This is safe. It's practice.

No one has to know she's pretending it's real. No one has to know she's preparing for the real thing with Malcolm later.

Maybe she should wear something Fox would also like. Or something she thinks he would like, since she doesn't know him well yet. She's never gotten ready for a date before but has seen her sister and former roommates do it. There's the shaving, the plucking, the running around with nerves, the outfit changes, the agonizing over which perfume to wear, the makeup and hair . . .

Joy used to love those nights—doing everything she could to help them feel beautiful, feel prepared and ready to conquer the world. Clothing and makeup as armor. Confidence and daring as their weapons of choice. And the way they would gas each other up, taking photos and laughing. That's what she remembers most: the laughter and happiness. How supportive they all were of each other.

Her very first date and she's getting ready alone. Being honest, that seriously bums her out a little. So, of course, she calls her sister.

"What are you doing?" Grace says when she picks up.

"I need help. I technically have a date tonight."

Grace's reaction goes from disbelief to screaming to full-blown witch-cackling when Joy tells her about Fox's idea. "That's diabolical and I *fucking* love it! Yes! Take me to the closet right now."

Joy's white floral lace maxi dress number won the night. The deep V-neckline on a princess-seamed bodice, the short cap sleeves, the delicate buttons in the back, the flowy skirt; no shoes, just summer fairy queen vibes; lips and toes painted a vibrant plum color—the perfect balance between casual and ethereal. She painstakingly piled her braids up into a high ponytail to show off her teardrop-shaped amethyst earrings.

"Okay," Summer says when she sees her. "Next time you go shopping, you *have* to take me with you. Please, please teach me your ways."

Joy isn't sure if she can trust the awestruck cadence in Summer's voice because she's been fooled before. But . . . it felt like a genuine compliment? If Malcolm hadn't looped his heartstrings around her, Joy suspects she might like her.

It just sucks that everything with Summer so far had to be viewed through so many different lenses. It's kind of exhausting. Stripping everything else away, and letting Summer stand on her own, she reminds Joy of Megan, who pops by her office every day just to wish her a radiantly cute good morning.

Fox enters the dining room, immediately stopping short. "Whoa."

"Hey, hey." Joy smiles as she watches him drink her in. His gaze travels from the base of her dress up to her face in one uninterrupted, leisurely motion.

"You look *great*. I, um, *wow*." Fox blinks in what looks like adoration masked by disbelief.

Times like these, when people suddenly get shocked into speechlessness, Joy usually makes jokes like *I hate to break it to you, but I'm very beautiful. Sorry you didn't notice before* to help them recover. A quick shot of too much self-aware confidence somehow always brings people back down to earth. She's learned, over and over and over, that no one likes a woman who thinks too highly of her looks and is daring enough to speak on it.

But not this time. For once, she wants to revel in the feeling of someone she wants to see her this way appreciating the work she's put in to look nice for them.

Joy meets his gaze with a pleased smile. "I feel great too."

Malcolm drops a metal spoon on the ground. It clangs against the floor, splashing sauce everywhere. "Sorry." He's looking directly at her—she knows it's not on purpose. He can't help it. All the attention in the room belongs to Joy now. "Slipped out of my hand."

Dinner is a fabulous affair courtesy of Malcolm's skill. Seared scallops with brown butter and lemon sauce, butternut squash steaks also with delicious brown butter, salad topped with blood oranges, and an impossibly creamy risotto with crispy roasted mushrooms.

"I made the salad," Summer says sheepishly. "The rest was too advanced for me."

"Don't feel bad." Joy sits in the chair closest to her at the dining room table. "This is too advanced for *everyone*. I'm sure your salad is amazing too." Fox takes the seat next to her, while Summer and Malcolm sit across from them, leaving the heads of the table empty.

Summer scrunches her nose. "You're just being nice."

"I am. Nothing wrong with that."

Malcolm begins by opening a bottle of wine, chosen because it pairs well with seafood. He pours everyone a glass, only hesitating for a moment when he reaches Fox. After, he holds out a hand for Summer's plate and she obliges, passing it to him.

Malcolm has always been that way. Cooking, plating, serving food—he happily allows the entire hosting experience to fall on him. Unfortunately, it's just another way his type A personality manifests. If he's in control, no one can disrupt his dinner. No one can taint all his effort.

Joy's been working on gently pushing Malcolm out of his controlling comfort zone in situations like this for years. She didn't want him to plate her food because she didn't like it. They eventually learned to meet in the middle. He always offers. She usually declines.

When he sets the salad tongs down, she picks them up and fills her plate. And for her next trick, she turns to Fox. "May I?"

"Oh, I can—"

"No, no. Please. Let me."

Malcolm watches her do it. She gives him a cheeky smile and wink for his troubles. Whatever he does for Summer, she'll do the same for Fox. She'll take her cues wherever she can get them until she figures this thing out.

Once their plates are full, Malcolm begins to bless the food by asking everyone to bow their heads. Religion is an essential part of Malcolm's life, affecting almost everything he does. He grew up Catholic but converted in college after he began to regularly attend a Baptist church near campus. Joy was mildly surprised to not see going to church on the agenda for the trip. He's done it before—researched welcoming churches they could visit during their travels. It's possible Summer isn't as religious as he is and he wanted to respect that. Joy doesn't know.

Malcolm concludes his prayer. "Let's eat. Enjoy."

"I can't believe how good this looks." Summer eats one of the scallops and pretends to pass out in her chair. "Oh my god. This is magic."

Joy snorts. "Malcolm the Magician strikes again." She takes her first bite—okay, Summer wasn't exaggerating. The risotto practically melts in her mouth, sending her taste buds to heaven and back again.

"Jesus," Fox mutters as he chews. "I think it's illegal for vegetables to taste this good."

Malcolm says nothing. Bragging isn't his style. He's always preferred to let the testimony of others speak for him and his work. But Joy, who can read him better than anyone, knows how pleased he is. Mission accomplished; his nervousness begins to fade. He sits up a little straighter, the worry lines disappear from around his eyes, the tension in his jaw relaxes. He pushes a button on a small black remote and melodic jazz music begins to float around the room.

As they eat, Summer starts to tell a story about a disastrous school play she had the misfortune to direct. Everything went wrong, from some of the plastic elements for the set design melting during a heatwave to a small outbreak of lice.

The entire time Joy keeps catching Fox staring at her. He turns away quickly—but not quick enough—whenever she glances his way. Suddenly, his plate, his wine glass, even the ceiling at one point, are the most fascinating things he's ever seen. His chaotic nervous energy electrifies her into giddiness.

Joy resists the urge to laugh at him, hiding her smile behind her napkin. People stare at her daily for a multitude of reasons: her face, her body, her skin color, they recognize her—and she's gotten used to it for the most part. Any problems they have with her are *their* problems. She's never given much thought to receiving attention like this before.

It isn't like when Malcolm admires her. He does so openly, and without embarrassment. With Fox it's almost like he feels guilty for looking at her too long. As if he's only allowed to catch glimpses of her while she's not paying attention, but it's not enough for him to hold on to. He has to try, try, try again until he can get the image of her to stick in his mind.

Feeling bold, she rests her elbow on the table and cradles her cheek in her hand (manners be damned). Keeping her voice low, she says, "Hi."

Fox wastes no time giving her his full attention. "Hey."

The lights in the room flicker—quickly turning off and on, accompanied by a loud buzzing noise. Joy looks at Malcolm, who seems just as confused. The music cuts in and out, like a record skipping, before shutting off completely.

"Power surge?" Fox asks.

Now it's as if someone is turning a knob, dimming the lights until they're almost out, leaving the room almost pitch-black. Joy can barely see Summer and Malcolm across the table. She reaches out, holding Fox's forearm for comfort and to make sure he stays near her. He covers her hand with his, bringing it closer to him.

Suddenly, the lights flare back on even brighter than before. The music starts playing again, picking up right where it left off.

Joy glances around the room. "What in the murder mystery—"

"Oh. My. God." Summer's jaw is practically near her plate. "Malcolm, did you rent a haunted cabin?"

"Uhh, not on purpose."

Fox says, "Ghosts aren't real."

"Mmm." Joy gives his arm a gentle squeeze. "They don't like it when you say that."

"You can talk to ghosts?"

"No, but I'd be pissed too if someone said I didn't exist."

"Everything seems fine now." Malcolm sighs, frustrated. "That was probably a power surge. I'll find the circuit breaker and look later. Let's just finish eating."

Joy lets go of Fox's forearm, laughing lightly. "Thanks."

"You know what could be fun?" Summer sets her wine glass down. "We should go buy a Ouija board—"

"*No,*" Joy and Malcolm say together.

# Ten

After dinner, they all move to the living room.

Malcolm sits directly in the middle of the sofa.

Clearly left with only one option, Fox sits alone on the love seat.

Summer doesn't even hesitate, positioning herself on the sofa—Malcolm's right and Fox's left, giving her access to both of them.

Joy watched all that play out, analyzing the scene like a long-suffering English major. The empty place at Malcolm's left is where she's expected to be. He's her homing beacon. Wherever he is, she won't be far behind. It's unconscious and habitual, and she needs to stop.

She pivots mid-step, heading for the love seat. Fox subtly adjusts himself to give her more space but doesn't remove his arm from the back of the couch. His fingers hover near her bare shoulder, close enough to caress. Struck by inspiration, she angles her body in hopes it reads as if she's waiting for him to put his arm around her.

He won't—she doesn't think either of them are there yet—but Malcolm and Summer don't know that. They're inching ever closer together right under their noses, one milestone at a time.

Joy checks in with herself constantly, waiting for discomfort to settle in. Personal body space has always been deeply important to her. She doesn't think of herself as a special untouchable snowflake— no one likes being touched without permission.

But she does obsess over it more than most—always considering how close she is to the next person. *Am I too close? Am I making them uncomfortable? Do they need more space? Should I back up?*

And now she's so aware of Fox, centimeters away, and it's driving her up a wall. He's a radiator disguised as a man. He's so *warm*, she feels the heat rolling off his arm onto her back. The flower game means she's uncomfortable. If she says one, he'll move, but she's fine.

She just needs to know if he's okay too.

Summer and Malcolm are scrolling through the movie catalog. Their words are for the room at large, assuming they're paying attention. Fox isn't. True to form, he looks bored. And grumpy.

"Hey," she whispers, attention split between him and Malcolm. The sofa is close enough that he and Summer'll hear if she's not careful. "Do you need a *flower*?"

Fox's attention snaps back from wherever he'd mentally gone. She can literally see his focus return as he stares at her, frowning in alarm.

"I'm fine," she assures him. "Are you? Is this okay?"

He nods. "Yeah. Sorry. I heard you say 'flower' and thought I did something."

Oh. "I'm sorry too. I realized you don't have a boundary word and got worried."

"I don't need one. You can do whatever."

Joy's eyes widen, completely aghast. What kind of trust— Who thinks like that? She's spent years building up her walls, setting boundaries, and making sure people *know* how it's going to be. And here's Fox You-Can-Do-Whatever Monahan—wild with abandon. She couldn't even conceive of wrapping her mind around that kind of freedom.

"What do you guys think?" Summer gestures to the screen. They'd narrowed it down to two popular movies: a dark comedy and a romantic thriller.

Joy votes, "Uh, thriller?"

"Thriller," Fox agrees, watching Joy again. He's so relaxed, half-reclined on the love seat without a care in the world. His head is cocked to the side, temple resting against his fist, arm propped up by his elbow.

"Majority rules," Summer says happily, and presses play.

None of them have seen the movie before. They speculate about what the infamous twist ending could be, trying to solve the plot together. About an hour in, the leading couple has their first kissing scene. Joy lets out an involuntary "Ew."

Fox asks, "On-screen kissing bothers you?" His amused tone makes a grand return.

"When it's fake. They have zero chemistry. It's the worst." Joy shudders. "Grosses me out. I hate watching it."

"Oh, because you're asexual?" Summer asks.

Joy freezes like a deer in headlights. She stares at Malcolm. *Did you tell her that too?*

His eyes are wide, shaking his head and looking as stricken as she feels. *No, of course not.*

A few tense heartbeats later, realization clicks into place for Joy. "*Oh*, right, you follow me online. Right, right."

Coming out online had felt like the second biggest mistake of her life. On a whim, she participated in a hashtag for aces to raise awareness by uploading a photoset of herself wearing outfits inspired by colors of the ace flag. She never for one second thought those pictures would leave her tiny bubble on the internet.

In less than twenty-four hours, her *entire account* had gone viral, and everything imploded.

Summer seems to recognize her faux pas, expression quickly shifting to embarrassment. Her cheeks darken with a creeping red flush. "Oh my god, I'm so sorry. I shouldn't have blurted that out."

"It's fine," Malcolm says.

*It's not.* Joy scowls at him. Suddenly, he doesn't see her, purposefully avoiding making eye contact.

Summer begins gently flapping her hands. "I just thought we all knew so it didn't matter. You two are the only asexual people I've met."

"That you know of," Malcolm says, kinder than Joy thought he should be. "Some people aren't ready to talk about it even if they've figured it out."

"Hey," Fox says suddenly. He barks the word, drawing the entire room's attention, but his gaze slowly slides from the screen to Joy. His face is completely neutral as he considers her. Strangely, she can't look away. She isn't sure how long he holds her captive like that, but it's beginning to feel excessive.

Joy's lips quirk into a smile. She can't read Fox like she can with Malcolm, but that buzzing exhilaration from earlier begins to return. Something is coming. He's planning their next move.

She's perfectly fine waiting for him to say whatever is brewing in that mind of his.

His lips part and he inhales before asking, "Which onscreen couple do you think has the best chemistry?"

"Julia Stiles and Heath Ledger in *Ten Things I Hate About You*," she says, not missing a beat. "Oh, and Max and Kyle from *Living Single*. I remember thinking if romance wasn't going to make me feel like that, I didn't want it. Which should have been a huge neon sign for later, but you know, hindsight and all that."

"I love that movie," Summer says with a nod. "I think *Mr. and Mrs. Smith* is a good example too."

Malcolm sucks in a breath. "Nooo—"

"See now, that's different," Joy says.

"Here she goes." Malcolm pauses the movie.

"Shut up, I'm right," Joy says playfully. She pulls her legs up onto the couch to sit on her knees, neatly arranging her dress around her so it doesn't snag. "Chemistry and sexual tension aren't mutually exclusive. If I see sexual tension, I can recognize it. Like in *Portrait of a Lady on Fire*. The *yearning* in that movie is off the charts. I've never seen it in real life, though."

Joy studied movies because she had to. She literally thought everyone was making sexual attraction up. She'd heard countless people describe it, read literally hundreds of romance novels—there's never any feelings low in her belly, no shivers down her spine. She doesn't have to cross her legs at the sight of veiny forearms, perky breasts, bubble butts, or perfect abs. It just doesn't happen. The day she realized it was, in fact, a *very* real thing absolutely blew her mind.

Summer asks, "This might be kind of crass, but have you ever been to a strip club?"

Joy nods. "Athletes, every one of them. Their bodies are so strong, it's incredible."

"Well, yeah, but you're talking about girls, right? At male strip clubs it's way different. I think you'd see it there."

"Doubtful. I've seen *Magic Mike* and that's not sexual tension to me. That feels like a performance of lust on both parts. The women in the audience are gassing the strippers up because they're doing a good job. That doesn't mean *both* parties want to have sex," Joy says. "It's like, uh, okay cool, you're very fit and there's your bulge. What's that supposed to do for me?"

Malcolm bursts out laughing. He doubles over, holding his stomach, absolutely losing it.

"Why are you laughing? I'm being serious," Joys says, unable to stop herself from smiling.

Fox has turned his face firmly toward the window, hiding his mouth behind his fist. Malcolm is wheezing now, crying for Jesus to help him.

"I thought we were having a serious conversation!"

"I'm sorry, but it's kind of funny," Summer admits, unable to hold back her giggles anymore.

"It's not!" Joy's mouth is slightly hanging open in performative shock. "I don't get it. I feel the same way about people sending nudes. Like, the one time I tried a dating app on a dare, my inbox got *flooded* with dick pics. Why?"

Summer recovers first. "Oh, unsolicited dick pics are super gross across the board. But. Like. If I'm dating someone and I ask for it, that's different. Then it's okay."

Malcolm has started staring into space. Every few seconds he almost loses the battle to another laughing fit.

"But why would you ask for it? It's just a picture. I don't get it.

What am I supposed to do with that? What is that supposed to do for me?"

Fox comes back and says, "Use your imagination."

"I've been doing that for fifteen years. I'm tired! I just want the answers! Give me cheat codes."

"No," Fox says, a mixture of frustrated and . . . embarrassed? Why would he be embarrassed? He runs a hand down his face. "I mean, that's what you do with it. You use your imagination. Sexting."

Joy watches him closely, processing what he's said. Softly, she replies, "No."

Malcolm loses it again.

"Will you stop?" Joy demands around her own pleased laughter. "Help me explain it to Fox and Summer, you jerk." She throws a pillow at Malcolm, who catches it.

"Okay, okay. Wait, hold on." Malcolm has to take several deep calming breaths before he begins. "Let go of the pictures for a second. Let's say you're with someone and they get naked. And then so do you."

"Hold on, let me stop you right there—"

"No, no, no. It's fine. I'm gonna explain it for them. There is absolutely no miscommunication, you both know what's happening, but this is where things stop for Joy. Seeing a naked someone, thinking about them being naked, does nothing for her. It doesn't happen even if there's an emotional connection between them. They're just naked."

"But if you know nothing is gonna happen, why would you get naked?" Summer asks.

"Because I don't care?" Joy shrugs. "Yeah, that trips a lot of people up. I like being naked. It truly doesn't bother me."

Malcolm tosses Joy's pillow back to her. "She's practically a nudist."

"Since I was twenty. Living in a dorm profoundly changed me. I'll get naked right now and be perfectly comfortable."

"And just to clarify," Malcolm continues, "nothing will happen without an active decision to have sex on her part."

Summer asks him, "Is it like that for you too?"

"Mostly. I've leaned demi enough times to make me question it."

"That's so strange to me," Summer says. "I understand what you said, and it makes *sense*, but I can't reconcile it in my brain." She makes a motion of trying and failing to link her fingers together.

Joy says, "And now you know how I feel. Two different sides of the same coin."

End scene.

Joy's seen that lightbulb moment so many times she's lost count. She became a pro at explaining by accident. If she treated everyone else like the special unicorn, if she pretended to be fascinated and baffled, if she stopped pleading and begging for them to understand, it stopped the questions. It makes them think. It's simply less emotionally exhausting to center their experiences.

"So you never think about sex? Ever?" Summer pushes.

"Oh, I think about it all the time, because I have to."

Understanding visceral sexual attraction will always be out of her wheelhouse. But she does try to understand it on an abstract and physical sensation level, like how Malcolm did. Sex is everywhere! It's inescapable! A lot of the time she felt like if she didn't get on the bandwagon she'd be left behind to die of cholera on the trail.

Joy continues, "Eventually you get tired of hearing 'stop leading me on' and getting violently threatened after accusations of
'being a tease.' I had to learn how to recognize situations like that.
I know what their expectations are. I know how to flirt, work a
room, and dazzle people. I also know my limits and how to keep
myself safe."

"Oh, I guess I didn't think about it like that." Summer glances
at Malcolm for help, but he shrugs. "There's good stuff too. Like
in a *you get turned on and you want to have sex* kind of way. Oh god,
you just said you didn't, I'm sorry."

"I never said that." Joy holds back a reluctant sigh. "For the
record, I do get 'turned on' in a manner of speaking. Attraction
has nothing to do with *my* libido. She wants what she wants when
she wants it, no outside influence required, if you catch my drift.
A few days before my period, it gets rough."

"What do you do? Just wait it out?"

"Pfft, no." Masturbation is a biological wonder. Sometimes, it
could be so good it would clear up a migraine. "Why suffer when
masturbation exists?"

Fox suddenly says, "I'm going to the kitchen, anybody want
anything?" and doesn't stop to wait for an answer. He doesn't even
stop in the kitchen, walking straight past it.

"Oops," Summer says, with a tiny laugh. "Fox is a little, um,
conservative. Very modest."

"We made *him* uncomfortable?" Malcolm asks, voice thick
with disbelief.

"Probably." Summer takes the remote from him and presses
play.

Meanwhile, Joy is *devastated*, feeling completely horrified. Fox
lied. She'd (rightfully) made such a big deal about boundaries and

flowers and within thirty seconds of him giving her carte blanche, she makes *him* uncomfortable. She turns back to the TV, trying to pay attention to the movie and not her racing thoughts. Her breathing is too fast, her chest aches, and regret won't stop pummeling her. Fox had been sitting right next to her—how come she didn't notice his uneasiness?

Joy endures five more unbearable minutes before leaving to go find him.

# Eleven

The front door is mysteriously cracked open. Joy spots Fox through the window next to it, sitting on the porch swing.

"Hey, hey." She aims for casual while lingering in the doorway. "In the mood for company?"

"Sure."

One-word answer, and it's like a stab in the heart.

Joy sits down, leaving a good amount of space between them. The temperature has dropped some, but the warm summer air is still winning. "So. About earlier."

"What about it?" He glances at her before turning back to the stars.

How conservative is conservative? The nudity was probably too much. Should she use euphemisms? She didn't want to risk upsetting him again by accident.

"I didn't mean to make you uncomfortable." Joy focuses on the sky too. Country dark is truly a sight to behold. The moon, stars, and constellations—everything so clear and close. "I, um, had to learn how to be, um, detached and, um, blunt, in conversations like that as a defense mechanism, you know? A sort of *get them before they get you. Make fun of yourself before they can do it* kind of situation."

"Okay."

Joy swallows, steeling herself so she can keep going. "The things that I said, I've been practicing saying them for years. They don't really bother me at all anymore. It's a script—those things about me are true, but they're also safe. I can say them because I have a general idea of how people will react and how I can steer the conversation as needed.

"I didn't want to be mad at Summer, but it was happening. And I didn't want Malcolm to be mad at me for being mad at Summer. She made a mistake, and so I ran with it to diffuse the situation for all of us. I know not everyone had to learn how to cope like that and are more, um, modest. I'm sorry."

Fox inhales, chest rising and then falling. When he turns to her, he's frowning. "Yeah, I thought I could fake my way through that. I have no idea what you're talking about."

*Huh?* "What? What do you mean?" she asks. "Earlier. We were talking about sexual tension and chemistry. I made the conversation take a turn, you got upset, and it's all my fault?"

Fox's laugh gets stuck in his nose—not quite a snort, but close. He even has to turn away for a second. "You didn't do anything."

"Oh," she says, leaving her lips in a thoughtful pucker. "Then what's wrong?"

He turns his entire body to face her, resting his arm on the top of the swing. The movement rocks them backward, making them sway gently. "Joy," he says, leaning closer. "Thank you for not getting mad at Summer. And it's very sweet that you're worried about me, but I'm fine."

Joy wishes she could believe the soft expression in his eyes, but there's something else there, drawing her in and trying to show her the truth. "Are you lying? I feel like you're lying."

"Do you always do that? Just say whatever you're thinking? You think a thought and it has to be said."

She shakes her head. "I like cutting to the chase. If I wanna know something I ask. If I have something worth saying I say it. Life's too short and I'm too old to hold back."

"Then why haven't you told Malcolm you want to be more than friends?"

"That's different." Joy sighs. "Asking if you're lying affects nothing whereas saying that to Malcolm could potentially shift the entire course of my life. Do you see the imbalance there?"

He goes quiet again, eyes downcast and focused on the stretch of wood between them. "I think that's your problem. He's used to you being open and not holding back. I'm just guessing here, but if you had something to tell him, he would expect you to tell him."

"Maybe with everything else. Not this. I've tried before and it's like he doesn't hear me. I want to find a foolproof way to get through to him before trying again."

"Hmm."

"You're thinking. I can see you thinking."

Fox exhales in a huff, eyes flashing with irritation. "You don't have to comment on everything I do or don't do. New rule: Is it possible for you to stop doing that? It's a bit much for me."

"Oh no, but that's my entire personality," she whispers, pretending to be hurt. It earns her the slight laugh she hoped for.

Joy often went where her thoughts led her. If something pops in her head and she wants to say it, she does. Doesn't matter if anyone else understands or not. If they went along with the conversation, she could keep it going. She discovered that it *was* annoying to some people, so she altered her behavior around them—toning herself down, keeping quiet—but Fox didn't seem truly annoyed.

"What if I kept my thoughts to myself fifty percent of the time?" she asks.

He counters with "Eighty."

She grins. "Sixty-five?"

"Deal."

"You got it," she says. "Can I tell you something?"

"Oh, we're asking permission now?" he teases. "Usually, you just let it rip."

"I'm glad I met you. I don't believe in fate, but"—she pauses, thinking back over the day—"you really made today worth it."

"Worth what?" His voice is so close to a whisper, the crickets nearly drown him out.

Joy smiles, her best and brightest. "Everything." Out of the corner of her eye, she sees Summer approaching the door.

"Oh, um, Fox, hey, Malcolm needs you for something in the bar room. Could you help him?"

"No," Fox rumbles.

"Please?" Summer pouts, placing her hands in the prayer position. That must be a favorite move of hers. "Come on."

"Fine." Fox heads inside without another word.

Joy lifts an eyebrow. "Cake time?"

"Cake time." Summer nods, barely able to contain her excitement.

In the kitchen, they work together, quickly placing and lighting the candles. Summer wanted to buy and use twenty-nine candles—fire hazard be damned. Joy convinced her to instead make the shape of a two and a nine with singles.

Malcolm's voice sounds through the kitchen, "OH LOOK, A CORNER."

"Here they come!" Summer jumps up and down, clapping her hands.

"No, really?" Joy laughs.

"Why are you yelling?" Fox stops short when he reaches the kitchen.

Summer immediately begins singing the "Happy Birthday" song *on-key*. No one ever sings that song on-key. She sounds so good Joy doesn't want to ruin it, and by the looks of it neither does Malcolm. He must not have known about this hidden talent of hers either.

When Summer finishes they all clap, and she says, "Blow out your candles!"

While Fox does, unable to help herself, Joy quickly sings three lines from the chorus of Stevie Wonder's version of "Happy Birthday." It's her family's tradition—she has to. Jazz hands and all.

Fox turns to Joy. "Is this the cake you were making earlier?"

"Mmhmm. Three-layer marble cake with buttercream frosting and raspberry ganache." The cake itself turned out pretty okay. It slopes slightly to the right and the buttercream accidentally has a pinkish tint to it, but Joy has faith it'll taste the way it's supposed to. Not too sweet, but still flavorful with a good, moist texture.

"It was for me?" He says it with such surprising tenderness, it stuns Joy into silence.

What kind of birthdays were he and Summer used to that they didn't even expect a cake?

"That's why we went to the store earlier." Summer hands him a knife. "I wanted to get you something and all the cakes were bad. Joy volunteered to make one instead. From *scratch*."

That isn't entirely true, but Joy lets it stand. Hey, if Summer wants to give her credit, she's in no position to turn it down.

"Thank you." Fox is practically bleeding sincerity. It's truly a sight to behold. "Both of you."

"En-*joy*." She grins as Malcolm loudly deflates.

Birthday Cake Time isn't on the agenda. He was being a good sport about the interlude, but Joy's pun seems to have pushed him over the edge. The solid line between his eyebrows that only appears when he's frustrated is out in full force. Did Summer not being the center of attention for five minutes really upset him that much?

Doesn't he realize Joy incorporated yellow cake for him because it's his favorite? When he eats it, will he notice how she held back on the sweetness for him too? That she chose tangy raspberries over ripe strawberries? This cake is for Fox, yes, but it's also for Malcolm. From Joy to both of them.

"I'll get some plates." Malcolm, still slightly frowning, reaches behind him and opens the cabinets.

Maybe Fox is right. Maybe Malcolm really does take her and the things she does for him for granted.

Joy tries to shake the thoughts away, pasting a smile on her face. It's not Malcolm's moment. She isn't going to let him ruin this. Not everything in her orbit needs to be about him all the time. She bumps into Fox with her shoulder, leaning into him. "Happy birthday."

And then, Fox smiles at her—Joy almost doesn't believe what she's seeing. Even when he laughs, the low grumbling scoffs and reluctant chuckles she manages to pry out of him, he keeps a near perfect straight face.

And now he's actually *smiling*.

At her.

And he has *dimples*.

ce

N ighttime routine complete, Joy turns off the lights before getting into bed.

That was a mistake.

When there are no city lights beaming in from the outside, pitch-black hits different. It instantly transforms into the kind of dark sleep paralysis demons and shadow people like to hide in.

Joy clicks the light back on to get her bearings, staring wide-eyed at every corner of her borrowed room. Her phone is charging on her nightstand. She brilliantly decides to leave the screen on all night, brightness turned all the way up. A MacGyvered night-light being better than nothing at all.

The second her head hits the pillow, she closes her eyes, but sleep refuses to show up. Instead, she replays the day over and over. Her memories mostly get stuck around Fox being surprisingly wonderful and Summer blurting out that's she's asexual.

In a perfect world, people would just say, "Okay. That's cool," but so far that hasn't been the case. Education goes hand in hand with coming out over and over and over . . .

What Summer did wasn't anything new. Her brain is just using it as an excuse to dredge up older trauma, forcing her to relive those moments.

After her hashtag miscalculation flung her right into the spot-light, aces from all over the world began leaving encouraging messages on all her posts, her follower count quadrupled, media outlets contacted her for interviews and guest posts, modeling agencies reached out to her—Malcolm had to help her sort through it all.

But everything wasn't all roses and cake. Trolls came out of the woodwork to harass her. Some even made videos about her, rating her pictures using disgusting made-up scales. A religious community even tried to make an example out of her, which was just weird.

Then, there were the comments that nearly took her out—the ones from other aces who *hated* her. Joy was "setting a bad example for the movement" and "confusing people" and "making it worse." She was "problematic" for taking her clothes off because "real aces don't act like that." She was faking and making it up for clout.

Instead of creating space for her at the table, they'd chosen violence—to serve her up and eat their own.

So she flipped that motherfucking table over instead.

Joy never asked to be anyone's role model or ace queen but became intensely anxious of letting anyone down anyway. She researched and boosted other voices and strived to be inclusive of the entire spectrum. No ace left behind.

If someone said they were ace, then that was that. They were welcome in her circle. She made room in her brand of bougie on a budget to include self-care, self-acceptance, education, and awareness. Joy isn't perfect, but she always, *always* does her best because it's the only way she knows how to hold on to people. The only way to keep them on her side.

Being accepted matters to her. Probably more than it should. She wants to belong and to be understood so badly it physically hurts. Her chest aches for it, every minute of every day. It's why having Malcolm in her life is so vitally important to her. He was the first. He's still the best.

Still unable to sleep, she decides to head downstairs for a midnight snack. She tries to be quiet, bare feet padding down the halls and then stairs. The lights are on in the kitchen.

Malcolm holds up a pint of ice cream and two spoons. "Took you long enough."

Joy mock-gasps as she joins him at the island. "How did you know?"

He rolls his eyes but answers seriously, "You almost never sleep on the first night of vacation."

"I'm in a new environment," she says, peeling off the lid. "I have to adjust. And I miss Pepper."

"I was shocked you didn't bring her. Mrs. Norman?"

Joy nods. "Pepper hated the drive to Arizona so much, and I didn't know where we were going . . ." she trails off.

Three months ago, they'd rented a camper to drive to the Grand Canyon. Pepper hated the road trip, spending most of it hiding in one of the cabinets, but she loved being outside and exploring the paths. Joy's current phone wallpaper is a picture of Pepper wearing her harness and perched on top of a boulder like she's the Queen of Pride Rock surveying her kingdom.

She continues, "It's fine. She loves Mrs. Norman and her one thousand hanging plants."

Malcolm nods toward the couch. They walk the few feet to the living room and get comfortable.

Joy has the first spoonful. "I didn't see this in the freezer."

"There's an extra one in the garage." Malcolm eyes her. "Don't go in there."

"More surprises for me?"

"I'll know if you do," he warns.

When they arrived at the cabin, her heart had sunk because it knew none of this was for her. And that was still true. The weekend belongs to Summer, but Malcolm remembers her here and there—little things like a room with a perfect shower, a window that will face the sunrise, hiking shoes, and midnight ice cream. So many tiny adjustments solely for her and her alone. She never has to ask. He always knows exactly what she needs to feel special.

"So what do you think?"

"I think it's delicious." Joy shoves another spoonful into her mouth.

"Joy."

She sighs through her nose. Guess they're doing this now. "Summer likes you. But."

"But?"

"But I think it's more of a *sure why not* kind of vibe instead of what you're looking for."

Malcolm doesn't look surprised. Or angry. "You always do this." His resignation is so complete Joy feels terrible for telling the truth.

"Do what? You asked my opinion and I answered. I don't see it," she says. "Do you want me to lie? Sure, okay, you two are great together. She's super into you and no one else."

"She's nice," Malcolm says. "And she really likes you."

"For now. It won't last because it never does." Joy sighs, weary and tired. "Eventually, she'll start thinking I'm around you too much, that you pay too much attention to me and not her, she'll get mad, make you choose, and then I get put on standby."

"I have never put you on standby," Malcolm says, snapping with sudden anger.

Not true.

One time. He did it one time, but it'd be unbelievably cruel to mention her right then. He also didn't even try to put a dent in the rest because he couldn't. That's how it always ends. An ultimatum and a goodbye.

He says, "I always choose you and you know it."

"I've never asked you to do that. You don't get to be mad at me."

"I'm not mad. I'm . . . frustrated."

"Because I don't see it for you and Summer?"

"Because you *never* see it for me and anyone I date."

"That's not true," Joy says, deciding to try and lighten the mood. She doesn't want to fight with him. She doesn't want him to be mad at her. She doesn't want to feel like shit for making him upset she doesn't she doesn't she doesn't—"There's also Summer's face."

Malcolm frowns at her, deciding if he wants to take the bait. "What's wrong with her face?"

"Forget Resting Bitch Face—"

"Joy, don't."

She couldn't resist. "—and get ready for Resting Princess Face. She's always smiling."

With teeth, mouth closed, with her eyes, smizing. Summer's entire body is one giant smiling superpower. She must not care about wrinkles—parentheses, crow's feet, and all that.

Joy doesn't either, not really. She likes cataloging the changes in her face, the new wrinkles, creases, and moles. That doesn't mean she's lazy with her skin care. She uses all the good stuff to help with things like replenishing elasticity and staying hydrated, but she isn't obsessed with smoothing, tucking, or hiding. She wants to look her best—the best version of thirty-year-old Joy that there can be.

Malcolm asks, "You have a problem with her because she smiles too much?"

"Did I say that? Did I say it was a problem? All I did was point it out." Joy grins.

Malcolm sits back, slumping against the couch. "I don't understand what the problem is, then. She likes you. She's trying damn hard to be friends with you"—he pauses—"and not like the others, okay? I know, I know. She's the real thing."

"Sure. If you say so."

"Would it kill you to be supportive?"

"Supportive?" Joy knew this would happen. "Look, I'm here, okay? You asked, I'm here, I'm spending time with Fox and keeping him away from you, just like you asked. I don't have anything else to give you right now. So I'm sorry if I don't feel like lying and saying *oh, you're so cute together, and me and Summer are gonna be best friends forever*. But don't tell me I'm not being supportive when you didn't even want me here in the first place."

Unless he did.

Malcolm sold this trip on the grounds of keeping Fox distracted. What if the true purpose was to keep *Joy* distracted? To make sure she didn't get in the way this time? She ruined things for him with Caroline, Summer convinced him all Joy needed was someone else to focus on, and what do you know, she has a friend—

And Joy fell right into the trap because she *does* like Fox.

All at once, her brain is sure this conversation is a test. He's checking to see if Joy will be a problem, checking if their plan is working. Joy not accepting Summer, who's just trying oh so hard, proves that it doesn't matter who Malcolm finds.

Joy is the problem. Joy has always been the problem.

The inside of her chest feels like it's crumbling to pieces. Is she really being supportive or is she desperately trying to convince herself that she is?

She doesn't want to believe it, but everything makes sense, falling into place like jagged puzzle pieces.

*He's used to you being open and not holding back . . . if you had something to tell him, he would expect you to tell him.*

Malcolm sighs, picking at the couch cushion. "I want to get married and start my family. I feel like I'm wasting time. I'm tired of searching."

Joy swallows hard, pushing down the sudden rising panic. For better or for worse, Malcolm's happiness has always been a priority in her life. But what she's doing now is the opposite. It's unhealthy and it's selfish. Her fixation on Malcolm isn't good for either of them. The longer she delays her confession, the worse off they will be. She breathes to stay focused and manages to keep her voice steady as she asks, "You really think Summer is the one?"

Malcolm bites his lower lip, pulling it through his teeth. He doesn't look at Joy when he says, "She could be."

# Twelve

## SATURDAY

Joy's mood lifts the second she swipes on the last coat of mascara.

Yellow sweater crop top (thin and breathable cotton).

Fitted high-waisted lavender shorts (tailored to her measurements).

White Air Force 1s (older and broken in).

Silver rings on her index and middle fingers with a matching bracelet on her right wrist. Small hoops on her ears. Braids half up with curly bangs freshly re-dipped in hot water.

Every day, step by step, from brushing her teeth and completing her skin care routine to inspecting her final look in the mirror, she concentrates on herself and saying her affirmations. But despite her best efforts, this morning all she thinks about is Malcolm. Her life and how Malcolm saved it, changed it, wrecked it. *Everything* he does affects her and vice versa. Part of her screams *that's Not Good!!!* but they reached the point of no return ages ago. And another part of her instinctually knows they're rapidly approaching another wall.

She needs coffee. Now.

No one else has made it downstairs yet. Kitchen all to herself, she plays some mellow morning music and dances, swaying around the kitchen while her coffee brews.

*You always do this*, he said.

*I want to get married*, he said.

*She could be*, he said.

Joy had tossed and turned and had full-body frustrated tantrums while she struggled to fall asleep. Upset with herself for fighting with Malcolm. Upset because he was partially right.

Fox ambles into the kitchen, eyes still heavy-lidded with sleep.

"Hey, hey," Joy says, aiming for cheery and bright, and not tormented by her unrequited emotions. "Do you like coffee?"

"Why?"

She places one hand on the counter and the other on her hip. "Oh, I don't know. I'm just standing here in the kitchen in front of a full pot of coffee and a cabinet full of mugs for my general health and well-being. Why do you think?"

He has the grace to look sheepish, features softening as he rubs his hands down his face. "Sorry. I didn't sleep well."

"Too loud? Too quiet? Too dark? Mattress not good?"

He takes a seat at the island. "I'm a tea person."

"Ooh. What kind?" She holds out the fully stocked tray for him. He picks one and she turns on the electric kettle. "This is my first time in country dark. I actually kept a light on all night."

"I grew up in it," he says absently while folding a napkin into increasingly smaller halves. "You get used to it eventually."

"Really? Where are you from?"

"Why?"

She rolls her eyes. "Because I wanna know you. *Obviously.*"

His *face* shrugs, nearly making Joy laugh. "I didn't realize that was part of our arrangement."

It must take his voice an exceptionally long time to warm up. He still sounds like he's been gargling gravel—rumbly enough to start an earthquake.

"Well . . . have you ever fake dated someone before?" She places her forearms on the counter, leaning over to be closer to him. He doesn't back away.

"No."

"Then why can't it be?"

Joy only knows how to give one hundred percent of herself. Once she took a pottery class, and surprise, surprise, she became obsessed with it. Within a few months she began selling her creations because they were good. Initially, working at Red Warren was supposed to be temporary. A stopgap job that paid substantially more than what she was making at the time until she figured out what she really wanted to do post-college. And yet she ended up devoting her entire existence to ensuring Malcolm's business was a success by taking classes and training courses, and learning everything she could about business to help him. She wouldn't know how to half-ass something even if she got paid to figure it out.

She continues, "I'm all in if you are. We get to make as many rules of engagement as we want. One of mine is I'd like to get to know you. The man behind the grump."

"I'm not grumpy."

"Oh yes, you are."

His face scrunches in disagreement. "Grumpy feels like a toddler who needs a nap."

"Or a pair of old men who've been neighbors too long," she says, referencing the movie. "Hmm. Yes." She begins to laugh, a deep and mischievous chuckle that refuses to be held back. "You're much closer to that because you're a Silver Fox."

"No."

"Oh my god. *Oh my god.*"

"Do not call me that. I mean it."

"But why?" She's trying, but she can't stop laughing. "You're beautiful. It's perfect. Not just anyone can be a Silver Fox. It's an extremely specific and dignified category."

"What?"

Joy's laughter begins to fade when she looks at his face. It's like she shocked the last remnants of sleep out of him. He's sitting straight up, alert and completely focused on her. His eyes bore into her like she has a secret and they're about to dig it out. "What?"

"You just—you just called me beautiful."

"Oh. Well. Um." Joy clears her throat. "Yeah. I mean, you're good-looking. Objectively speaking." She gestures toward him. "Your face and stuff. For an older gentleman."

"I'm not old." He bristles.

"We all are," she says seriously. "It's fine. Getting old is mostly great. I might change my mind once my knees give out on me, though."

"I'm not old," he insists. "I just have gray hair. It's genetic."

"Clearly that's a touchy subject for you so I will drop it."

Fox runs his hands through his hair, pushing the longer pieces back from his face. It's a good head of hair, thick and layered with a slight curl. It looks better this way instead of that slicked back thing he tried to pull off yesterday. "I used to dye it for a while, but eh. My grays are gonna gray."

"It suits you," she says, meaning it. "Really brings out your eyes."

He scoffs. "Thanks. I've almost made my peace with it."

The electric kettle beeps. Joy heads back to the counter, placing a tea bag into a mug and pouring the water so it can steep. She sets the timer on the microwave and presses start.

"A timer? Really?"

"Time is relative. Trusting my brain's version of five minutes will result in cold tea." She opens the condiment cabinet. "Sugar? Honey? Non-dairy creamer?"

"I'll do it," he says, getting up. And then he's standing behind her.

His skin is radiating heat again—he must be one of those scalding-hot-water-shower people because he feels even warmer than last night—and he smells nice. Aloe? Roses? She doesn't want to sniff him, but he's wearing something way too subtle to be cologne or aftershave. She asks, "Do you use lotion?"

"Yeah?"

That's what it is. Must be. "Good."

Joy tries to not seem shocked. She's long since accepted that not everyone takes moisturizing as seriously as Black people. If her skin has even the tiniest speck of ash between her fingers, her mom rocket launches hand cream at her. She learned the hard way what happens if she waits too long after taking a shower to put lotion on. Her skin literally itches as if she's having an allergic reaction, and when it gets too dry it looks like she's been kicking flour.

"Okay." He says with a lift of his infamous eyebrows. A look that means *this girl says weird things all the time, let it go*. A *go with the flow* kind of resigned eyebrow raise. He caught on quicker than most people and didn't hate her for it. He bargained with her instead.

Sixty-five percent.

"Why are you staring at me?" he asks, with a sideways glance.

Because she likes watching him.

Joy feels herself softening toward him. She can't stop slouching closer, leaning into the space between them, ready to curl around him like an overly friendly cat. She realizes she *really* likes watching him. A man of few words but infinite interesting reactions. And she wants to catch them all.

Continuing to gaze up at him, she asks, "Does it bother you?"

"If I say yes, will you stop?"

"Mmhmm." She nods.

He's quiet as he pulls the tea bag out of the mug, gives it a squeeze, and tosses it in the trash. "Then no. It doesn't." He picks up his drink—no additions—and turns away. "I'm gonna go for a walk."

Fox is *such* a delightful grump. Joy smiles into her coffee, watching him outside until he disappears from view. She moves to the living room and lounges on the love seat while checking the news and her mentions on her phone. The size of her platform being what it is made it somewhat impossible to keep up with comments and new followers. She's used to it for the most part. Besides, burner accounts exist for a reason.

Joy scrolls just to reset the number to zero as she often does, but an interesting username catches her eye—MonahanWoodland had followed her.

Fox has a decent following for a small business. His pictures are mostly scenic shots and wood furniture because he's a *carpenter*. Is that the right word? Or is it *woodworker*? She isn't sure, but there's a time-lapse video of him building a cabinet from start to finish—shopping for wood in a huge warehouse to proudly standing next to it once it's done.

Joy's jaw drops as she clicks a picture of a beautiful coffee table. His captions are straight and to the point: *Coffee Table. Red Chestnut finish. Completed January 6th. Available. Etsy and Monahan Woodland.com*

His main grid keeps to theme fairly well, minus a few pictures. She spots Summer and another woman who looks so much like Fox they must be related. There's only one non-work-related picture of him with a golden retriever. Joy laughs—even with a very happy dog by his side, Fox looks as grumpy as ever. She doubletaps that one and follows him back.

Malcolm finds her like that about thirty minutes later. Still lounging on the couch, systematically liking all of Fox's posts to freak him out. She's never understood why people get so skittish when a new follower likes all their old photos. What's the point of having a public archive if everyone is expected to like it in secret?

"Hey," Malcolm says.

Her heart clenches at the sight of him. He heads straight for her, lifting her legs, sitting down, and lowering them onto his lap.

Joy rests her phone facedown on her stomach.

Malcolm doesn't say anything else, and neither does she. They just . . . stare at each other because that's what they always do. Both feeling terrible. Both wanting to apologize first. Neither one wanting to make the other feel worse. He wants her to go first because he needs her to. He can't react until she chooses the direction their conversation will go in. Just looking at him makes her want to cry and it's just so *stupid* that they're like this. There's always some external pressure wedging itself between them.

He's been this way since he was a kid—a sensitive Black boy surviving in a world where all its stereotypes tried to beat that softness out of him. He feels so deeply and intensely, she doesn't understand how he hasn't shattered into a million pieces already.

But she knows he survived because he's so much stronger than he gives himself credit for. He took those beatings, and he took their slurs, and he refused to let it break him. Growing up he learned how to be quiet, how to hold it in and protect himself. He let other people project their thoughts and feelings onto him to survive. Only people important to him, like Joy, know the truth.

People like Summer don't know. They just see the result and want it for themselves, but they wouldn't know the first thing about caring for someone like Malcolm.

Joy asks, "Do you really feel like I'm unsupportive? Don't tell me what you think I want to hear. I really want to know."

He hesitates by placing his hand on her knee. She knows his answer and he doesn't want to say it.

"Answer me," she presses, voice whisper soft.

"Sometimes."

"Okay." Joy's face feels too hot. Her jaw begins to hurt as she nods in acknowledgment. Her bottom lip pokes out as she screws her face up to keep from crying, but she pulls it back in. "I'm sorry. I didn't know I was making you feel like that."

"I'm sorry too. I really did spring this on you last minute. You were right—you weren't supposed to be here, and I've been trying to make up for it, but I don't think I'm doing a good job."

"You are." Joy places her hand over his. "I'm just . . . frustrated too. We haven't been being honest with each other lately. Why did you keep Summer a secret from me?" She pauses to breathe and find her courage. "Is it because of Caroline?"

Joy wants him to say no, needs him to. She's waiting, holding on to hope as if it's a life raft because it's the only thing between her and drowning. And when the denial doesn't come, Joy turns away in shame. Outside, the lake looks as serene as ever, mocking her with its tranquility.

"I don't blame you for what happened, Joy. When Caroline told me she thought you were in love with me, I told her you weren't. Then she said it again. And again. And she kept saying it until finally, she added that she thought I was in love with you too. That's why she left me." Malcolm stops, jaw flexing as he swallows down the bitter memories Caroline left behind. "She thought I didn't love her more than I loved you. And I don't know if I can honestly say she's wrong. It's just . . . I don't know how to do this anymore."

Joy's next breath catches in her throat as she freezes in place, suddenly terrified. She loves him, she will always be there for him, never leave him, and he always says he feels the same. This can't . . . He can't . . . She manages to force the words out of her. "Do what?"

"Have you in my life and be with someone else. I don't know how to balance it, so everyone is treated fairly. I don't think I ever have."

"So that's it? You're trying to choose between me and Summer?"

"No." Malcolm shakes his head. "There's no choice because it's not either or. I'm trying to figure out how much I'm willing to let go to move forward. We can't stay like this. It's not working."

His responses are so quick it's clear he's been thinking about this for a while. He must have been biding his time, waiting for the right moment to lovingly push Joy to the side. She knows him well enough to know when he's made up his mind and she's already tried telling him the truth.

But she can't give up. Not yet. If she tries to confess now, what if he misunderstands her again? He'll hear what he wants, what he expects, and not what Joy is saying. So what if she flipped it? What if she tried to get an answer from him in another way?

"Why have you never asked me out?" The question tumbles out of her, bold and unyielding. No room for miscommunication.

"I wouldn't do that to you." Malcolm's eyes widen in surprise. "I would never put you in a position to choose between our friendship or something more just to make me happy. My issues are just that—mine. Because of me, not you. I have to figure this out on my own."

"But what if that's what I wanted too? We can just cut everything else out and be together."

He scoffs as if he's insulted. "Joy, I *know* you. You don't have to ever pretend for me. I love you just the way you are. I don't need *more* from you. You give me enough."

Well. That's certainly an answer. Malcolm only cares for her one way—the same way he always has. Joy takes a breath, numbness flooding in. "Okay."

"But I would just like it if you could try with Summer."

"If that's what you want, sure."

*She could be*, he said.

He'd rather settle for Summer than take a chance on Joy.

"Good morning!" Summer shouts as she enters the room, bright-eyed and with damp hair. "Ooh! Coffee!"

Joy closes her eyes. She tries to clear her mind, counting to five and focusing on her breathing. When she opens them again, she forces herself to smile. "Game time," she says to Malcolm and jumps off the couch.

# Thirteen

G ood morning, Summer. You're very loud," Joy says.

"Sorry," she says, before gasping. "Oh my god, I have to tell you guys what happened. This cabin is *definitely* haunted."

"I don't want to know," Joy says to Malcolm, who joins them in the kitchen. "You ask."

He snickers. "Why is it haunted now?"

"So I'm in the shower. Everything is fine. Good temperature. Water pressure is wonderful. Then out of nowhere the water suddenly turns cold. *Cold*, cold. Like, so cold I almost screamed. I jumped back to get out of the way and that's when I noticed *everything* is cold.

"All of a sudden, the entire room felt like Antarctica. I could see my breath. I couldn't touch the tiles. At this point I'm freaking out because there's obviously a ghost in the bathroom with me while I'm naked and shivering for dear life. Ten seconds later, it's gone. Everything begins to heat back up and go back to normal. That's so weird, right?"

"I'll give you weird," Joy agrees.

*"Haunted."*

Malcolm says, "Or the AC is broken and maybe the cabin just ran out of hot water. You were the last one to take a shower."

Summer pouts. "Don't use logic for hauntings. That's no fun."

Breakfast arrives shortly after—a giant spread of fresh ingredients and baked goods. The delivery driver wheels a palette into the kitchen and three more into the garage under Malcolm's strict supervision. He bought enough to last the rest of the trip, making this the only morning delivery.

Once the dining room table is set up, Summer begins piling food onto a plate. She reminds Joy of a guest at a hotel because an air of expectation wafts around her. Of course, breakfast is there. Of course, coffee is ready. *Of course.*

To be fair, the way she's acting isn't all her fault. Malcolm always sets the bar impossibly high. It's easy to fall into being accustomed to being catered to—Joy would know. But whereas Summer's excitement yesterday was peppered with thank-yous, they're non-existent this morning. She's settled in for the ride.

But Joy promised to try harder.

At the moment, though, she doesn't think she has it in her to watch them get married someday. Suddenly, Jules's actions in *My Best Friend's Wedding* don't seem so far-fetched anymore. Her tactics were still horrible, but Joy intimately understood the drive behind them now. Incredulity and desperation taking turns repeatedly sucker-punching you. The dawning horror of realization. A frantic voice screeching, *You're going to lose him forever, you stupid woman.*

It's enough to make a person lose all rational control, that's for sure.

Fox joins them in the dining room not too long after. Joy is sitting at the head of the table this time, and as he passes her he sets something down next to her plate. She picks up the woven circlet threaded with white daises and long-stemmed tiny purple flowers.

Joy is speechless for a full five seconds. "You made me a flower crown?" He went for a walk to go pick flowers and find pliable branches to make her a crown, *dear god*. This little gesture from Fox completely breaks through her drowning anxiety spiral. She gets up from the table, heading for the giant decorative mirror on the wall. After placing it on her head, she fixes her hair around it. It fits perfectly and looks good enough to be sold in a store. Feeling giddy, she adds, "And it matches my outfit?"

"That's why I made it," he grumps.

"Where's mine?" Summer asks, grinning at him. She punches him gently in the arm when he sits next to her.

"Uh, sorry."

"Well, thank you," Joy says, trying to keep her preening under control. "I love it."

"Hmm."

"Always so grumpy," she whispers, watching him. His lips *twitch*.

"So," Summer says, "what are we doing today?"

Malcolm finishes chewing before answering. "We have a couple of reservations for a couple of places I think you'll like."

"Can I know what they are?"

"I thought you wanted to be surprised?"

"I do. Sometimes." Summer picks aggressively at her muffin. "Can I at least know what time we're leaving?"

"Not too long from now."

Summer's smile stays put but her eyes have gone flat, losing some of their shine.

Interesting. Or as Fox would say, *Hmm.*

"Do I have time to go for a walk?" Summer pushes her plate away. "I want to make sure there's no residual ghost energy on me by spending some time in nature."

Fox asks, "Residual ghost energy?"

Joy taps his arm and whispers, "Oh, there was a ghost in Summer's bathroom this morning. Huge ordeal." She speaks quickly, not wanting to interrupt what's happening between Malcolm and Summer.

Malcolm asks, "And how is walking in nature going to help?"

"It clears my mind, gets the blood flowing, burns some energy. That kind of thing," Summer says. "And I was thinking maybe Joy could come with me."

Joy chokes on her orange juice. "Me?" she manages through a slight coughing fit.

"I know, I know, you're not an outdoorsy person, but this trail is really easy. I promise. So do we have time?"

Joy can feel Malcolm's eyes on her. She makes a show of whistling while looking around the room. He's on his own for this one. She said she'd try and she'll go on the damn walk. But if he doesn't want them to go, he'll have to be the one to say so.

Malcolm reluctantly checks his watch. "Will you be back in twenty minutes?"

Joy mutters, "It'll be a miracle if my body lasts that long."

"We'll be quick. I promise. *Ah,* this is going to be so fun."

And that's how Joy ends up walking on a dirt road to get to a thicket to get to a trail in her most cherished Air Force 1s.

Once they reach the start, Summer begins limbering up, as she puts it, stretching her arms and legs. Meanwhile Joy is trying to decide if she should too. She ends up settling for reclining against a tree in the shade. Limber by association is probably a thing.

"Ready?" Summer asks, swinging her arms back and forth in wide arcs.

"My non-sporty body and I are good to go. Nice and prepped to have a cramp attack midway through."

"It shouldn't be too bad. See?" Summer points to a green star in the top corner of the large wooden map. "Green means super easy."

"How thoughtful."

Each trail has markers to ensure travelers don't get lost on their way to the destination. The path Summer chose appears to involve going uphill, something immediately upsetting to Joy and her muscles.

They depart on the winding trail, Summer setting their pace to something a lot faster than Joy's expecting. She watches a spot in the bush like a hawk as they pass it. "Did you hear that?"

"What?"

"It was like a rattling sound."

"There aren't any rattlesnakes here."

"Who said *anything* about snakes?"

Summer giggles. "There might be snakes but not dangerous ones."

"I really hate the woods."

"I know—uhh, I mean, how come?" she says, pairing it with a timid smile.

"Too many things that can eat you, kill you, or bury your body somewhere it will never be found. Don't even get me started on the bugs."

"Bugs are pretty unavoidable. Danger is danger no matter where you are, but we're not in it."

"There could be bears."

"There's definitely bears but they don't care about us. Not unless we go mess with them. They probably know lots of people come through here, so they steer clear."

"Are you trying to make me feel better?"

"Is it working?"

Joy can pretend with the best of them, compartmentalizing so well all in the name of functioning normally. Because inside, she's still reeling from her talk with Malcolm. All those feelings are swirling within her, manifesting the perfect storm, just waiting to be unleashed. But not yet.

She chooses to grin and keep their small bubble of friendly conversation going. "Little bit. Okay, so you made a point about animals and bugs. You seem to be an authority on ghosts, so what about serial killers and witches?"

"Oh, if you think that's what that noise was, it probably is a bear, then. Witches wait until night," she says. "Um, do you like horror movies?"

Joy holds back a sigh. She gets the feeling Summer knows she does. Malcolm must have talked to her about last night, resulting in the idea for Summer to pretend like she doesn't know Joy at all. This is going to get old, fast.

"Maybe."

"Do you ever wonder why horror movies take place at night?"

The incline begins to kick in. Joy has to pace herself, focusing on deep breaths in and out. "Because it's scarier."

"Right, and it's also a cop-out. It's easier to build tension with the unknown if you can't see it. The sun is a timer. Once it sets all bets are off. Gotta make it home before dark, you know?" She's taking deep breaths too, but she's not sweating like Joy is. "But things in the light can terrorize you just as well as things in the dark."

"That's a good point."

At the top of the hill, the trail makes a sharp right, leading to a semi-circle clearing overlooking a long stretch of the woods below. The sun is climbing steadily toward high noon.

"Wow." Summer's mouth is hanging open. "It's so beautiful."

It really is. Joy climbed a mountain! Sure, it was really a hill with a steep incline, but Grace wouldn't know that! She sits down on a bench, happy for a chance to catch her breath. She's (hopefully) not infected with any residual ghost energy, but the walk *did* help her mood a little. Summer sits next to her, unclipping the water bottle from her belt and offering it to Joy first. She tilts her head back, pouring the water without touching the rim. "Thanks."

"You're welcome." Summer takes a drink too. "I'm sorry about last night."

"Water under the bridge."

"Is it really? You're not mad? Malcolm said you were."

"He's not wrong. But I made the choice to not be." Joy leans over and picks up a dandelion. "It puts me in a difficult position when you talk like you know me. It honestly makes me feel weird. There isn't anything we can do about it so no point in dwelling on it."

Joy hasn't decided how much she's willing to trust Summer, how many faces she has, what her motives are. But it costs her nothing to be nice to her for the time being. And it could cost her everything if she doesn't try.

"Here." Joy offers the dandelion to Summer.

"What's this for?"

"I'm not making you a crown. That's as good as it gets from me."

Summer laughs and takes the flower. "I see. Thank you."

Joy stands up, stretching her legs and arms. "We should head back before Malcolm sends a search party to come find us."

# Fourteen

ev

Joy spends the entire drive to Fable's Barnyard Animal Sanctuary in surly silence.

At one point, she feels the eyes of every single person in the car drift her way. Summer keeps trying to bring her into the conversation. Malcolm asks her if she has enough legroom and if he needs to roll up his window. Even Fox attempts to cheer her up by making a horrendously wonderful pun about elevators and stairs.

Misery beat them all, decisively winning Joy's company.

It's too early in the morning to feel so many emotions at once. Too numb to feel sad. Too disappointed to feel angry. Too shocked to feel hurt. Actually, no. There's never a good time to be this conflicted about anything.

Joy promised herself she would quietly step aside.

Past Joy was clearly an overly optimistic fool who believed in her own righteousness a little too much.

What did Fox say about her? That she's honorably devoted? Well. No time like the present to prove it.

After checking them in, their assigned instructor, Savannah, leads the group to a stable near the trail they'll be taking. She's white, tall, has long brown hair, and exudes big horse person energy. The bridge of her nose is red and freckled from a healing sunburn and contrasts with her otherwise pale skin.

Before heading in, Joy pulls Fox to the side. "Did you really have your heart set on horseback riding today?"

"I wouldn't phrase it like that, no." His amused and questioning grin warms her heart. Instantly, she feels exactly how she did earlier that morning in the kitchen. Warm. Compelled. Eager.

"I kind of want to sit this one out. Stay with me?"

"Yeah. Sure." Fox nods. "Everything okay?"

"Not exactly. I'll tell you later."

It'll be easier for Malcolm to let go if Joy steps back. They function the way they do because she almost always goes along with his plans. If she stays behind, nothing will be ruined. In fact, this is probably the most helpful thing she could do. He'll get to spend time with Summer alone.

Joy doesn't like this. She doesn't want to have to do this. It burns her up inside like an uncontrollable wildfire to give up, to step aside, but this is what she said she would do. Being stubborn and selfish won't help either of them.

At least now she isn't going to be alone. For the second time in as many days, she's glad Fox is there with her. Questionable setup situation be damned.

"Joy?" Savannah is gesturing for her to rejoin them. She points to the first stable. "This is Molly. You'll be riding with her today."

Oh, she's *beautiful*. Brown with patches of black, she eats treats out of Joy's hand and nuzzles her face for more when they're gone. One look into Molly's giant dark brown eyes almost changes her mind. It physically pains her to say, "I think I'm too scared to ride. I don't want her to feel my bad vibes. But rumor, and your website, has it there's an open barn and petting zoo around here? With animals in need of scritches, which I happen to be fantastic at giving."

"Yes. Most of them are pretty friendly." Savannah laughs and gives her directions for where to find them.

"You're not coming with us?" Summer asks, helmet already on. Fox is standing next to her.

"Nope."

Malcolm says, "Joy, cut it out."

"I'm serious. I read there are rabbits here."

"There are," Savannah says.

"I *need* to see them."

"We can do that after," he promises.

Not according to the agenda. The schedule is skintight today with barely more than a couple of hours between Fable's and a trip to a vineyard for lunch. He won't be willing to show up late for that. Unless it's for something Summer wants.

Joy tries to communicate with her eyes: *This is what you asked for this is me being supportive you're welcome.* "You two have fun, okay?"

"Two?"

Fox clears his throat. "I'm going to stay with Joy."

Summer's alarmed, "*What? Why?*" startles one of the horses— a small white mare with a blonde mane. Savannah soothes her with some apple slices.

"To keep her company."

"But you love riding."

"It's fine. You go with Malcolm. I'll stay with Joy. We'll meet back up later."

Summer wilts like a plant turning away from the sun. "Oh. Okay, then."

Joy blinks at her. That wasn't the reaction she'd been expecting or hoping for. Didn't she want to be alone with Malcolm?

"Flower time," Fox mutters under his breath before raising his voice. "See you guys at lunch." Then, he wraps his arm around Joy's shoulders. He doesn't pull her closer or press down with any semblance of pressure. His arm delicately encircles her like a light scarf. "Ready?"

"Ready." Joy giggles with utter delight. He's hovering for show, and it absolutely tickles her. Right there on the spot, Joy decides to meet him halfway. She grabs his arm, pulling it tighter around her. "And we're off."

They walk away together, neither of them looking back. The dirt trail leading away from the stables begins to incline upward. Once they reach the crest of the hill Joy says, "I think we're in the clear."

Fox nods, dropping his arm. The promised structure is still a small rectangle in the distance. "Did something happen?"

Joy nods. She tells him about her conversation with Malcolm, the way her reverse confession backfired, and the aftermath.

"Hmm." Fox considers her for several heartbeats—and her imagination jumps the gun per usual.

"You're thinking I'm right, aren't you?"

"Sixty-five percent."

"What's that supposed to mean? I'm not prying. We're having a conversation!"

"Reading my face is cheating."

"I didn't—"

"You did," he says with another smile, slightly mocking, mostly a challenge. His smile last night had notes of sunshine after a rainstorm—warm and welcome but all too fleeting. "You have this way of looking at people. It's pretty intense, like you're searching for something important."

"People," she repeats, skeptically. "I look at *people* like that?"

Fox is trying so hard not to stretch that smile into a grin. Joy can't help but see that as a challenge on her life and namesake.

Any time she can assert her comedic prowess, Joy takes the chance. She likes to live up to her name because she thinks it's funny in a *her parents subjected her to a lifetime of irony* kind of way. Trying to make Fox smile is quickly becoming her new favorite hobby. Getting that sentient grump to laugh satisfies her in a way she hadn't really thought about before.

"No," he admits.

"It's like I said, I want to know you. You have my full attention. For better or for worse."

"In sickness and in health."

Joy's comedic heart stammered in her chest. That's *exactly* where she was going with that. Yesterday, she made a quip about a proposal. This morning, she said rules of engagement and what comes after that? Marriage.

"You have no idea how refreshing it is to be around someone who gets my terrible jokes. Malcolm just sighs at me like he's dying."

"That's why I like them," he says. "Because you know they're terrible and you say them anyway."

"Because—"

"Because they bring you joy. Yes, I know."

Joy laughs. "You better *stop* that before you give me a heart attack."

The Barn Hall is a massive one-level structure. It's painted dark green and has professionally shot portraits of the blue-ribbon animals mounted out front. There are two entrances, one on each side, and they enter from the right.

Joy says, "I love the smell of a barn in the morning."

Fox raises an eyebrow.

"It's a joke. It smells foul as hell, but the cows are adorable. I heard they like to be petted. I probably shouldn't try."

"Probably. You can't exactly ask them for permission. Like how with a dog, you can put your hand out to let them decide. I don't think that works with cows."

"That's an excellent point." She stares at him, considering his response. "You've thought about that before, haven't you?"

"I have," he says with grave sincerity. "I wanted a cow when I was younger, but my parents wouldn't go for it."

Joy makes her way down the line of pigs, saying hello to each one. If they seem friendly and interested in her, she takes a picture with them. "Did you grow up on a farm?" she asks Fox, who's trailing her.

He shakes his head. "We just had a lot of animals. Dogs, cats, chickens, a couple of goats."

"And where was this? Hmm?" She snaps a photo with a bright pink potbellied pig who keeps sniffing her sweater.

"Virginia."

"That's where you're from originally?"

"Yeah. My parents are still there. My sister moved here with me."

"Is she the other girl on your RoT account? The one with the blue hair?"

He nods. "And yes, she's gray too."

"I wasn't going to ask," she lies. "What's her name?"

"Fiona."

"So Fox and Fiona from Virginia move to California for college? Work?"

"College."

"And loved it so much, they decided to stay."

"Something like that."

Moving on, the cows are also friendly and surprisingly *do* want to be touched. A reddish-brown cow who likes to have her ears rubbed ends up voluntarily resting her head in Joy's arms. "Take a video," she whispers near tears. "*Quickly. Please.*"

The rabbits and other small animals are next. Off to the side, in a room with open windows, their large pens are lined up in neat rows. All their ribbons are proudly pinned next to their name tags. There's a large sign that says: *Please do not open the cages or interact with the animals unsupervised!*

"They must have seen you coming," Fox jokes.

"That sign can't stop me if I don't read it." Joy turns her phone over and over in her hands, eyeing Fox. "You wouldn't be interested in taking some pictures *with* me, would you?"

"You want me in your pictures?"

"I didn't say that." She looks into the cage of a gray rabbit with long floppy ears named Umji snacking on some sprouts. "It's just I'm having a really shitty day and the past half-hour has been significantly less so. I'd like to capture the moment. Accurately."

In fact, she hasn't thought about Malcolm once since they entered the Barn Hall. A new record. Being with Fox made her feel less sad—the wildfire reduced to a smolder. Spending time with him and these adorable animals distracted her in just the way she needed.

"So." Fox stands next to her, leaning against the edge of the cage. "You want me in your pictures?"

"Fine. Yes." Joy gives in, pretending to be exasperated. "Please?"

"Sure. Whatever you want."

Joy positions him next to her with Umji in the background. She takes a few pictures and each one makes her frown harder than the last. "So, idea. What if you smiled?"

"Hmm."

"Don't *hmm* me. See, look." She shows him her screen, swiping through the pictures. "Here we are. Beautiful, photogenic, but we look like we're having a good time, not a great time. Umji? Adorable. Me? Excited ball of sunshine. You? Possibly constipated."

This earns her a spontaneous snicker. Fox tries to turn away but isn't quick enough.

"That look! Right there! That smile!" Joy matches his movements to face him. "Imagine I said something funny before every shot. That's all we need."

They try a few more test photos that still don't pan out. Joy gives up and changes course. "Videos," she says.

"What?"

She poses them for each take, makes sure they're in frame with a furry guest star behind them, hits record, and tells him awful knock-knock jokes she stole from her dad. It works. By the end of their time in the Barn Hall, she's the proud owner of five videos, actual photographic evidence, proving that Fox's smile exists.

"Let's do one more," he says. "I have one for you."

Joy chooses a beautiful pair of brown dwarf rabbits, Mable and

Dipper, saying hello before standing in front of them. "Ready?"
She positions her phone.

"Knock, knock."

"Who's there?"

"Aardvark."

She eyes him. "Aardvark who?"

He says, "Aardvark a million miles to see you smile."

*"Oh my god."*

After washing their hands and disinfecting their phones, they follow the signs directing them to the adjacent area, where the rest of the animals are. It isn't the kind of small pen you'd see at a county fair or at a tiny tots thing for elementary school kids. This is a wildlife reserve for barnyard animals. They walk into a giant field full of small animals running around and having the time of their lives. The worker gives them a few bags of treats—the animals can all eat the same thing and are used to it. A small flock heads straight for them as soon as they clear the gate.

They're instantly surrounded by a small donkey, alpacas, calves, lambs, goats, a couple of dogs, chickens, and what Joy is positive is an actual capybara, the internet's favorite lo-fi animal. When all the treats are gone most of the animals lose interest, wandering away, to Joy's endless disappointment.

"Want to take a walk around the perimeter?" Fox points the area out—it's one giant circle. "We have time." Surprisingly, a pair of goats and a lamb follow their lead as they walk around the fenced edge of the field until they find a tree to sit under. Fox coaxes the lamb onto his lap and it promptly goes to sleep, tucked in close to his body.

Joy takes a few pictures of them for posterity and her heart. "The jokes I could make right now. Fox and a lamb."

"I appreciate your restraint."

"As you should. Can I ask you something instead?" She gives one of the goats scritches to stop it from nibbling on her sweater. "Why don't you like Malcolm?"

"Is that what he told you?" Fox shakes his head. "The only problem I have with him is that he's wrong for Summer."

"If she wanted to get back together, would you?"

"No."

"Why not?"

"Sixty-five percent."

"I haven't done anything! Again, this is a conversation! That requires back and forth! We're building rapport! At least give me something to go on."

"Why do you even need something?"

"Because I've been thinking. The whole point of this, *us*, is to show Malcolm a different side to me, I guess." Joy sighs. "That doesn't matter now. I got my answer straight from the source. But you're still here with me anyway. Why?"

"So Malcolm can realize he's in love with you."

"He's not," Joy insists. "But for the sake of the conversation, then what?"

"If he realizes he's in love with you, he'll leave Summer alone."

"Which is important to you because?"

Fox averts his gaze, focusing on his lamb. "I have my reasons."

"Which are? Stop grumping with me."

"Grumping?" He doesn't bother trying to hide his smile and Joy's heart *soars* when she sees his dimples again.

"Yes, you're grumping around. Face it: you exude grump energy. Resting grump face. Forrest Grump. Oscar the Grump."

"Please stop."

"Sorry. My daily pun quota is behind schedule. I got carried away." And now . . . Joy is definitely searching. She tells herself to stop, but she can't help it. It's like she's obsessed with his face. He's focusing on the grass now, lips pursed slightly.

"When I said we're better off as friends, I might have let you believe that she decided that. She didn't. I did," he says. "She's my best friend's little sister."

"Oh." Joy's gaze flicked to his thumb ring.

"Yeah. And he died in a car accident five years ago."

"*Oh.*"

"Grief makes you do things you normally wouldn't. She didn't have anyone else. I was there and—" He exhales in a huff, waking his sleeping lamb, who bleats in distress before closing its eyes again. "Within a month, we both knew it wasn't going to work, but I'm the one who broke it off. I made a promise to myself. I would always, always look out for her. Me and Fiona, we take care of her, you know? She's family now. So no, we're never dating again. Neither one of us wants that."

"Oh."

"If Malcolm asks to make things official, Summer will say yes. I can't stop that. If it's going to happen, it'll happen. But I can try to help you before it gets to that point because I know I'm right."

"Oh," she says again and then shakes her head to make herself stop. "*Oh*, no. No. Fox, I don't know if this is a good idea anymore. You don't have to do this with me. Malcolm and I are . . . complicated. You just met me. You don't need to be dragged into our mess."

"I'm already here. Tell me, what did he say exactly? Because I think he's assuming you're not interested in dating, period. When you first told me you were asexual, that's what I did until I asked questions to clarify."

"We honestly haven't talked about it in years."

"Well, there you go. To me, it sounds like he's assuming that's still true."

"Even if that's what he thinks, he's fine with it. I feel like if I say anything now, it'll be a burden on him. I'd be making him responsible for my feelings when he just told me he needs to stop doing that. I have to respect his wishes."

"Then don't say anything to him. Let's keep going, me and you, see what happens. I'm telling you we're not out yet." Fox leans in as close to her as his lamb allows. "Joy."

His deep rumble softened into that tender cadence she heard the night before. She wants to ask him to say her name again, and almost does, but stops herself.

"I've been hearing about you nearly non-stop for a month," he says. "And the thing is, Malcolm didn't lie. Not once. The terrible jokes, how smart and stubborn you are—it's all true. I tried to call you out for eavesdropping and you wished me a happy birthday because that's the kind of person you are."

"Petty? Passive aggressive?"

"*Thoughtful* and attentive. You *care* so much about other people's well-being it's practically bleeding out of you."

Joy balls her hands into fists to stop them from shaking. Her mind feels like a hamster on a wheel, just running in circles for dear life. Why does her chest feel so tight why is he looking at her like that why is he saying such nice things why isn't he freaked out why does he want to help her why why why why why why— "Summer said you were emotionally closed off," she says. "This is not that. I want a refund."

He laughs. "You want to know me and I want to help you. You're a good person, Joy. You made me, a stranger, a birthday cake, the best cake I've ever had in my life. I owe you one."

Joy turns to the goat. "You can eat my sweater now." She deserves that because she certainly doesn't deserve someone as wonderful as Fox so committed to helping her. "I got it during Nordstrom's Anniversary Sale. I hope it's delicious."

"And," he says with a grin, "you're not exactly unpleasant to be around."

"Not exactly? Don't know how I feel about that."

"Good." He laughs again.

# Fifteen

Going to Glass Bead Winery & Vineyards sounded great in theory—until Joy saw the helicopter waiting to take off.

In the car, she drifts toward the front seat like a vengeful ghost. "The agenda didn't say anything about a helicopter, Malcolm," she seethes into his ear. "I thought we were driving and stopping by the cabin first. I smell like *goat*. Adorable baby goat."

He turns to her with a smirk. "That's your fault, darling."

"I can't go to a fancy winery smelling like *goat* in *wrinkled* clothes."

Summer giggles in the front seat.

"First time for everything."

"If it helps, I also smell like goat," Fox says, tone completely flat. "We can make up a cover story about how we rescued them from near death on the freeway and returned them to their farm. We had to hold them the whole way to keep them calm and came straight there to make our appointment. We even have the pictures to prove it. People love animal rescue stories."

"Your grumpy mind," Joy says. "I love it."

It's a short trip from the parking lot to the launch pad walkway. Their pilot meets them there, shaking Malcolm's hand and confirming the registration and destination, and goes over the particulars of the ride.

"It's even smaller than I thought." Fox has suddenly gone full grump—tense jaw, furrowed brow, and angry glare.

"Careful there or you'll make the jump from grump to grinch," Joy teases.

That earns her an amused side-eye. "Grinches are very misunderstood creatures. Green ones hate Christmas. My nemesis would be that." He gestures with his chin to the helicopter just as the blades start up. The sound is a lot to take in—loud, uncomfortable, and almost piercing.

"Are you scared of flying?"

"No." His worried face implies otherwise.

"No?"

"Maybe."

Joy raises her eyebrows. "Maybe?"

"It's heights more than flying. That thing is small. There's no way to avoid looking out a window."

"You could keep your eyes closed the entire time. You could also hold my hands. I've been told they have incredible comforting powers."

Fox scoff-laughs as Summer runs from Malcolm and the pilot over to them. "Okay, so they don't have a helicopter available that will fit all four of us, so we have to take two. Who do you want to ride with?" She's asking Fox.

"I'm fine with Joy."

"Are you sure?" She turns to Joy. "He's afraid of flying. I was just thinking he might be more comfortable with me being there."

"Oh. I had no idea. Hmm." Joy can feel how bad her acting is but keeps going. "Malcolm went through all this trouble for you so you should probably stay with him. Don't worry. I'll take good care of Fox."

Their helicopter is bright purple with two tan seats for passengers in the second row. It *is* small, nearing claustrophobic levels. Their seats are so close together their shoulders touch. The sound is surprisingly more bearable once they're inside, and the pilot hands them each a headset and instructs them to put on their safety belts.

Joy holds out her hand. Fox takes it, then promptly squeezes his eyes shut. "Feeling better already."

Takeoff feels more like being on a roller coaster than an airplane—anticipation builds low in Joy's stomach as they begin to ascend into the sky. Except there's (thankfully) no drop. They move forward, the helicopter balancing out and staying in the air.

Fox might be afraid to look down, but Joy isn't. She takes in the view of the wide sparkling lake on the opposite side of their cabin as the pilot gives a guided tour, telling them facts and history about the area. Once upon a time, this area boomed during the California Gold Rush. The tops of the trees look like green bushes instead of a small forest, and even though they can't see it there's also a river that winds straight through. Farther in the distance she can see the freeway, neighborhoods full of blocky streets and houses, and large buildings jutting out of nowhere to create the downtown business area. The most breathtaking part of the trip is the horizon. A light blue sky slashed with wispy white clouds covers everything like a sheer blanket. There's no end to it, no mark of delineation between the sky and everything else. It's just simply there and perfect as they fly through it.

Thirty minutes later, they touch down on the winery property. Joy taps Fox's shoulder. "We made it! We're alive!"

He cracks one eye open, staring directly at her. "Is this a trick? I can't feel if we landed or not."

Joy squeezes his hand. "We landed. You can see the vineyards from here."

Fox opens his other eye, but it takes several heartbeats before he's willing to look past Joy's face. Outside, a worried Summer is standing anxiously next to Malcolm, bouncing on the balls of her feet as she stares at their helicopter. Fox waves at her before carefully taking off his safety belt, hands still slightly shaking.

Golf carts are waiting to take them on a tour of the flat vineyards, then down to the winery itself. There's a museum and a separate restaurant where they have a lunch reservation, which would be followed by *another* tour of the elevated vineyards.

"Was it okay?" Summer stands in front of Fox, concern written all over her face. "Do you need anything?"

The changes in Fox post-flight are subtle. His skin has a slight greenish-gray tint, his forehead is damp, and there's a slight tremor when he inhales.

He touches the top of Summer's head affectionately. "I'm fine."

"I'm so sorry. He didn't know—"

"It's okay."

"—but if he had told me what we were doing like I asked—"

"Summer."

"—this never would have happened."

Joy feels like she shouldn't be watching them like this. Summer looks like she's caught in that delicate middle between crying and rage. And Fox is doing his best to comfort her, but he's the one who just went through the traumatic event, so the reverse should be happening.

Quietly, Joy wanders away to where Malcolm is standing near one of the golf carts.

"Is he okay?"

"I think so."

"I didn't know it would be that bad for him."

"Well, it's not like you talk to him. Directly. About anything." Malcolm scoffs. "Whose side are you on?"

"Love and justice, at all times." Joy laughs. "You need to apologize."

"I know."

"And you need to give him a chance."

"Next."

"No, no next, Malcolm. What is your problem with him? Did he do something to you?"

"Why didn't you come horseback riding with us?"

Joy sighs. Of course he changed the subject. "Because I didn't. I thought it'd be better if you two were alone."

"Well, it wasn't," Malcolm snapped. "Summer wanted you there, both of you. I told you to just stick to my agenda. What is so difficult for you to understand about that?"

The second he finishes talking, Joy enters a state of perfect fury. Her eyebrows go up, her eyes go wide, her entire body goes still—she doesn't even blink—and the iciest fire known to man begins to brew in the back of her throat.

"You know what, Malcolm? You and your damn agenda are starting to get on my goddamn nerves." She steps forward. "You got one more time to talk to me like that. Do that again and I will intentionally wreck all your shit. I'm not your fucking doormat."

"Joy—"

"Don't you *Joy* me. Go apologize to Fox. Right now." She points to where they're standing.

The golf cart driver looks from Malcolm to Joy and back again. "I'd already be over there if I was you," he mutters. He's an older Black man, sitting behind the wheel wearing a tan uniform.

Malcolm regards Joy for a few moments, gaze steely and unwavering. Joy knows that look—he has something to say and he's weighing whether or not it's worth pissing her off more to make his point.

"You really don't want to try me today," Joy seethes. "You really, truly don't."

That last threat did it—the scales tipped in her favor. Malcolm drops his gaze, saying, "Fine." He marches over to the others, steps stiff and hands balled at his sides.

"*Whew*," the driver says. "You remind me of my wife. He must not know how close he was to death right then."

Joy tries to calm down, laughing softly. "It's not a side I let out often." It's hard to reconcile how powerful the heat of the moment feels, where you're nothing but raw, reckless rage. Fighting with people she loves always gives her the worst anxiety spirals. Stuck for hours, sometimes days, reliving every harsh word, cold stare, and idle threat. Suffering through her brain painting her as an even worse person, making her believe she said more than she really had.

She'll apologize to Malcolm sooner or later. Sometimes it's better to let her threats sit so the memory lingers and he'll think twice before talking to her like that again.

When she rejoins her group, Summer is calm and sunny once more, Malcolm seems to be grappling with remorse, and Fox looks stable. He's the one who says, "Are we ready to go? Joy?"

She nods.

"Our carriage awaits." Fox takes her by the hand, interlocking their fingers. Joy glances up at him just as he looks down at her. "This still okay?"

"It's more than that," she says, feeling too somber to smile.

"Wait, don't tell me you're afraid of golf carts?"

"We'll be in a moving vehicle with no doors, no seatbelts, or any kind of shocks to speak of. You should be too."

Like the helicopter, each cart only seats two people so they have to take separate ones. Their driver is a younger Mexican man with a generous smile. "Welcome to Glass Bead," he says.

Fox says, "Thank you," followed by Joy who says, "Nice to meet you, Miguel," after reading his name tag. They depart as soon as they're situated in the back seat. Miguel is a smooth driver; however, the dirt road is anything but smooth.

A few bumpy minutes later, Fox taps the back of Joy's hand. "I heard you," he says. "Everyone did, actually. I guess he must have made you mad."

Joy glances at him. "That happens from time to time. Did he talk to you?"

"He did. He apologized, as ordered."

"Good."

Fox leans over until their shoulders are touching. "I think I understand why he's desperate to keep you in his corner now. I don't think I've ever met anyone quite like you."

"What do you mean?"

"I can't describe it, so I don't really want to try."

"Hmm."

Fox laughs.

"Hey." Joy pushes back on his weight, just enough so she can turn and lean on him instead. To be fair, he started it. He opened the door she didn't realize she wanted to sprint through until she saw the light on the other side. "Have you ever been in love before?"

"Why?"

"I've been wondering about it. I thought asking a random question about you might make me feel better." Joy sighs. "I know fighting with someone doesn't automatically mean you love them any less. Logically, I know that. But I'm kind of struggling." That familiar prickle is starting behind her eyes. "I just feel like I was really *mean* to him. Even if it was for a good reason, I should've handled it better. You shouldn't yell at people you love."

Grace does it all the time. It's practically her default setting because she's just a loud person. Joy isn't. So when she yells, it feels different, more potent. Like she's choosing to cross a line even though she knows it will hurt someone. It's intentional and awful and every time she does it, she can't help but hate herself.

"You shouldn't," Fox agrees, "but it happens. That's hardly something unique to you. I hope it doesn't feel like that?"

"It does. I'm a selfish monster with a bad temper." She laughs bitterly. Anxiety is such an unfair mind-fuck because sometimes it can even make her believe Malcolm only brings out the worst in her. If they get together and all they do is fight—about kids, about the future, about sex, about work—it'll be the worst thing to ever happen to them because they don't want the same things. They'll never see eye to eye, never find a way to compromise or agree. She'll browbeat him, wear him down, yelling and screaming and fighting until she gets her way . . .

"If there's one thing you're not, it's that. You shouldn't be so hard on yourself." Fox's frown intensifies, quick and angry, but it smooths back out into his grumpy neutral like it never happened. "I thought I was in love. Once. But I don't think I was."

"Why did you think you were?"

"I don't know."

"Yes, you do."

Fox actually begins to fidget—right leg bouncing, free hand tapping the seat. "I don't like talking about this kind of stuff." He shakes his head as if that's the end of the conversation.

Joy scoffs quietly, partially hiding her face behind their joined hands. She presses the back of his hand directly to her cheek. "When it's about you. Let's be specific: You're fine to analyze and talk about me and Malcolm, but when it's you? Instant reversion to a grumpy potato."

"Hmm."

"That's what I thought."

They enjoy the rest of the ride in a comfortable silence. There isn't much to see—if you've seen one vineyard, you've seen them all. A million rows of vibrant green leaves, dark brown stems, plump purple and green grapes. It only takes ten minutes before they pull up to the front of the restaurant.

Before they get out, Fox says, "Remember, the goal is to have fun. Nothing else."

Joy nods.

"If he notices, if he says anything, then we'll take it from there. Otherwise, no pressure. This is a completely passive play."

"Aye, aye."

"You still want to do this, right?"

"Oh yeah." Joy gives his hand two gentle squeezes. "I do." *For me.*

# Sixteen

The air conditioning inside the restaurant is a welcome relief from the outside weather.

A host, Mary—with flaming red hair, light brown skin, and a face full of freckles—sits them at a table on the second-floor balcony under an oversized umbrella. She explains the details of their packages and how the wine tasting works, encouraging them all to not actually imbibe the wine if they don't wish to get drunk *very* quickly. The food that will be brought out will all be complementary to whatever wine group they're sampling at the moment.

"This should be fun," Summer says, slightly bouncing in her seat. "I'm going to go to the restroom first."

"Me too," Fox says. And they leave together.

"Joy." For once, Malcolm wastes no time. "I didn't mean to talk to you like that. I'm sorry."

"Okay. Thank you." Joy smooths the napkin in her lap as if she's trying to get rid of the permanent pleats.

"I'm just feeling really stressed out today. I didn't mean to take that out on you too."

"I know."

"Do you forgive me?"

Joy sighs, finally looking at him. "I always do."

Lunch lasts for nearly three hours. Slowly, Joy's anxiety recedes, inch by inch until she's able to relax enough to have a good time. Fox smiles often. Summer's infectious drunken giggles charm everyone. And Malcolm, oh Malcolm, he seems so happy. As far as anyone knows they're just four friends having a great time together.

As they're descending the stairs on their way out, Summer says, "We should skip the museum. It looks boring." Her face flushes as another drunken hiccup bursts through.

Joy is already sitting in the golf cart and in the middle of situating her purse when she hears, "I'm riding with Joy. You go in that one. With Malcolm. Over there." She looks up in time to see Summer gently pushing Fox away before plopping down on the seat.

"Hi," Summer says.

"Hallo."

"I made an executive decision."

"I see. Malcolm *really* loves those, by the way."

Summer shrugs. "That was a total boss bitch move earlier. I'm going to be more like you."

"Oh, you don't want to do *that*." Joy's sarcasm will hit a fever pitch any second now.

"They need to spend some time together. Haven't you noticed they've barely said anything to each other all weekend? I'm sick of it."

Drunk Summer apparently doesn't fuck around. Joy gives her an appraising look. "Is that something you do often? You know, meddle. Interfere. Set people up and push them together?"

Summer's innocent, wide-eyed look doesn't quite work as well after drinking the equivalent of two bottles of wine. "What?"

"Uh-huh."

The golf cart lurches forward as Miguel begins the second tour. It doesn't take long to reach the first patch of incline. The golf cart struggles at first, their pace noticeably slowing down. The entirety of the "tour" is once again looking at an incredible amount of vineyard rows, this time curved against a landscape of endless rolling hills. The next turn is sharp, but Miguel takes it slow, and the road that follows travels along a steep drop-off.

Summer glances over the side. "Oh yikes." She grabs hold of the safety bar.

"So," Joy says, "tell me your life story."

"The whole thing?"

"The CliffsNotes version is fine."

Summer gasps, eyes going wide. "Oh my god, Joy! You used a pun on me!"

"And you seem very excited about it."

"Because you only joke around with Fox and Malcolm." Summer starts crying—actual tears streaming down her face. "I felt so left out."

"If I knew I had such an eager audience for my bad jokes, I would have told them to you too." Joy gapes at her, unsure what to do. She really went from zero to waterworks in .02 seconds flat. "Summer, that wasn't personal at all. I promise."

"I know. I knew that." She sniffles, wiping her eyes on her sleeves. "I'm just a really emotional person, you know? And I cry sometimes. It just happens. I can't help it. It's not you. I'm also kind of drunk."

"Kind of." Joy waits patiently for Summer to calm down by avoiding looking at her, figuring she wants some privacy. Malcolm and Fox are in front of them, which is a true shame. Joy would have paid good money to see Malcolm's face now. She wonders if he's thinking what she's thinking—that Summer might be too chaotic for him to handle. So many deviations from his agenda must have him reeling since he willingly admitted to being "stressed." It's possible he hasn't told her how important order and control are to him yet. Maybe she doesn't know how much each disruption to his agenda upsets him.

"It's so beautiful here." Summer's wistful sigh makes her smile lose some of its wattage. "I'd love to get married somewhere like this."

Joy's hackles immediately rise, putting her on high alert. Is that supposed to be a hint?

"There's something I want you to know about me. I think it will help things." Summer sniffles a few times before she continues. "Ever since I was a little girl, I've wanted to get married." She gives her a tight smile. "I used to line my stuffed animals up in a straight line to bear witness as I walked down the aisle wearing one of my mom's white nightgowns. I was obsessed with the idea of being the center of attention and at the end of the line, there would be someone who would love me forever. We would eat cake, dance with all our friends, and drink what I thought at the time was grape juice. Happily ever after."

"That's really adorable," Joy says carefully.

"Except I kept believing it, you know? I just knew someday I would reach the end and get my happily ever after. So much so that I maybe wasn't as, um, discerning? Is that a good word? As discerning as I should've been." She takes a deep breath. "I've been engaged six times."

"Six?" Joy almost chokes on air. "Six? Five plus one, six?"

"Yep. It's pretty bad, huh?"

"*No.* No, not bad. I wouldn't say *bad.*" Joy searches for the right thing to say but unfortunately her brain has abandoned her in favor of screaming *six!* repeatedly. "Everyone moves at their own pace, even if that's the speed of light."

Summer giggles, face brightening. "I really loved them all. At one point, I thought they were all the one. I was positive I was making the right decision, you know? They said they loved me too and I believed them. I felt loved. Turns out, I was wrong every time except the last one. When he left me anyway, I was done. No more love. No more marriage. It just wasn't in the cards for me."

Joy suddenly has an idea where this speech is heading and she's not sure she wants to hear it.

Summer continues, "I was looking for a husband. I'm not ashamed to say that. I want to be married. I want to have a family. I want to be a housewife, throw parties, and take care of our kids and teach them, you know, homeschool them. That's the job I want. I want motherhood to be my *actual* job. Taking care of my husband, our house, and our family.

"I'm not willing to settle for just anyone anymore, you know? Malcolm knows that about me, and I fit what he's looking for. But you don't have to worry." Summer nods as she speaks. "I know how much he means to you. I'm not trying to steal him away or anything like that. I think our bubbles could be good together. We're all really compatible."

And *boom* goes the drunken dynamite. "Is that why you invited Fox? To test your little compatibility theory."

"Um. Well." Summer looks away toward the vineyard. "Malcolm and Fox avoid each other, interacting as little as possible. I thought that maybe if we were staying in the same place, they wouldn't be able to anymore. But Fox is spending all his time with you and they're still not talking."

Wait . . . didn't Fox say Summer *asked* him to spend time with Joy?

"I really think they'd be good friends. Just like we could be."

Joy sighs. Honestly, she still doesn't know why Malcolm claims to not like Fox. And Fox doesn't have a problem with Malcolm, per se, just the complicated circumstances, and if Joy told Summer about any of that, she'd have to tell her everything and . . . no.

"I don't dislike you, Summer. Things are . . . complicated."

"But they don't have to be, do they?"

"I had a talk with Malcolm and we . . ." Joy trails off. God, this is so hard. How can she be honest with Summer while still protecting herself and her feelings? "We have—we've been friends for a really long time. For a lot of that time, we only had each other. No one understood us the way we did. We had a bubble, like you said, and it just kept getting smaller and smaller and tighter and tighter and now, there really isn't room for anyone else.

"But Malcolm keeps trying to make room. It's important for him to do that. And I agree. We have a lot to work on that we've been ignoring because it's easier that way, I guess. I just don't know if I can do that work with someone else in our bubble." Joy whispers to herself, out loud, "Wow that was a weird metaphor."

"No, that was really good." Summer grabs her forearm. Her

face is practically exploding with encouragement. "Have you ever tried? I mean, really, really tried to make it work?"

"No offense, but I really, really don't want to talk to you about that."

"Oh." Her face falls. "Okay."

Summer sits back in her seat, hands in her lap, wistfully looking at the vineyards. The ride is only a couple of minutes longer anyway.

The first thing Malcolm asks is "What happened? Is everything okay?"

Summer's face is splotchy, and her eyes are bright red. Joy waits for her to answer because anything she says, as a joke or seriously, probably won't go over well since Summer has clearly been crying and she has not.

"I think I drank too much." She looks to Joy for confirmation with a watery smile that says: *We'll keep that between us.*

"Where's the other helicopter?" Fox asks.

Joy searches the small blacktop. He's right. Why is there only one?

"I ordered a car to take Fox and Joy back to the house," Malcolm says. "Me and Summer will fly back and get my Jeep."

"Thank you," Fox says, surprised. "I appreciate it."

"Sure." Malcolm clears his throat. "No problem."

Joy and Summer exchange a look. There might be hope for them yet.

The car arrives a few minutes after Summer and Malcolm take off in their helicopter. When the driver gets out, Fox waves him away and opens the rear door himself for Joy.

"Why, thank you," she says, sliding into her seat. Fox follows her shortly after. The ride is supposed to take significantly longer than the twenty-minute flight due to traffic and required slower speeds, thanks to some dangerous cliffs.

"I'll never understand why trails are cut *into* mountains. Surely there's a better way. It's as if someone decided the best thing to do was just pave over the original gold rush trails people used with wagons."

Fox snickers. He's facing her, using the headrest as intended. For the most part, he'd made it through lunch without any issue, but alone together in the car he looks tired and overwhelmed again. Joy guesses he put on a show for Summer to convince her he felt fine and stop her from fussing over him, when in reality he's still reeling from being in the air.

"How are you holding up?" Joy asks. She brushes a lock of hair back from his forehead. He catches her hand in midair, interlocking their fingers.

"Need more comforting," he says.

"That's what I'm here for." She gives his hand a squeeze and situates herself so she's facing him too, pulling her legs up on the seat and readjusting her seatbelt.

"I can't stop thinking about what you said earlier." His voice is a soft rumble of concern. "When you called yourself a selfish monster."

"Ah no, don't do that."

"You don't strike me as a liar, but you can't honestly think that's true."

"Shows what you know. I lie all the time."

"Not about that."

Self-loathing is sneaky. Even on her best days, when Joy is positive she's a long-lost goddess, there's no outrunning how awful she can feel about herself.

She shakes her head, then exhales into a sigh. "I don't like yelling at people, period. Yelling at Malcolm feels like I'm committing some unforgivable crime. It's hard to explain. I guess, part of me feels like I'm not allowed to get mad at him. Because if I do, then I'll lose him."

There's no expression to read on Fox's face when he says, "That's, uh, an interesting way of looking at it."

"I *said* it was hard to explain." Joy chuckles darkly. "Grace says I'm hung up on some self-inflicted morality clause and if that's all it takes for Malcolm to leave me, then I shouldn't be with him in the first place."

"Hmm." His brows come together. "I take it Grace and Malcolm don't like each other much?"

"I think they do," Joy says, nodding. "But as we got older, they started growing apart. Grace thinks he's all wrong for me, same as how you think he's wrong for Summer."

"Hmm."

"She hates that I'm just 'waiting around for him' instead of living my life or whatever."

"Hmm." Fox breathes deeply, gaze drifting from Joy to the window. His attention isn't on her anymore. She has a feeling he's chasing after his runaway thoughts.

Joy waits patiently for him to come back, taking note of every movement he makes. A quick bite of his lower lip. A slow blink. A nose scrunch. A scratch of his chin.

When did people watching become *so* fascinating? She's never been shy, but she can't remember the last time she purposefully paid this much attention to one person before. Does it always feel like this or is Fox just a special case?

"Would you ever consider dating someone else?" Fox is still looking out the window.

"I have," Joy reminds him. "I *am*."

Her answer captures his attention. All his focus is hers again. Fox laughs, short and breathy. "I meant for real. Do you think that's something you'd ever be interested in?"

Joy's heart has been set on Malcolm for so long she doesn't know if that's even possible. If it is, where else would she find someone handsome, ambitious, successful, Black, *and* asexual? Someone who her family loves? Someone who cares so deeply about her, they're practically drowning in each other?

"I never told anyone this before. Don't laugh at me," she warns.

He immediately replies, "Wouldn't dream of it."

"I don't like thinking of a future without Malcolm because it's too hard to picture. I'm pathetic, I know, but I'm also just . . . scared. If someone as perfect for me as Malcolm, who feels like my match in every single way, doesn't want me, what possible chance do I have with anyone else? I'm not willing to let my heart get broken over and over again to find out. I'm really scared of getting hurt and being mistreated and getting called broken or worse."

"Hmm," Fox says, and then adds, "I understand."

Joy blows out a huff of air, raising her shoulders and letting them fall as if she's shaking off a weight she's been carrying for far too long. "What about you? Why are you single?"

"I'm not." He grins.

"Ha. Ha."

"No particular reason. My job is physically demanding. After work, I don't really want to do anything else. I'm a *have dinner, watch a movie, and just rest* kind of person."

"Me too! I let Malcolm drag me to places but really I'd rather stay home and hang out with Pepper."

"Pepper?"

"My cat."

"Right. And on the weekend, I'm usually building pieces for my business. I don't really go out or try to meet new people. If it weren't for Summer's weekly get-togethers, I probably wouldn't go out at all."

"So you're not interested in using dating apps or anything like that?"

"I have before. Don't get me wrong, I don't mind going on dates. I've just been too busy lately."

"Hmm."

Fox laughs. "Plus, I've been worrying about Summer nonstop. I know I'm being overprotective, which she hates, but I can't stop myself. She's . . . *very* unlucky in the romance department."

There it is again: Fox talks so freely about everyone else but never himself. He's so closed off, she could practically feel the door she slyly managed to weasel open slam shut in her face as he changed the subject to Summer.

Joy wants to ask him so many questions—what made him pick his trade, what's his comfort movie, can he cook or is he a takeout enthusiast? Asking now would feel selfish, as if she's purposefully ignoring his candid confession about Summer. She's already said she wants to know him. Maybe he just really doesn't want her to.

She says, "I heard. She told me."

"Every time it goes wrong it feels like it's partially my fault for not protecting her. That's why I'm here. I couldn't just stand by and let it happen again. I had to at least try to save her from making another bad choice. I want her to be happy. *Safe* and happy."

"You think Malcolm would do something to hurt her?"

"Not on purpose."

"I don't think you have to worry about that. He's . . . They're, um—I think they're further along than either of us realized. Standing in their way might not be the way to go."

"That's not what we're doing."

"It's not?"

Fox shakes his head. "All we're doing is spending time together like they asked us to. I don't know about you, but I'm having a wonderful time. Minus the flying."

"Really?" Joy tries to keep her smile to a tolerable cheese level. "With me?"

"You've seen my RoT account. You think I take pictures with just anyone?"

Joy snort-laughs. "In that case, I have no choice but to cherish them forever."

# Seventeen

ord Jesus, Joy is desperately in need of a shower.

And once she's done, for her afternoon ensemble . . . she's over it. She picks out a multicolored pastel tie-dye hoodie and matching short set. The fuzzy material feels heavenly soft on her skin and perfect for a low-key, cozy evening. The agenda lists game night and campfire dinner—probably hot dogs and s'mores. Quite the contrast from lunch, but that's Malcolm too. He'll never be too good to pass up beer, pizza, and hot dogs.

The game room is located just past the living room. It feels dark and cozy, like a dive bar, with brick red walls, a pool table, a dartboard, a large TV mounted on the wall, and a fireplace. The left wall is lined with standing tables and stools, and the back wall hosts the actual bar and shelves fully stocked with boxes and bottles of all kinds of alcohol. Malcolm likes to be prepared, but that's an excessive amount of booze. There's no way four people could drink all of that in a weekend. Not if they want to keep their livers.

There's also a sliding glass door leading to the backyard. The fire pit has already been started, crackling fiercely in the dying afternoon light. Summer is out there with Fox, each holding a beer. Malcolm pops up from behind the bar and smiles when he sees her.

"Hey, hey," she says, strutting to the music playing from the speakers mounted in the corners near the ceiling.

"What can I get you?" he asks.

Joy makes a show of twirling the rest of the way to him and leans on the bar. "Read my mind. What am I in the mood for?"

He closes one eye, turning his head to the side. "Rum?"

"No, but I'll take it," she says. "Malibu and pineapple juice?"

Malcolm starts making her drink, and it instantly takes her back to college. On the nights when he worked as a bartender, she'd stay for his entire shift to keep him company. But instead of sitting at the bar, delirious and lovesick, she danced for hours, having the time of her life. Eventually the club offered her a job, the start of her illustrious go-go dancing career.

Every memory and every story. My friend Joy this and my Malcolm that.

"We haven't done this in a while," she says.

Malcolm places her drink on the bar with a coaster. "I know. We've been busy." He doesn't look at her as he wipes the counter down and goes back to prepping the food.

Busy growing up, working, and building their lives up from nothing. Side by side and alone, together. "You look tired," she says.

"Yeah."

"Everything okay?"

"Yeah."

"I guess I'll leave you to it."

"Okay," he says. "I'll see you out there."

Joy approaches Fox and Summer, joining them near the edge of the lake. Her hoodie has bear ears on the top—Fox tugs at one of them, and she doesn't mean to look up at him with sad eyes and a pout, but she can feel it on her face and see it in his eyes.

"What's wrong?" he asks immediately.

"Are you okay?" Summer looks concerned . . . and wobbly. She's flushed from the chest up and her eyes are glassy.

"Are you?" Joy asks. "You're kind of red there."

"I'm *perfect*." Summer drains her beer and hiccups. "I think I need another one."

Fox sighs. "I'm cutting you off at five."

"Ew. No," she says with a snort, already walking away.

Joy's eyes widen in surprise. "Does she always get so . . . *sassy* with you when she's drunk?"

"Yeah, and it's all downhill from here," he says. "Now, what's with the sad face?"

"Something's up with Malcolm. It's like he doesn't want to talk to me," she says, watching the water. "Did something happen while I was upstairs?"

"Not that I know of."

"He should be happy. They're going to flit away to some festival together tomorrow for his big confession. Oh god," she says with a groan. "And that's *why* he's upset. He's stressed about that *especially* considering what happened today. He gets like this at work too." She rolls her eyes and sets her drink down. "He's impossible to deal with the night before important meetings or presentations. I'll be right back."

Malcolm is beside the bar now, preparing to carry the meat

out to the barbecue. Joy takes the tray out of his hands, sitting it back down on the bar. "Hey, hey, I have returned. I need to talk to you."

"What?"

"Now." Joy grips his arm, pulling him into the hall and taking him to the living room couch.

"Joy, I need to finish—"

"Malcolm, you need to sit down. Now, tell me what's wrong." She hasn't let go of his arm, nor does she plan to.

"Nothing."

"Oh really? You know, today was a lot of fun. I had a semi-wonderful time. Did you?"

"Yeah."

"Don't lie to me. You're obviously upset, and we should talk about it so it doesn't fester."

"I don't want to do this right now."

All Malcolm needs from her is support. She can give that to him. She can give that and *mean* it. Straight from her heart.

Joy takes a deep breath, decides on a tactic, and goes for it. "Okay, fine. Let's talk about tomorrow. Are you ready or are you having second thoughts because Summer keeps messing up your perfectly choreographed trip?"

Malcolm seems surprised. "Who said that?"

"No one needs to say it because I know you. I ditched you during horseback riding, Summer tried to ride with Fox in the helicopter, and she did ride with me in the golf cart after deciding to skip the museum. I know you're upset about that."

He frowns. "'Upset' is a strong word."

"A word that fits." Joy squeezes in closer to him until their shoulders are pressed together. "I shouldn't have to say this, but

I'm going to: you can't force people to always follow your lead. People are unpredictable, Malcolm. Plans will change. Things can go wrong."

"It's not about force." He grimaces. "It'd be nice if *people* would just trust me. When I plan things a certain way, it's for a reason."

"If people don't know what those reasons are, you can't blame them when they decide to do what they want. It doesn't mean they don't trust you, but it does mean you're not communicating with them." Joy laughs, breathy and fast. "Only one person can read your mind and she's sitting next to you. Even I'm only right eighty percent of the time."

"It is kind of creepy how we can do that."

"It's not creepy. It's practiced. We just know each other well. Too well." She sighs. "Why didn't you email Summer an agenda too? Why didn't you ask for her input or help on anything? You can't treat her the way you treat me. I know I can trust you because it's been ten years. You've known her two months. You can't jump into the deep end without doing the work first just because your endgames align, Malcolm."

"Endgames?"

"We had a talk today. You want to get married. She wants to be married. Honestly, you two are a hop, skip, and a jump away from a marriage of convenience. If that's what y'all want, cool. More power to you. But I don't think it is?"

"It's not," he confirms with a half-smile. "I want the real thing."

Joy loves Malcolm. She's in love with Malcolm.

And she's beginning to understand that her life has revolved around him for too long, because all their bubble is doing now is damaging both of them.

Joy waits for the pain to come. She waits for the longing and reluctance that will taint her every word; for the hurt to coax her into being selfish; for any opening to insert herself so he remembers that if all else fails, she'll still be there. But this time, they're not there.

All she feels is hope.

She hopes that this, what she has to say, is enough to help him, really help him. She hopes that he's making the right choice for himself. And she hopes that Summer is everything *he* hopes she is.

The overpowering feeling of her hope fills up every inch of her, taking over everything. It makes her want to smile and cry at the same time, but she knows if she does both it'll only worry him.

So she smiles, and she says, "I don't know, I'm just guessing here, but I think Summer's willing to do the work. The least you could do is meet her halfway."

"That's not the *least*."

"You know what I mean."

When Joy heads back outside, Fox hasn't moved, but he's alone this time. She briefly wonders about where Summer has gone as she walks down the small sloping hill.

"Did you miss me?" Joy jokes.

"Do you like hugs?"

Surprised, she stares at him, but as usual his face reveals almost nothing. "Depends. Are you offering?"

"If I am, would you say yes?"

"If I say yes, will it be any good?"

This stumps him for a second, but his grumpy frown doesn't last, giving way to a knowing smile. It's a good one. "Shit. You are fantastically annoying, you know that?"

Joy laughs. It feels like some of the residual weight on her chest from talking to Malcolm disappears, bubbling away. Being with Fox makes her feel better. It *always* makes her feel better, she realizes. Since she met him, every time she's feeling down, there he is distracting her somehow. "I'd like that hug now, please."

As expected, he's warm and smells good. He holds her firmly, arms at her waist, and she rests her head on his shoulder.

"It's okay to be sad." His whispered words brush across her temples.

"I'm not sad."

"You looked like you were earlier." When he's not whispering, the rumble of his voice vibrates through his chest.

"Gotcha." She laughs. "Why are you being so nice to me?"

"Because I like you, Joy. And I'd like to see you happy."

Joy lifts her head. This is the closest she's ever been to him and it feels . . . nice. She examines his face, one feature at a time, seeing him for the dozenth time and the first time. He blinks slowly. Or maybe it just feels that way.

"Oh my god," Summer yells. "Why does he get to hug you and I don't? I give way better hugs than he does."

Fox answers without taking his eyes off Joy. "Probably because I asked first."

Joy laughs, planning to tell Summer she can have a hug too—she's feeling generous—but her gaze finds Malcolm instead. He's staring at them like he isn't sure what he's seeing, blinking rapidly in disbelief. His brow furrows into a deep frown. He snaps out of it, shaking his head, and takes the food tray the rest of the way to the fire pit.

"Iris," Joy says quickly.

Fox drops his hands immediately and takes a half-step away from her. "Sunflower."

"Sunflower?" Summer asks, taking another pull from her beer. He nods. "Sunflower."

"Whatever. I don't care." Summer has hit that stage where she drunkenly wobbles when she walks, but it looks purposeful when she does it, like she's dancing to music only she can hear. "I'm starving," she says to Malcolm. "Are there veggie dogs?"

"I didn't forget." He says it like it's an inside joke and she responds the same, "Remember, that was all your fault."

They position the chairs around the fire in a circle, and Malcolm passes out roasting skewers. Hot dogs and links are the primary attraction, but at some point, Malcolm also cooks hamburgers and a slab of ribs. The dessert station has ingredients for s'mores neatly laid out. Two more pints of Joy's favorite ice cream are chilling in ice buckets next to more beer.

"We should play a game," Summer says, turning her veggie dog over the fire like it's on a manual spitfire.

"What kind?" Malcolm asks.

"Something fun but easy."

"Whatever it is, I'll win," Joy says. "I get really competitive. It's one of my worst traits."

Fox asks, "Worse than your pervasive honesty? That's still number one for me."

"Not quite that bad," she says, playing along. *Pervasive*, she thinks, trying not to smile. *That's a new one.* She figures he's thought up his own new game where he gives her creatively strange compliments. "But it's up there. Malcolm, remember the Great Beer Pong Disaster, when I flipped the table?"

Malcolm is sitting back in his chair, arms crossed, and very much not looking at her. "Yeah."

Summer asks, "On purpose?"

"Oh yeah. I'm a very sore loser."

Summer *hmmm*s for a few seconds. "Have you two ever played Chain Story?"

Fox explains, "You start with a random prompt and whoever goes first has sixty seconds to tell a true story from their life. They then pick one element from their story, usually a single word, and the person who goes next. That person then has to do the same thing. Whoever tells the best story wins."

"But there's less time each turn," Summer says. "There's four of us so the first person gets sixty seconds. Second will get forty-eight seconds, then thirty-six, then twenty-four."

"Drunk math. I'm impressed," Joy says kindly.

"Really?" Summer grins.

"It's true. You should go first. How do we pick the prompt?"

Summer ends up telling a story about the first concert she ever tried to go to alone but got the dates mixed up for. She went to the venue on the wrong day, but the doorman let her in, and instead of seeing the Jonas Brothers she watched a metal concert. It turned out to be quite the formative experience for her—her nose got broken in a mosh pit.

"Is that true?" Joy asks Fox.

"Could be. It was before my time."

"That's why I have a lump here." She points to her nose—and accidentally leaves a smear of mustard behind. "The doctor set it weird so it healed crooked. Anyway, I choose you, Joy. Your word is"—she mimes a drumroll—"*crush.*"

"Ooh, okay. Crush." Joy tries to think quickly and snaps her fingers when it comes to her. "Crush. Celebrity crush. This is the story of my brief but incredibly intense crush on Naomi Campbell, and how it ended with my dad fighting the pastor in the sanctuary because he told me I was going to hell. Forty-eight seconds on the clock, please?"

"And go," Fox says.

Long story short, when Joy was six she became obsessed with Naomi Campbell. She told everyone she was going to marry her, because young children say things they don't understand all the time. Her pastor, however, heard her, condemned her to hell for being gay, and then her dad punched him in the middle of service. Her entire family switched to a more accepting church after that.

"Your dad is badass," Summer says.

"Yeah, he is," Joy says proudly. "Someday, I'll tell you what my mom did." The petty apple doesn't fall far from the petty tree.

"I'm going to forfeit. It doesn't matter what word I get, I don't have a story better than that," Malcolm says, grinning.

Fox says, "Me either."

"So I win? Why am I surprised? Of course I did."

Summer comes up with another game and they play, following her lead. Once again, it feels like earlier in the day—just four friends on vacation together. The weather around them has that perfect balance of cool air blowing off the lake mixing with heat from the fire. Fireflies drift in the distance between the trees and a chorus of frogs echo one another's songs. They finish dinner, make dessert, and drink as if they won't get hungover.

Well, Summer does, anyway.

# Eighteen

Malcolm trails Summer as she slides from tipsy to drunk because she asks him to. She also firmly tells Fox to stay away from her because he's no fun. They swap the backyard for the bar room to sing karaoke—she wants to and has to *right that second*.

"How are you feeling?" Fox asks Joy.

"Not nearly that sloppy," she jokes.

Two drinks are hardly enough to send her over the edge. She barely feels enough of a buzz to declare her love for everyone. That used to be her signature. One cocktail too many and everyone within her immediate vicinity needed to know exactly what she loved about them. Their glasses, their shoes, their cool shirts, and their good energy—anything would do.

"I want to try the hammock. Do you know how to use it?" Joy pushes down on the middle of the fabric, unsure if she trusts it.

Fox stands by one of the poles. "Pretty sure you just lay down."

"If I fall, you have to promise you won't laugh."

"Can't do that," he says. "After I make sure you're not hurt and I help you up, I'm most definitely going to laugh."

"Jerk. Feel free to go back to being grumpy."

Fox snorts. "Just sit horizontally like it's a swing. You don't have to get in it like it's a bed. Here," he says, moving to the middle and placing the fabric at his back. It's large enough to cover from his neck down to his knees. "I'll hold it steady and you climb on."

Joy waits for him to get into position—at an angle, legs bent, and feet planted—then stands next to him, leaning backward until she feels cradled.

"Here we go." He's taller so her legs lift off the ground before his do. She grabs his arm, gasping as they gently begin to rock back and forth. "So here you are, not on the ground."

"My hero." Joy laughs and turns her face to the sky. "Did you major in woodworking? Is that even a major?"

"Where did that come from?"

"My brain. It moves at the speed of light sometimes. In high school, I really leaned into that whole *I'm so random and quirky!* thing to get away with it."

"I can see it," he says.

"Anyway, I meant to ask you earlier but got distracted when you changed the subject. So, school? You?"

"Fiona did the university thing. I went to trade school for carpentry. I work in construction."

"Not to brag or anything, but I refinished an entire dining room set."

"Did you, now?"

"Sure did." She laughs. "But you actually make everything? From beginning to end?"

"Everything I didn't learn at school or on the job is self-taught from the internet," he says. "It was a hobby that accidentally turned into a small business."

"Wow. That's so cool."

"It's no different from what you do. We all have a side hustle these days, you know?"

"For real. They're required to have even the barest minimum of anything."

"Did you always dream of being a model?"

"No. I mean, I knew I was pretty," she said, only half-joking, "but I was more interested in the ocean."

"Marine biologist?"

"No, that's for plants and animals and stuff. I wanted to study the actual ocean. It didn't work out."

Joy stretches her arms upward, then twists her body closer to Fox until her head lands on his shoulder. "How are you so warm all the time? It's weird." She snuggles closer, drawn in by his rumbling laugh.

*You can do whatever*, he said.

Joy tentatively traces the veins in his arm again, starting at his elbow and trailing down, down, down until she reaches his palm.

"That tickles."

"Sorry," she whispers. "I'm just gonna rest my eyes for a minute."

"We should go in before you fall asleep."

"I'm not asleep. I said I'm resting my eyes."

"Okay." He laughs again. "If everything went perfectly and you became Joy, the oceanographer, what else would you have wanted?"

"That life doesn't exist at all anymore." Joy yawns. "I might've had an answer for you when I was eighteen, because if I didn't go to SJSU with Grace, I never would've met Malcolm. You know how in games you have a save point? No matter what happens you go back to that point when you run out of lives. Meeting him that day was too important. I can't go back beyond that moment."

"Hmm," he says. "What kind of life do you want now, then?"

Joy inhales—

"Besides Malcolm."

—and exhales a snort of laughter with enough force to shake the hammock. "Surprisingly, I wasn't even going to mention him."

"Sure."

"It's the truth." Joy yawns, covering her mouth with her free hand. "Let me think for a second."

But she doesn't. Joy drifts off to sleep instead.

Feeling the warmth of his body, the calluses on his palm.

Listening to waves lap gently against the shore.

Watching the rise and fall of his chest through half-closed eyes.

⁓

Malcolm's voice snaps Joy back to consciousness. "She's asleep?"

Fox says, "She's resting."

"She's asleep."

"I am not." Joy can't quite open her eyes. "I find your lack of faith disturbing."

"And she's quoting *Star Wars*. She's gone." The hammock stops moving and familiar hands touch her arms. "I got her. Come on, Cinderella."

Joy's feet are on the ground now but she's not sure how they got there. "You haven't called me that in forever."

Malcolm wraps his arm around her waist. Joy leans on him, letting him hold her up. She blinks and they're upstairs in her room. On the bed. Shoes gone.

"Shower. Makeup. Moisture."

Malcolm laughs. "You can do that when the Ghost of Wrinkles Past wakes you up in two hours."

"Shut up." Joy swats at him. He catches her by the wrist, kisses the back of her hand, and then places it on her stomach.

Suddenly, she's awake.

"Thank you for talking to me earlier. You were right. As always."

"Oh? Did you talk to her?"

"Somewhat. There's this tiny snag in that she's super drunk right now, but I think I said enough so that she knows the conversation train is moving."

"Good."

Malcolm kisses her forehead and says, "Good night," face hovering just above hers.

"Don't move." There's an eyelash on his cheek. It takes a few tries, but she picks it up and shows it to him on her index finger. He gently blows on it until it flutters away.

Joy raises her hands, pressing them to his cheeks, holding him there. "Malcolm."

"Hmm."

*He sounds just like Fox*, her brain thinks.

Malcolm raises his eyebrows to punctuate the patient question. He's not anxious to be anywhere else. She brushes the soft tops of his cheeks with her fingertips. Her palms cradle his jaw where the stubble has already begun to grow in. He shaves every day—he hates the way he looks with a beard.

They've been here dozens of times before, right on the brink of what comes next. So many times, in fact, that she can choreograph exactly how every scenario will go.

*If I say I love you, he'll say I know.*

*If I say I mean it, he'll say I do too.*

*If I say you don't understand, he'll say then tell me.*

And that's when it all falls apart. Joy can't predict what he'll say or how he'll react.

She doesn't know what will be left of her at the end.

It's jumping off a cliff. It's soaring until she's falling. It's being willing to crash to the ground, to lie bleeding and broken and alone even though she knows he won't leave her. He'll still be right there by her side looking at her the exact same way he always has. Helping her up with reassuring hands.

He's never going anywhere, and they'll always be at this standstill, balancing on the precipice. Unless they begin to let go. Together.

Joy's so afraid of life without him, tears begin to prick at her eyes. She tries to steady her breathing because he will ask what's wrong and she will lie.

She knows this part.

*He'll joke and say, is it me?*

*And I'll say yeah.*

*He'll laugh and say, Okay. I'm sorry.*

*And I'll say it's me too.*

*He'll ask if I want to talk about it.*

She's almost there. Just not tonight.

But for now, Malcolm takes her wrists and kisses her left palm. He puts her hands down again and says, "Good night, Joy."

"Night."

She watches him stand and walk to the door. He pauses there, half in and half out, leaning against the doorframe, saying nothing, but looking at her like he wants to.

She knows that face. She knows all his faces.

But he doesn't because Malcolm keeps his secrets, same as how Joy keeps hers—right below the surface where they can both see that they're there but not what they are.

"Off or on?" he asks softly, hand over the light switch.

f Joy is going to be sad, it shouldn't be on an empty stomach. Rummaging for snacks it is.

Downstairs, she raids the fridge, swiping all the fruit within grabbing distance until her arms are full. She shuts the door with her hip, turning to go back upstairs, when she does a double take. Fox is still outside on the hammock. Alone.

Joy sets her food treasures down on the counter. He might not want company, but it won't hurt anything to ask. She opens the sliding glass door and softly calls out, "Hey, hey."

"Joy. Hey." He props himself up on his elbows, legs bent, and feet planted to keep the hammock steady.

"What are you doing?"

He holds up his phone. "Reading. Thinking. Resting my eyes."

Joy laughs. "Are you planning to sleep out here?"

"Nah. I'll go in eventually."

"Ah. Hold on one second." Joy dashes back to the counter, grabs a container, and walks outside. "I come bearing pineapple in exchange for company."

"You don't have to do that."

"Bring pineapple or keep you company?"

"Both. You can sit here for free. You can also go back to bed if you want."

Joy shakes her head. "Second wind. I'm up now." She crawls back onto the same spot she had lain on earlier, curling up next to him again. "What were you reading?"

"A memoir. I prefer non-fiction and how-to books, usually."

"Ah, no torrid romance novels, then? I don't know why, but I feel like you'd really like those."

"Recommend me one you like. I'll give it a try."

"Deal." Joy laughs, snuggling closer to him. She rests her head back against the fabric, lids beginning to feel heavy again. Not even five minutes ago, she had felt wide awake and ravenous, but now the sleep that's been avoiding her seems to want a truce. Yawning, she says, "I really can't get over how clear the skies are here."

"On nights when there's no moon, you can't even see an inch in front of your face."

"No thanks. I'll stay indoors, then." Joy laughs.

In the eerie quiet, Joy listens to Fox's breathing, closing her eyes and searching for comfort in the sound, in the rise and fall of his chest.

"When she asked me if I loved her, I said yes. Of course I did."

*She?* Joy opens her eyes, immediately frowning. Damn, she fell asleep again.

"She said to prove it, and I had no idea what the hell she was talking about because I proved it every day. I was there—we moved in together, we shared everything, I took care of her. We were building a life together. How was I supposed to prove I loved her if that wasn't enough?"

Joy tries to be still, scared to make a sound or even breathe too hard and distract him. He's not talking to Joy. He's thinking out loud *for* her. At the winery she asked him if he's ever been in love and he's answering now. *Why?*

"She asked how that was different than how I treat Fiona or Summer. I said I don't have sex with my sister, and she rightly shot back with 'So you love me because you can have sex with me?' I didn't know what to say, because of course that wasn't true, so I didn't say anything. She said, 'You're not in love with me, Fox. You never *tell me* that you love me. You just care about me enough to convince yourself that you are.' The last thing she ever said to me was 'I hope you find someone who makes you see the difference someday.'"

Joy isn't sure if Fox is finished so she continues to hold still, keeping her breathing even.

"I'm sorry I waited until you were asleep to answer you."

He thinks she's asleep! Oh lord . . .

Fox turns his head, resting his cheek against her forehead. "You were right. It's hard for me to talk about myself like that out loud. But I wanted to tell you. You're always so honest with me. You make me wish I could do the same."

God, romance isn't easy for anyone. Still pretending, Joy grabs hold of his shirt and snuggles closer to him. She breathes in deeply, as if she were sleeping, and exhales into a sigh.

# Nineteen

ﾧ

## SUNDAY

Joy's heart isn't into getting ready for the day. She keeps it simple: a blue and white floral sundress with a square neckline and puff sleeves.

Downstairs, she keeps her routine, making a pot of coffee and waiting for Fox. The cabin doesn't feel old—it doesn't creak or groan with dead secrets. It's eerily silent save for the soothing sounds of the coffeemaker. Outside, the water looks as calm as ever and the sun shines like it's never seen a cloud in its life. There's so much peace all around her and she can't feel any of it.

Joy hears Fox's footsteps before she sees him. "Hey, hey. Welcome to the second meeting of the Early Morning Risers Club."

He laughs. "Is that what we are?"

"I like naming things."

Fox is next to her now, standing while she sits at the island. "How are you?"

"Mostly okay." She scrunches her face in discomfort. "Feelings are a little raw. Exposed. Like a pack of wolverines went to town on my chest, you know?"

"That's . . . okay. Wolverines. Got it."

"And, um. Would you laugh at me if I said I was scared?" she asks. "I'm scared."

Fox moves closer to her, until their arms touch. He places his hand over hers, thumb caressing her skin. He speaks softly, voice so low and a comforting murmur at her ear. "What are you scared of?"

"He'll finally leave me."

"I don't think he'll do that."

She won't look at him, but she heard the gentle smile in his voice. "Yeah. I know."

"What are you really scared of, Joy?"

She doesn't even have to think about it. "Everything will always be exactly the same."

"Hmm."

Joy turns to look at him. For once he's searching her face, trying to find something, his eyes the kindest she's seen them so far. "We can't keep living like this. He realized it before I did, and he's right. But he also needs me? I don't know what to do. I wanted to be able to wake up this morning and say, Yep, totally over him. Completely detached now. And it would happen with, like, accelerated manifestation. Instead, I got wolverines."

And at that, Fox has nothing to say. He sits with her in the quiet caused by releasing that piercing truth she's refused to accept for so long until she's had enough. He goes for his walk, and she heads upstairs. She lays on top of her made-up bed, swaddled in a quilt. Since Grace isn't awake yet and Joy's life is in shambles, the only logical thing to do is sit there until she turns to stone or her problems magically get solved on their own. That could happen.

Maybe.

"Hey, Joy?" Summer stands in the doorway waiting to be invited in. "Can I talk to you for a second?"

Maybe not.

Joy checks the time. "Aren't you supposed to be leaving?"

"Malcolm says the car is like fifteen minutes away."

Ever meticulous, instead of leaving Fox and Joy stranded he decided to leave them the Jeep.

"I'm not feeling all that great."

"Oh, I'm sorry. It'll be really quick. It's about Fox."

"Fox?" Joy asks, surprised.

Summer walks into the room, shutting the door behind her and surprising Joy again. All she needs is anything that resembles an opening and she barges straight in. She doesn't get too close—if she turns back the doorknob is in reaching distance—and her stance is plagued by fidgeting nerves. She asks, "Do you like him?"

"Yeah. He's great."

"I think so too. He's always looking out for me, even when I don't want him to. And he's the absolute worst when he's right about something. There's people who say I told you so, and then there's Fox."

"Okay."

"It's just um, I've noticed that you two have been really getting along," she says. "I saw the pictures in your powershots. He's, umm, really private, you know?"

"It's not like they were candids. I asked his permission before I posted them. He said it was fine as long as I didn't tag him, which I didn't, so."

"Right. And it's just, he never poses for pictures." Summer's wavering smile dips. "For anyone."

"I feel like this is going somewhere, *very slowly*, and I have a bit of a headache, so if you could hit that fast-forward button for me, I'd appreciate it."

"I can't remember the last time I've seen him this interested in someone this fast. So either you're some kind of magical love goddess"—her smile grows and then shrinks—"or he's faking it."

"Faking it?" Joy repeats, careful to keep her tone even and not give away how confused she feels. She figures this can go one of two ways.

One: intentionally admit to everything and play it off like a ridiculous joke.

Two: call a spade a spade.

Joy makes a guess based on Summer's body language. "You think Fox is pretending to like me? I'm not sure what I'm supposed to say to that. Why would he do that?"

"No. No, that's not what I'm saying." Her face screws up in consternation. "Shit. That sounded horrible. I'm sorry. I mean, he's very reserved, you know? Seriously emotionally closed off. The way he is with you isn't him—at least it's not the Fox that I know. I'm not saying it couldn't be him, just that it's . . . different. And it happened really fast."

"And," Joy begins, holding on to the word, "you're warning me about this because?"

"No, not warning. Just . . . saying. I know you don't like dating and—"

"I don't?"

Summer hesitates, unsure. "You do?"

Joy's temper flares hot and fast, scorching through everything else she'd been trying and failing to deal with. She's had enough of people thinking they know everything about her, drawing conclusions from assumptions they made on their own.

"Did Malcolm tell you that? Or are you guessing based on—what, exactly? We *talked* about this. You don't know me, Summer. Stop acting like you do because you have direct access to a source of secondhand information about me. And you know what else? I know Malcolm. I know exactly how hurt and vulnerable Caroline left him. I know exactly how rich he is. And now suddenly he's inviting some stranger he met two months ago into our bubble. That's pretty damn fast too, don't you think? What did *you* do? Maybe you're the one who's pretending."

Summer begins blinking rapidly like she doesn't understand—or maybe that she does. She starts crying before she even makes it out of the door.

Joy falls back on the bed in defeat. "*Fuck.*"

hey're gone," Fox says.

"Great."

Joy sighs, retreating further into her quilt. She's added two blankets to her cocoon, hoping to create the same sensation as a weighted blanket, but no dice. Overwhelmed, and full of regret and fury, she resisted calling Grace, who would make her feel better *but* also yell at her for not listening.

Fox lingers in the doorway.

"Are you here to start shit with me too?" Her mood hasn't recovered, stuck somewhere between dejected Sour Patch Kid and snapping turtle. She didn't mean what she said to Summer but that doesn't change the fact that she lost her temper again and said it anyway. The words rolled out of her like a bomb being dropped from a plane—no way to abort or stop it.

He blinks, suddenly very fascinated with the floor.

"Oh my god, you are," she says, temper burning again. "What the fuck—is it Make Joy Feel Like Shit Day or something?"

"Definitely not here to do that." His morning vocal fry still hasn't warmed up to his usual rumble just yet. He looks squinty and tired, like if the room gets too quiet, he'll fall asleep standing up. "What did you say to Summer?"

She looks him dead in the eyes. "The same thing she said to me."

"But she's the one who's crying."

"I'm crying on the inside," she deadpans. "You don't know me."

"You're right. I don't." He rubs his hands down his face. "Can I come in?"

"I don't want to talk about Summer."

"Okay."

"Or Malcolm."

"Okay."

Joy nods him in and watches him as he sits on the bed. "What do you want to do today?"

"Wallow in a vat of misery." She laughs, hollow and defeated.

His eyebrows fly upward. "Or we could do something fun."

"Like what?"

"Whatever will make you happiest."

"I don't deserve to be happy."

"I don't deserve to be miserable," he says. "We're spending the day together. Might as well meet in the middle at content."

"We are?"

He nods.

Why is he so concerned with *her* happiness? So far, the best parts of the weekend for Joy were all with Fox. Now here he is again, wanting to spend his one free day with her. She made Summer *cry*—surely that's a few points in the evil column that he should take into consideration.

And why does he keep putting everyone else first?

The entire trip was built around Summer—everything she loved and wanted, everything Malcolm could give her. He even included Joy in some of that planning by making a modicum of space and buying her gifts. Nothing for Fox at all except that damn cake.

He could do anything: sleep, go for a seven-hour walk, swim in the lake, take the boat out for a joy ride to give Malcolm a heart attack, but no. He's choosing her.

Not for show. For them. He *wants* her company.

Joy makes up her mind and asks, "What do you want to do?"

"Me?"

"There's no one else here except for my shadow person in the corner but I don't think they count in daylight," she jokes. "What do you want to do, Fox? It's your day. I hereby decree it. Whatever you want."

He's surprised—staring at her like she just tried to sell him the moon. "I don't know."

*I can't remember the last time I've seen him this interested in someone this fast*, Summer had said . . . *he's faking it.*

They had agreed to pretend to like each other, but there's nothing fake about what has resulted from it. Wanting to know him, to talk to him, to make him laugh and trick him into smiling—all of that is real. Joy genuinely likes Fox.

"Pick something," she says, crawling out of her cocoon and

across the bed. She stops directly in front of him, sitting on her knees, hands on his shoulders. "You've been nothing but good to me this entire time. Let me do something for you."

"You already did."

"Birthday cake doesn't count. Everyone gets one."

"It was a really good cake," he says solemnly.

She laughs, moving closer to him. Her arms are draped around him now, their faces inches apart. "Fine, let me do something else. There's no quota on good deeds. Let me take care of you by spoiling you with all my luxurious riches I managed to fit into two suitcases," she says, nodding toward them. "The third one is for shoes."

"How?"

"We're going to have a spa day."

No Malcolm. No Summer.

Just her and Fox.

# Twenty

Joy stands in front of him, pulling at her bottom lip while she considers where to start. "Facial," she decides. "Do you want clips or a headband?" She holds up both for him.

"Clips, I guess," Fox says. "This is interesting."

Joy pins his hair back, careful not to use too much tension. "Close your eyes."

"Why?"

"Because I'm asking you to." When he does, she adds, "Tilt your head back. Hold still."

"What are you going to— OW!"

Joy plucks a second eyebrow hair, and his eyes snap open. "Shh, shh," she whispers, climbing on top of him to keep him still. "Just let me help them a little. A good clean brow can do wonders for your face." She doesn't wait for him to respond and continues working, while watching for any indication that he doesn't want her there on his lap.

"Why are you so obsessed with my eyebrows?" He flinches instead of yells, and glares at her to *hurry up*.

She moves as quickly as she can without getting too tweezer-happy. She doesn't want to alter them too much, they have *character* after all, but she does disconnect them from his hairline and define his arch.

"I can't believe you do this," he says.

"You shouldn't because I don't. I get my brows microbladed."

"What's that?"

Joy explains the process to him. "Are you looking at my brows?"

"Yeah, since you pointed them out."

"Want to know my deepest, darkest beauty secret?" She grins and then whispers, "I have a unibrow. It's not super thick but it'll grow in if I'm not vigilant."

He scoffs. "My condolences."

"Thanks. Lots of people look amazing with a unibrow. Unfortunately, that's just not in the cards for me. All done." She smooths his brows out with her thumbs, slowly, to soothe him. "I have a cooling face mask that'll help prevent irritation as well as pay some attention to your pores." Between her expert fingers, the stiff gel warms into a viscous paste that smells like cucumber and mint. She drops small dollops of it along his T-zone, over his cheeks, and on his chin. "You have good skin," she says. "And you're being a very good sport about this."

Fox closes his eyes as she takes her time massaging the planes of his face in sections with small circular patterns.

"Relax," she murmurs. He has one major frown line, right between his eyebrows, just like Malcolm. She presses against the skin there in hopes of coaxing it to soften.

"I am relaxed."

"You're still frowning."

"That's just my face."

Joy keeps her cackle to a neutral witch setting. Fox's hands are hovering again, this time over her hips as she straddles him, fingers splayed and his touch light.

"You're very handsome," she says quietly as she works.

"Hmm."

"It's true. Objectively speaking. And personally speaking," she says. "You look extremely grumpy and bored a lot of the time, like absolutely nothing is worth being interested in. Sometimes, though, I catch you in these moments where you're so deep in thought I don't think you'll ever come back. It makes me want to chase after you. I want to see what you see, find what you find because I know it'll be brilliant, whatever it is."

Fox opens his eyes, finding hers.

"Get used to it," she says, smiling. "It's all a part of the Joy spa experience. I'm going to shower you in compliments too. All the things I like about you so far."

While the mask dries, she moves on to his hands. For this she abandons his lap in favor of sitting beside him. "How do you feel about nail polish?"

"Never thought about it," he says. "Not really interested."

"Not a problem." She puts the clear polish away and begins his manicure. The steps are basic: clipping, filing, buffing, prepping, and then attacking his cuticles with an almost religious zeal.

After exfoliating his hands and wrists, she's massaging them with a custom-made body butter to prevent dryness, when he asks, "How did you learn how to do all this stuff?"

"I taught myself. It's not hard. You should try it."

"I don't have time for all this."

She quirks an eyebrow. "You think I do? I make time."

"Because you're expected to."

"Because I *want* to. I'm only ever going to have one body. I wanted to learn how to take care of it in a way that works for me, so I did. No one else was going to do it," she says. "You should at least be doing the bare minimum. Do you wear gloves when you work?"

"Sometimes."

"Yeah, and every letter of that 'sometimes' shows on your palms. You should take better care of your hands," she says. "Personal care isn't a gendered thing. You can be rough, crusty, and ashy if you want, but why? There's a better way, I promise."

"That's harsh." He laughs.

"So are your hands." She laughs too. "Get help."

"Sure," he says. "What's next?"

"Well, we don't have a sauna, but we do have a hot tub."

Joy cleans the dried face mask off and moisturizes his face before they head downstairs. They raid the kitchen, ending up with a platter of leftovers, breakfast pastries, and fruit, and snag a bottle of champagne from the bar room to make mimosas.

It isn't quite warm enough outside to worry about heatstroke just yet. In fact, the last few remnants of the overnight chill still hang in the air. It prickles at Joy's bare skin, and coats the grass she walks on, tickling the bottoms of her feet. She opted to wear her second bathing suit—one-piece, all black, with geometric cuts of fabric in clever places.

Joy sets up the table for their food so it's within reaching distance, while Fox peels back the hot tub cover.

"I think it takes a couple of minutes to warm up," he says as the jets kick on.

"I can take it." Joy climbs the steps and gets in immediately, feeling perfectly fine and chilly.

"Isn't it cold?"

"Freezing," she says, excited. "I love it."

Fox, on the other hand, waits until he can see steam rising off the water. He settles in next to Joy, who immediately asks, "Have you thought of anything else you'd like to do?"

He shakes his head. "This is okay."

"You should still pick something," she says. "How do you feel about massages? Would you like one?"

*"From you?"*

"That had a tone." She laughs.

"No, no tone. Just surprised," he says, completely blush free. Either he never turns red or he truly isn't embarrassed. "Would you be okay with that? That's a lot of touching."

"I'm okay with you, Fox," she says. "If you're cool with it, then so am I."

And she is. She doesn't even have to think twice about it. Ever since that first moment in the kitchen when he let her touch his hand to see how comfortable she felt, she's been openly inching toward him, closer and closer.

Fox nods and Joy moves to sit behind him. He scoots forward, giving her room on the bench.

Joy says, "You don't have to sit so far away. Come here, please." She only has the basics down: effective ways to use her hands and which muscles to look for. She hits a knot right between his shoulder blades almost immediately and tries to work it out, but she can't. He doesn't seem to mind how bad she is at it, leaning into her touch and exhaling in delighted surprise when she hits certain spots. She's glad he can't see her face—her pleased smile is practically criminal.

Fox says, "You didn't answer my question last night."

"I didn't?" Joy plunges her hands under the water to reach his lower back. He sits up a little straighter with a tiny noise of acknowledgment that sounds low in his throat.

"About what kind of life you want. You fell asleep while you were thinking."

"Wrong, I was resting," she jokes. "I really want a house. Something small with a yard so I can get the kind of dog Pepper will like. I love my jobs, so I think I'd still want those to keep me productive. Travel a couple times a year to see the world with my family. That seems really basic, I know, but it also feels really fucking impossible and far away."

Between student loans and systemic racism, it's hard to feel hopeful about something even as standard as that. The American dream came in different flavors of privilege. Some people could never even hope to taste a single one of them. But being shut out was becoming more and more common—eventually the jig will be up for *everyone*. Maybe things would change then.

"Yeah, I know what you mean," he says. "My parents bought a house for dirt cheap in the seventies and my dad put himself through college with a minimum wage job while taking care of a family. He doesn't understand why I can't do the same thing. My mom gets it. She understands, but not my dad."

"Do you get along with them?"

"Sometimes. My dad is . . . difficult."

Joy can't relate—her parents are unbelievably supportive. They even call her every week only to say, *I didn't want nothing. Just saying hi. How's the weather?* "Your turn," she says.

"My life is good," he says. "I'm happy."

"Being happy is great. Most people can't even get there."

"You think so?"

"That most people aren't happy? Oh yeah. Definitely."

"It'd be nice if I made more money or the government did something that would balance out the economy and help people. It'd be nice if I didn't have to work six days a week, but it's not a deal breaker. My sister finally feels happy too. I signed a lease for a small shop to display and hopefully sell some of my pieces."

"Really?"

"Grand opening next week." He nods. "Other than that? No real complaints. Definitely not ready for kids, but I think I'd like to be a parent someday. As long as I can afford it. They're adorable money traps."

"Circling back to that first 'it'd be nice,'" she says, "that's a big part of the reason why kids are expensive. It doesn't have to be that way."

"It's all connected. One shitty knot of stagnation," he says.

Joy slides from behind him to sit at his side again. "I think if there was a way for me to do it without signing off on massive amounts of debt, I'd go back to school too. I still really love the ocean." She grabs one of the mimosas she prepared. "For now, I have to settle for making science puns, but only periodically."

Fox snickers. "What do you love about the ocean?"

"We don't know what the hell is down there."

"I think we have a pretty good idea."

"No, we really don't. So much of the ocean is unexplored. We, as a species, can go to the moon and send rovers to Mars, but we're just fine not knowing what's happening on our own planet? Bullshit. I have this really stupid theory"—she rolls her eyes—"I thought of it when I was a kid and it's just always stuck with me. I think we, as a species, could find out more about the ocean but we have this deep-seated, unspoken fear that stops us from going too far. We're never, ever supposed to find out—like it's a part of our DNA. We're born afraid of the ocean deep. But there are some people, like yours truly, who didn't get that fear gene. And James Cameron."

"Hmm." He considers her for a moment, a teasing twinkle in his eyes. "So you're the kind of person who would open the sacred cursed tomb without hesitating that it might end the world."

"Well, my middle name *is* Pandora."

"No, it's not."

Joy smiles at him.

"Wink or something, because I know you're lying."

"Joy Pandora and Grace Cassandra." She shrugs. "My parents have a prophetic sense of humor."

"You know, if Malcolm were here, that one might have actually killed him."

*Malcolm.* Hearing his name shatters the bubble of ignorant bliss she'd taken the past couple of hours protecting. Near instantly she thinks of him and Summer and where they are and what they're doing. She remembers last night and her fear. She thinks of later tonight when they return and tomorrow when everything might be different. The uncertainty returns just as fierce, settling into its familiar haunts for the long haul.

"We had a deal. We're not talking about him." Joy stands up, muttering, "And I'm turning into a raisin." She carefully climbs out of the hot tub, and instead of drying off, she walks down the small slope of grass and lays out her towel in a perfect patch of sun.

Fox joins her a few minutes later with a towel as well, setting up shop next to her. "Can I give you some unsolicited advice? You two need therapy."

Joy snorts. "Grace would love you."

"I mean it. I'm sure there's a couple's therapist that will take your case. I've never seen two people so dedicated to honesty not being able to be honest with each other. You don't communicate at all, you just think you do, and then you get trapped in this weird back-and-forth cycle. It's not good for you."

"That's not fair."

"I'm not judging you, Joy. I just get the feeling you don't see what's happening clearly because you can't. You're too close. I'm not and I do."

This is exactly what Joy meant when she called Fox brilliant. He portrays himself as one way, and one way only: the precise way he wants to be seen. Where one-liner quips and *hmm*s and hesitant smiles are the most anyone can get out of him. He's not reserved as in conservative—he's reserved as in *hidden*.

But he keeps giving Joy glimpses of his insightful mind, keeps letting his guard down just enough for her to be surprised, and then it's back up again.

Maybe he's like Malcolm—so sensitive he had to learn to hide it. What could have made Fox want to shut his brilliance away?

"You understand, but you also don't," Joy says. "I don't think it's something I can explain. If you never experienced a relationship like what Malcolm and I have, you'll never fully understand. You physically and mentally and emotionally can't. You don't just walk away from something like what we've built." She sits up suddenly, rolling her neck and stretching her arms upward until her muscles feel too tight and protest.

"Okay," he says. "We don't have to talk about it."

And with that, she closes that door again and all the lights cut off. Compartmentalizing until she can't anymore.

Her and Fox. Nothing else.

"How do you feel about pie?"

His eyebrows raise immediately. "You can make pies too?"

"Someone has a sweet tooth. Apple okay? There's a bunch of them in the breakfast pallet we can use. Come on."

Joy collects her towel, and they clean up their uneaten breakfast feast before heading inside. She begins as she always does by turning on music. Apple pie requires slow jams: crooning, soulful ballads, and mid-tempo bops that make you sway in time to the rhythm and move your hips. Not sad enough to make you cry, but sappy enough to make you smile and feel nostalgic.

"The secret ingredient is the singing," she whispers dramatically. "Dancing is optional for the uncoordinated."

"Hmm."

She shows him how to wash, cut, and prep the apples, giving him stern warning to use *exact* measurements. They make the dough together too. She puts him in charge of kneading with the instructions, "Be gentle with the dough. Make sure you and your sexy forearms don't go overboard."

"Excuse me?"

She laughs. "I hate to break it to you, but you also fit that very exclusive and specific category. My sister is obsessed with forearms for some reason. Especially when the guy is wearing a collared shirt and rolls up his sleeves. I don't get it, but according to her you have good ones."

"You don't get why your sister thinks forearms are sexy or sexiness in general?"

"The forearms. They're just arms. What's appealing about them?" She laughs. "I understand sexiness on an abstract level. When something or someone is considered desirable to the eye of the beholder and all that."

"Does it bother you that people find *you* sexy?"

"Are we going there? Really?" she teases. "Occasionally. Oh, and thank you, I guess? I'm assuming you meant that as a compliment."

"I did."

"Do you think I'm attractive, objectively speaking? I get called ugly and a whole lot worse on the internet. It's been . . . interesting to deal with."

"You're not ugly, Joy."

"There'd be nothing wrong with me if I was," she clarifies as she halves the dough and begins stretching it for the dish. "I don't view myself like that because it feels so negative. I feel like when people say 'ugly' they're either trying to hurt you on purpose, imply you don't fit conventional beauty standards as a fact, or bully you into being ashamed until you do something about it."

"Hmm."

"*I* like the way I look, so *I* don't think I'm ugly. But I know not everyone feels that way."

"Hmm."

"When I was younger, I used to stare at pictures for hours trying to figure out the difference between people's faces. I remember sometimes I'd be like, 'Oh yes, this is a good face that makes my brain happy,' and then there'd be others, 'Now, people are saying this one is sexy, but *why?*' and just on and on and on. I finally gave up, decided everyone is beautiful, and called it a day."

"Hmm."

"Am I talking too much?"

"No."

"Then how come you aren't saying anything?"

"I'm listening."

Joy stops pouring the filling and sets the bowl back down. "I want to talk to you, not at you. All you say is *hmm*. I'm tired of hearing *hmm*."

"Hmm." He grins.

"Don't be funny. Actually, yes, continue to be funny, it's great. But my point still stands. I'm interested in what you have to say, what your opinions are." She tilts her head back, pressing closer to him, her front flush with his side. "I want your thoughts. Give them to me."

The left side of his mouth quirks upward, making his dimple pop.

"You know, every time you drop that *hmm* wall, what you say blows me away."

"That's why I don't do it that often. I want to make sure you stay right here."

"Oh, that's awful, and I walked right into it." Joy begins to *wheeze* with laughter. She drops her forehead against his shoulder. "I love this for us. I really do."

# Twenty-One

P ie assembled, top crust weaved with Suzy Homemaker precision, Joy places it into the oven with an encouraging, "You're
going to be amazing."

The opening chords of a sweeping ballad begin to drift through
the kitchen. Joy twirls in time to the music, right past Fox, holding her apron like a corner of a dress. Growing up, she wanted to
be a Disney Princess—one who didn't get turned into an animal
twenty-five percent of the way through her movie. Her favorite
clothes to wear were dresses for that very reason. You never knew
when the right song would play and require you to dramatically
twirl on a moment's notice.

"Joy," Fox says. And then he's there, taking one of her hands in
his, one hand at her waist. She automatically places her hand on
his shoulder, assuming the position before she realizes what she's
done. He spins her in a circle, and she squeals with glee when he
dips her quickly before bringing her back up.

Alleged Romantic Bucket List item number 12: slow dancing in an unconventional place.

A kitchen had to count for that. And okay, it may not have been romantic, but pretending it's real feels as good as the real thing.

"Okay. This is probably, definitely why Summer accused me of casting a love spell on you," she says with a completely straight face.

". . . What?"

Joy hadn't meant to bring it up. It just popped into her head. Summer was right—Fox really is different when it's only the two of them. There's no way the grumpiest grump to ever grinch would be dancing with her in the kitchen if they weren't alone.

"Did Summer tell you *everything* about our fight this morning?"

"She didn't tell me anything. I caught her coming out of your room, crying, but she didn't tell me why."

Joy tells him what happened with Summer. She peeks around Fox's shoulder to check on the pie. It's already turning golden brown with fifteen minutes to go. "I guess it's not possible for you to honestly like me. Something *must* be wrong."

"And what if I did?"

"Huh?" She didn't mean to say that—it just slipped out.

Fox doesn't repeat himself. No smile. No laugh. He's not joking, and he knows she heard him.

And then, she realizes he's waiting for an answer.

*what if what if what if*

This moment feels familiar, like the time she and Malcolm kissed at the bar in college. Doubt had plagued her almost immediately. Did he mean it? Was it real? She'd wanted to ask Malcolm, but nothing changed after because they were already close.

He never tried to kiss her again, and she couldn't shake the feeling he was waiting for *her*. Was there something she was supposed to do? Malcolm had adjusted faster than she had—was there some kind of social rule she hadn't learned yet that she was supposed to follow? She never got an answer. That kiss lingered between them for days, then weeks, and then a month later he went on a date with someone named Dylan. Joy had cried for a week straight.

Now, that same yearning gulf is widening before her, except this time there's a bridge, with Fox waiting on it. He's giving her a way to reach him if she wants. All she has to do is accept.

Does she like Fox?

Of course she does. Yes. If she thought about it . . . no wonder she was so determined to get to know him and make him smile. Friendly at first, they're technically dating after all, but this . . . isn't that. Her brain had made the leap from friendship to romance and she hadn't even noticed.

Slowly, she stretches her fingers against his chest near his shoulder. Her thumb reaches his firm collarbone, and she runs her fingers along it, back and forth.

Joy has rules for moments like these. She needs to be sure first. See what he wants. *It's okay*, she thinks. *It's Fox. He knows.* She asks, "Can I kiss you?"

He nods . . . and then doesn't move. They're still slow dancing in the kitchen, swaying lightly to the music, surrounded by smells of flour, baked apples, sugar, and spices. She waits and waits and waits . . .

Joy almost laughs when she gets it. He took her literally—she's supposed to kiss him. She stands on her tiptoes to reach him and smiles through their first kiss. When he kisses her back, he doesn't linger at all. It's quick, efficient, and strangely enough, she does laugh then, a disbelieving and breathy sound as she presses another kiss on his dimple, because he's smiling too.

Oh, she's sure all right. Damn sure.

The song ends, breaking the magic spell. They automatically part, backing up half a step, hands falling to their sides.

"So," Joy says. "That happened."

"I was surprised you asked."

"You didn't seem surprised."

"I was surprised on the inside," he says. "Or maybe I've adjusted to your impulsive ways."

"No, it's not that. It's not possible to get used to me," she teases. "We should clean up." After the pie finishes baking, Joy sets it on a cooling rack just as Fox finishes drying the last of their dishes.

He asks, "Do you know how to play pool?"

"I know the basics. I think."

"I could teach you."

"That sounds fun."

In the bar room, Joy refuses to play fair. She does everything she can to sabotage his shots, including (but not limited to) sneaking up behind him, cackling maniacally before every shot he makes, moving the balls around when he's not looking, and even lying on the table and demanding he shoot around her or forfeit his turn, which he thankfully refuses to do.

All part of her master plan.

"You're absolutely ridiculous," he says, shaking his head.

"And you're absolutely laughing. That's all I wanted," she says. "I'm not above making a complete ass of myself to see you smile."

"Please don't."

"I have to." She rises onto all fours, crawling across the table to him, praying to any god listening that it won't break. "I get it.

You're grumpy. You have a grumpy reputation to uphold, but I need those smiles. Brightens my whole day."

"Hmm."

"That too. Just love those *hmm*s."

"Maybe we should play darts instead."

"Oh good, then I can compliment your form and your forearms again."

"Or not."

"Look, this is happening no matter what game you pick. I need you to accept the fact that you're getting these compliments. You're gonna take them and your gonna like them."

"I do like them," he says. "They're, umm, very sweet. Thank you."

"You're welcome. Now, teach me how to play."

For lunch, they return to the outside, armed with a throw blanket and a basket Joy randomly found in the closet of the bar room. She kicked Fox out of the kitchen while she packed it full of sandwiches she made, chips she found, an assortment of drinks, and, of course, their pie. The side of the house where a group of trees separated them from their borrowed neighbors had the best patches of early afternoon sunshine—not too direct as to burn them to a crisp, but just enough to engage in lazy cat mode. Stomach full and good mood rescued from the depths of despair, Joy began to roll around on the warmed blanket, stretching and making tiny happy noises.

"Is sleeping part of the Joy Spa Day experience?"

"I'm *resting*. Y'all are so rude about my old lady internal timer," she says. "You should try it. Pretend you're a cat or a solar panel. Let the sun recharge you, make you feel warm and whole again."

"What are you even talking about?"

"I don't know," she says with a laugh. "I'm warm and sleepy, shut up."

Fox sits with his knees bent, arms looped around them. From where they are, there's still a good view of the lake and he seems to be enjoying the idyllic scenery, but Joy knows better by now. He's off somewhere, thinking again. She turns onto her side, tucking her hands under her head as she gazes up at him. He has freckles all over his body—she noticed while massaging him—but none on his face. Strange.

Lifting one hand, she presses a small cluster on his forearm, then traces a line to the next, deliberately spelling out a short word with three letters.

"Why did you ask to kiss me?"

Unbothered, she answers, "Because I wanted to. Happy to report, I've been thinking about asking again."

"Hmm."

"Hmm? Why hmm? What's going on? Talk to me."

"He's not here."

*Malcolm.* "Nope."

"But you asked anyway."

"That had nothing to do with him," she says, dropping her hand. "And everything to do with you. Kissing other people doesn't mean I love Malcolm any less. It's nice to connect with someone lovely and pass the time with them for a little while."

"Hmm."

"And it's not like I'm saving myself for him or anything like that. That'd be beyond stupid."

Nothing about his body language changes in the too long silence that follows before he finally says, "How long is 'a little while'?"

Joy sits up, placing her chin on his shoulder. His gaze slowly slides to her as he turns his head ever so slightly so he doesn't have to look from the corner of his eye. She murmurs, "Just for today?"

Fox lowers his head, frown out in full force. "Then no. I don't want to do that."

"Oh." Joy backs away quickly, like she's been burned, to give him space. "Okay. That's okay too." Her mind goes blank—complete hard reset. She has to make sure her mouth is closed and not hanging open in shock because she wasn't expecting that.

He rejected her. Fox rejected her.

But he likes her—she knows he does. They have chemistry and jokes and understand each other. Why no? *No?*

Joy blinks rapidly as she stares at her thighs because she's in the damn twilight zone. How did—

"Until we go home."

Her head snaps up at the sound of his voice. "What?"

"You want someone to pass the time with and I want it to be until we go back home," he says.

Joy isn't sure if she should trust her voice just yet. If she opens her mouth, it would be equally likely to result in laughing, screaming, or calling him a very un-Joy-like name because he did that on purpose. Deceit and mischief are practically glittering in his eyes, and the restraint he's using to not wickedly grin at her is truly something.

She settles for stalking toward him slowly like a cat about to pounce. "*How dare you,*" she says, launching herself at him.

Fox laughs through her kiss attack, expertly holding them both up instead of falling backward. "Is that a deal?"

"Shut up and kiss me, you jerk."

Oh, and he does.

And the thing is, Joy feels safe, which doesn't always happen. Without breaking the kiss, she climbs onto his lap. This is a danger zone—always has been, always will be, but it's her favorite way to kiss someone. Her on top and in control.

Sometimes she held her kissing partners' wrists to keep their hands from wandering. Because she knew they saw kissing as a prelude—hands touching her breasts, her ass, trying to slide up her skirt, without permission. Kissing didn't imply anything other than that she wanted to kiss them.

Fox doesn't do that. As they kiss, his hands rest on her hips, firm and warm, but very still, until his right thumb begins to brush the tiny patch of skin left uncovered by her swimsuit. She runs her fingers along his jaw, brushing against his stubble. He inhales as she does it, his chest rising and pressing against hers— she squeezes closer to him as tight as she can until she feels the faintest thrum of his pounding heartbeat.

Joy pulls back to look at him. His lips are slightly parted, gaze unfocused and yet still so sharp. She's searching him now, trying to find in his eyes the look she knows all too well, that says *Too much. Not fair. You can't do this to me.* The one that tells her the party's over, to detangle herself before he tells that lie about blue balls. But it's not there either.

He brings his face close again, but not to kiss. His breath fans out over her cheek as he exhales and places a kiss at the corner of her mouth—the start of the trail. Down, down, down the kisses go, to her chin, along her jaw, in front of her ear, and down her neck, each one more welcome than the last. His hands still haven't left her hips.

Joy smiles, biting her lip and ducking her head to hide it because she doesn't want him to see how giddy he makes her feel, like champagne bubbles under her nose and the first perfect taste of decadent chocolate cake. It's not only his careful, delicate kisses, soft, perfectly sized lips, and scratchy stubble scraping against her smooth skin. It's thinking about all of him, all at once, holding him in her mind and in her arms.

Hesitantly, she touches his hair, stroking his loose curls and then diving in, fingers lightly massaging his scalp. He makes a noise when she does this—and she stops, assuming she's gone too far.

Joy tries to peel herself away, quick like a Band-Aid, and he says, "Wait. No," eyes intense and on hers. "It's okay."

Fox takes her hands, kissing her palms and each of her fingers, and when he finishes, he presses them to his chest. Thoughts un-muddied, she realizes it's firmer than she'd thought it'd be—the give of pliable skin and hard muscle underneath. And he's still so warm, truly like a furnace. He runs his hands from her fingertips to her wrists, touch so light it feels positively silky, like freshly shaved legs on clean bedsheets. He keeps his gaze down. That line between his brows appears.

Joy wants to ask him what he's thinking but something tells her it's a sixty-five percent moment. If he wants to tell her, it'll be when he's ready and she'll wait because he's wonderful. There are worse people in the world to kiss and Fox Brilliant-Grump-Extraordinaire Monahan is nowhere near that list.

"Do you want to go up?"

Fox looks at her face. "Up?"

"Stairs," Joy says. "To my room."

# Twenty-Two

Whenever Joy talked about sex with Grace, her sister focused on emotions and connections and selfish partners not worth her time. With Malcolm, he talked about the act itself, focusing on the physical sensations and the learning curve for how to be a good partner.

Both of those conversations merged in Joy's mind.

Fox holds her by the neck, bringing her face to his. Joy curves her entire body around him—she's on his lap, hands in his hair, legs wrapped around his hips. He's touching her back now, warm hand sliding under her shirt and splaying flat against her skin. But that's all. He doesn't move anywhere else. He doesn't try anything else. He just kisses her and kisses her and kisses her while her hands are all over him. And oh god, he gets it. Fox understands and it's not unfair or selfish. It just *is* and he understands exactly what she needs. When she can firmly feel his erection, she stops, pulling back and trying to catch her breath.

"Is something wrong?" He's equally out of breath and blinking in confusion as she slides off his lap.

"No." She kisses him once, twice, and then moves to the head of the bed, holding out her arms for him. "Let's take a break."

Fox sits next to her, and she curls around him again, unable to stay away. He's so warm and strong, and breathing him in makes her feel so calm.

"Was it too much?" he asks carefully.

"No." She laughs into the crook of his neck. "Not even close."

Joy is sure he knows his limits. If he needs a break, she's confident he'll tell her. But part of this includes being attentive to his needs too. She doesn't *want* him to have to get to that point. She could keep going on forever like that, especially with him, but he can't. Not without wanting more.

Fox touches her elbow, fingers dancing up her arm to her shoulder and then to her face, urging her from her hiding spot. "Joy," he whispers. It doesn't take much more to coax her back onto his lap and to kiss him again.

This time, Joy's hands find their way under his shirt. She murmurs, "Lift your arms, please," against his lips. He does, helping her take off his shirt. She presses her forehead against his as she looks down. His nose brushes hers, and he lightly nudges her head up to kiss her again.

Fox has a tattoo on the side of his rib cage—two words written in cursive. Joy traces them with her fingertips before making her way across and down the rest of his chest. Washboard. She gets it now.

"What's so funny?" he asks, smiling like he can't wait to know the joke too. His lips are swollen, a brighter pink than usual, and just as wonderful.

But Joy shakes her head. She moves her hands back up his chest and over his shoulders, down the curve of his biceps and forearms to his hands on her hips.

"I didn't really notice you on the boat or even look at you in the hot tub. It's just not something I care about looking at. Does that bother you at all? That the way you look doesn't—"

"No."

"But I do like touching you."

"I can tell."

Her fingers skip along his collarbone like she's delicately plucking guitar strings. "Does that bother you?"

Fox takes a deep breath, pulling his bottom lip into his mouth, and just shakes his head. He's patient, but she can see his eagerness too. She can see that he wants her to stop talking.

Joy's hands fall to her sides, and she sits back on his thighs. "This is what it's like with me."

There's the tiniest bit of strain in his smile. "I'm not complaining."

"Please listen, okay?" She cups his cheeks and gives him a quick kiss. "I view sex very rationally."

Joy is grateful for growing up the way she did, because her high school taught comprehensive sex education. They drilled it home that no matter how you felt or whom you were attracted to, deciding to have sex was a big choice for everyone to make.

Being asexual wasn't a choice for Joy. Deciding to have sex would be.

There are too many things to consider, so many potential outcomes like pregnancy and STIs that could change her life forever. She doesn't see it as fun like Malcolm, and she doesn't feel a desire to have sex with another person. The cons simply outweigh the pros.

If she ever decides to have sex, she wants it to be an informed and active choice. And she wants to feel safe.

Joy continues, "I need someone who'll be okay with me laughing, asking too many questions, being weird, and cracking jokes. Someone that can calmly explain things to me in the moment without getting frustrated or overwhelmed.

"One of my worst nightmares is having sex with someone and then they get mad at me because they think I'm not taking it seriously or because I don't automatically turn into a puddle of moaning mush. When if they knew me at all, they would know I *am* taking it seriously. It's a big deal to me—I just express it differently because I want to understand what's happening while it's happening."

"I could do that," Fox says too quickly. "You can trust me."

Joy manages to not laugh. "Let's think with our big brains, not our little brains." She places her hands on his neck, stroking his jaw with her thumbs. "You're a great person, Fox. I really do like you, but I also met you three days ago. I don't know you well enough to trust you like that. I'm not having sex with you tonight."

"Hmm."

"That's exactly what I wanted to hear," she whispers, mouth near his. "I can see you thinking."

"I am." He gives her a quick peck and rests his forehead against her chest. "Big brain needs a minute to catch up."

Joy holds him there, rubbing his back. "Cool. I'll wait here."

He laughs and mutters, "*God*." His expression is solemn when he says, "I really like you too, Joy."

"Okay." She inhales, holding it to prepare herself to be disappointed. It always ends like this.

"I'm very attracted to you." He lifts his head.

"I know." Her gaze flicks downward and up again. "I can tell."

That makes him smile. "I hear you. I understand what you're saying."

"But?"

"No buts," he says. "I understand."

"No buts? No questions? Nothing?"

"I said I understand. Is there something else you need to tell me?"

"No. That's it."

Fox kisses her again, softly at first and then harder and with more urgency. She's not overwhelmed but she gets close when he squeezes her thighs. Her hands are on his wrists in record time, holding him firmly. He breaks their kiss and looks her in the eyes—still soft, still understanding.

He asks, "Can I touch you?"

Touching makes it intentional. Kissing combined with touching creates the shift from kissing to arousal to sex. Joy only wanted the first part. Maybe not forever, but certainly for right now.

"Depends where."

He thinks about it and answers, voice low in earnest, "Is everywhere too much?"

Joy laughs, wrapping her arms around his neck and repeatedly kissing his cheeks. "It might be, so let's start slow."

"What are you doing?"

She pauses, holding the hem of her sweatshirt. "I'm taking off my clothes. I'm okay with some touching. Unless you want me to keep them on?"

"Hmm." Fox squeezes his eyes shut for a second, shaking his head. "Can I just?" He touches her at the waist. "Maybe I should do that."

"Oh," she says, understanding him. "Panties on unless I say otherwise."

"I understand. Lift your arms." His voice is firm, a rumbling command. She does and he slides her sweatshirt off with one hand and unclasps her bra with the other.

That's . . . skillful.

Fox kisses up her neck and ends with nibbling her earlobe as his fingers trace the outline of her shoulder blades. Joy places her hands on his shoulders, trying to concentrate on how each sensation feels so she can remember what she likes but it blurs together, everything sending signals to her brain at once.

He stops, moving to kiss her chin. "You don't like being on your back."

Joy bites her lip in surprise. When did he figure that out? He said it like he already knew the answer, so she nods to confirm.

"If I'm next to you will that work? Not on top or over. Just right next to you, like we're side by side."

"I've never tried that."

"Do you want to? You can say a flower if you want to stop."

Joy kisses his forehead. "Let's try it." She lies back in the bed, head propped up by pillows.

True to his word, he stays next to her, completely to one side as he kisses her. He creates a path, touching and kissing and tasting down her body—her neck, her shoulders, each of her arms and all her fingers, her chest, down, down, down, down. When she laughs because it tickles, he does too. When he takes off her shorts, lifting her legs in the air and kissing down the length of them, she holds his gaze. On the way back up, he pays special attention to all the spots he missed on the way down, like the backs of her knees, her elbows, and her waist—

Joy shivers and gasps, back arching. There's a slight tremble low in her abdomen. The same kind she gets when she masturbates.

"You okay?"

"Kiss me again. Right there."

He does and the same thing happens—she laughs this time, absolutely delighted by the sensation.

"Ahh," he says. "I think you have a spot."

"What's that?" She giggles and feels stupid for doing it but can't stop.

"Think of it like a cheat code," he says, laughing too.

Fox lifts himself up, and she holds her arms open for him, bringing him close. He kisses her mouth and says, "You're too beautiful. I almost can't believe you're real."

"Fox, no. Don't say that." She buries her face in his neck, practically her new favorite spot. "It's so cheesy and I love it."

Downstairs after dinner, Fox and Joy are still wrapped up in each other, snuggled under the blankets on the couch watching a movie. She shifts to the left, head landing perfectly in the crook of his neck.

Fox says, "You should go to bed."

"I'm not sleeping."

"You're resting, yes, I know."

Joy groans in complaint. "It's not my fault. If I hold out a little longer, my second wind will kick in."

Malcolm and Summer are still missing in action. The sun went down hours ago, it's so far past her bedtime her shadow person is probably pissed that's she's late, and everyone knows you can only watch so many Nicolas Cage movies before your hold on reality begins to slip. If Joy hasn't lost count, the credits for their third completed film are rolling on the screen. She snuggles closer to Fox, breathing in deeply. "I'm fine."

His hands are on her thighs and her back.

"I'm awake." Joy closes her eyes again. "We're moving?" she says, voice thick with sleep. "Where did the couch go?"

"It's still there." Fox is carrying her up the stairs.

"This is cheating, *oh my god.*"

"Cheating how?" He sets her down in front of her door, holding her steady by the hips.

"I don't know." Joy rubs her face in defeat. "It just is."

Fox leans in, and she tilts her head upward to meet him in the middle. At the last second, he bypasses her lips in favor of her ear. "Good night, Joy," he whispers before leaving a kiss on her cheek.

Joy supposes that's acceptable. Not what she wanted, but it'll do. There's still tomorrow. She still has roughly thirty-plus hours left to spend connected to him. Not that she's counting. "Good night."

Joy flies through her nighttime routine in record time and collapses into bed. She's asleep before remembering to turn off the lights and turn on her makeshift nightlight. And she's in full-blown snoring mode when someone knocks on the door.

The sound jolts her awake, heart racing with the sudden fear that only being caught unaware and defenseless can bring. "Yeah?"

It's Malcolm. As expected. Hasn't he visited her every night so far?

"Hey. You asleep?"

"Not currently. Come on." Joy waves him in, moving over to make space for him on the bed. It's only after he shakes his head no and sits on the floor that she remembers. Today was the Big Summer Day. She presses the heel of her hands into her eyes and takes a tired, shaking breath. The physical separation is starting. She stretches back out onto the bed to get comfortable. "How did it go?"

"Not at all like I expected." Malcolm moves closer, resting his forearms on the edge of the mattress inches away from her.

Joy fills the gap, pillow folded under her head. "No?"

He shakes his head.

If that's all he wants to give, she doesn't feel right asking for more. The fact that he isn't on the bed with her now tells her everything she needs to know anyway.

Malcolm asks, "What would I do without you?"

"Depends." She covers her mouth to yawn. "Is it an *if we never met* situation or an *I died* situation?"

"Jesus, Joy."

"What? You asked a question. I'm asking specifics." She pauses for a moment to blink away the tendrils of sleep tugging at her. "If I died, you'd be devastated, obviously. Weekly visits to my grave tree to talk to me, a sort of memorial shrine in your house full of your favorite pictures of us, and so on. Now, if we never met . . . I don't know. I think you'd still be successful. And happy."

"I'd miss you." His voice is soft, and his touch is softer as he quickly brushes his nose against hers. "I wouldn't know you, but I would miss you. Even if I was successful, happy, all my dreams came true, everything would always feel slightly off because you weren't there. I wouldn't know why, but I'd always feel sad about it. I think I'd always feel incomplete."

"Don't." Joy wipes a tear from the corner of his eye. "What's wrong? It was your big day. Everything's good, right?"

Malcolm sniffles. There aren't any more tears—just the one Joy caught. "Hey, do you remember how we met?"

Joy smiles. "I do. At the LGBT Alliance mixer." This is one of their rituals and why she can remember it so well—out of nowhere, he'll ask if she remembers and retell the entire ordeal. She loves listening to him, as if she doesn't star in the story too, and seeing herself through his eyes.

Malcolm begins, "The club president decided to set up informational booths for each letter. I was the only ace member, so they put me in charge of the A-station."

"Naturally."

"You walked in wearing the shortest pair of jean shorts I've ever seen in my life, to this day, and a practically see-through tank top."

"They weren't *that* short."

"Everyone could see your cheeks."

"It was hot outside. I wanted to stay cool and not get tan lines." Joy giggles at the memory. The audacity of College Joy was truly unmatched. "Continue."

"I watched you the whole time as you worked the room, going from table to table and leaving a trail of dazzled people in your wake. I didn't even notice that there was a girl who had your exact face right next to you. It was you. You were the one." Malcolm touches her hand. "Finally, it was my turn. You walked up to me and said, 'Hey, hey, what's this mean?' smiling like you already knew."

"Nope." Joy shook her head. "I was smiling because you were cute. You and your little bow tie—you were so serious too."

"I was. Still am," he agreed. "When I told you what asexual meant your smile started to disappear, getting smaller and smaller, and your eyes were getting bigger. I thought, *Great, she's gonna laugh and say that's not real.* So I start steeling myself because I'd been dealing with that erasure bullshit all day and I was fucking tired. But then, you looked at me and said—"

"*Oh shit,*" they say together and laugh.

Malcolm continues, "'Oh shit. That's a real thing? There's a word?' You snatched up one of the pamphlets I made, mouth completely hanging open."

"I started asking you a million questions. I was such a rude little shit about it. 'Do you feel like this too?'" Joy covers her eyes in embarrassment, groan turning into a yawn.

"Then you said, 'Gimmie your number.' Not a request, a full-on demand. I was so shocked I just gave it to you."

"Excellent choice."

"I waited all day for you to text me. Constantly checking my phone, getting my hopes up that maybe you wanted to hang out or something."

"Wait, you never told me that?" Did he? Joy doesn't remember, but she's so sleepy and trying so hard to focus on her parts of telling the story. That *feels* new, though. It must be.

"It took two weeks for you to remember I existed. I got a text in the middle of organic chemistry: *Hey, hey it's Joy! If you're not busy let me buy you lunch.* I knew it was you. You never told me your name, but immediately I just knew."

"I was so wild back then." Her voice is muffled by sleep. "Couldn't tell me nothing. Anything I wanted, I went for it. No shame. No doubt. Just balls-to-the-wall confidence." She laughs. "God, I was amazing."

"You still are. Just older."

"No. Now I'm an almost old lady who's scared of everything."

Something warm touches her face.

"Joy?"

Her eyes flutter open, but she's fading fast. Only Malcolm's face is in focus—everything else is a blur.

"Joy?"

She didn't realize she'd closed her eyes again, but there he is. Still there, still perfect.

"Hi, Malcolm," she mumbles, sleep finally overtaking her.

His laugh sounds broken—too short and gasping.

# Twenty-Three

MONDAY

Overbearing sunlight wakes Joy up in the morning. She half-expects Malcolm to still be there next to her bed, but he left at some point during the night. Memories of what happened while he was there are fuzzy at best. Too tired to hold on to images, the details wash away, leaving only vague impressions.

Malcolm was sad about something.

They talked about how they met.

Things didn't go the way he expected with Summer?

Joy gives up with a sigh while rolling out of bed.

The day's agenda had been modified to include making an appearance at the neighborhood holiday party Summer wanted to go to after getting the invitation from the boating invaders. Before that, they're going downtown, and then hiking after lunch.

Joy retrieves the bag Malcolm gave her to assess the items and figure out how to tailor them to her style. A pair of soft brown leather hiking boots that aren't terrible to look at. A couple of high-rise breathable leggings in a few different colors. Some pants she would donate to a shelter when she got home. A black long-sleeved shirt that doesn't look like anything special but according to the tag has "special moisture-wicking technology built in."

Joy would just . . . change her clothes in the car when they got there.

Her outfit of the day is a simple teal gingham top with puff sleeves, a deep V-neck, and thick ties that wrap around her waist to make a bow in the back. The top matches well with flared jeans, letting her live her best seventies disco chic life. She dresses quickly—well, quickly for Joy—and barely restrains herself from running down the stairs to meet Fox in the kitchen.

Was she maybe a little too excited to see him? Yes.

They're the real deal now, until they say goodbye at the end of the trip tomorrow. And Joy doesn't want to waste a single second.

Fox appears, rounding the corner to the kitchen. Joy ambushes him. "Let's go." She hands him a still-hot mug of tea.

"Where?" he asks, a smile in his gravelly voice but not yet on his face.

"I'm coming with you on your morning walk." Joy unlocks and opens the sliding glass door. "Which way?"

Fox points to the left. They set off for the lake's edge, walking along the path. The mornings have all been uniform in their weather and beauty. Partially cloudy skies. Gentle waves. The barest hint of chill. Early morning birdcalls and other wildlife noises Joy doesn't recognize but has a healthy fear of. There could still be bears out there. Overall, though? She could really get used to a place like this.

He slings an arm over her shoulders and kisses her forehead.

She leans into him, hoping he doesn't notice how deep of a breath she takes through her nose. God, he smells so good.

At the midway point, they stop at a wooden bench with a gold dedication plaque. It's stationed right in front of what appears to be an entrance that leads straight into a denser woodland area. It's so thick with stick-thin saplings, flourishing ground plants and bushes, and trees with trunks bigger than Joy, it's only possible to see a few feet inside.

Won't be going in there. Nope.

Fox sits down, and so does Joy, except sideways to keep an eye on that entrance. That's *absolutely* where Hansel and Gretel went to get eaten. Trail or not, willingly going that way is no different than flat-out asking for the universe to test your will to live.

"Any word on how the festival went?"

"Malcolm came to my room last night—"

"He did?"

"Yeah, he does that all the time. Anyway, I asked, and he said something like it didn't go the way he expected it to. Have you talked to Summer?"

"No." Fox takes a sip of his tea. "This is just a question: You think it's perfectly fine and platonic that he goes to your room every night?"

"All we do is talk, so yes."

"Hmm."

"You don't think it's okay?"

"Just a question. Not a judgment, Joy."

"Okay, I'm going to lose it if I don't say it: you're thinking, and I can see it, so just come out with it." Joy swats at a bug that flies too close to her face. "Come on."

Fox actually laughs. "Sometimes I'm not thinking about anything. I pretend like I am to see what you'll do."

"You *diabolical* dick." She kisses his cheek to let him know she doesn't mean it.

He laughs again. "This time I am—thinking, not a dick. You two bother me."

Joy's eyebrows raise in surprise. "Me and Malcolm?" He nods and she asks, "Why?"

Fox exhales into a sigh. He raises his head, looking at the sky and frowning before his gaze lands back into his cup of tea. His lips twitch, either ready or reluctant to speak. Joy can't tell which it is.

"You love him," he says through nearly clenched teeth.

*Reluctance*, Joy decides. He really didn't want to say that.

"Yes." Keeping it simple feels best. No qualifiers necessary.

"He loves you."

"Yes."

"And is in love with you."

"No."

"*Yes*." He turns to her so quickly, so exasperated, and insistent with his furrowed brow and grumpy line between them on display. Frustration and confusion are written all over his face.

Feeling calm, albeit a little surprised, Joy caresses that small, lovely wrinkle with her thumb until it relaxes. She has an idea, a way to make him understand. There's no fear here, no hesitation. Nothing ever stops Joy from saying what she wants to Fox.

Even if she's repeating something he said to her while he thought she was asleep.

"I've known Malcolm for ten years and you've known him a

month, but here you are, fabulously and brilliantly grumpy, so firm in your belief that you are right, that you were willing to be my fake boyfriend to prove it." She drops her hands to his shoulders. "Fox, you don't see something I don't. You're projecting."

"Projecting?"

Joy leans to the side, draping one arm over the back of the bench. "Sometimes you have to tell the people you love that you love them. Showing them isn't enough."

Fox's eyes widen, bigger than she's ever seen. His face is nearly slack with shock. "I didn't ask to be attacked like this."

"Hmm." Joy laughs. "Malcolm and I don't have that problem. We know we love each other. We say it and show it all the time. Our problem is that love is fucking complicated. We bother you because you think a declaration will change things for us because it could've changed things for you."

"He should be in love with you," Fox insists. "I don't understand why he isn't."

"Welcome to the club, I guess." Joy kisses the back of one of his hands and holds it to her cheek. "You know about Caroline, right? When she left him, she flat out told him that he's *in love* with me. Malcolm denied it. Even now, he still does and he wants to be with someone who isn't me. Right now, that's Summer. And I have to accept that. We both do."

Back inside, Malcolm sits on the couch alone. His gaze completely slides past Fox as if he isn't there, settling on Joy. "Where did you go?"

"Morning walk. Not far."

Silence descends around them with a quickness, transforming into a tense stalemate. Malcolm continues staring at Joy like he's waiting for something. The tension is so overbearingly thick, Joy almost wishes Summer would giggle her way into the room to help diffuse the bomb sizzling in Malcolm's eyes.

Something must have gone wrong. Inexplicably, desperately wrong.

Joy voluntarily stands between Fox and Malcolm. "I think I'm going to hang out down here for a bit."

Fox takes the hint, God bless him, nods, and walks into the kitchen. After he places his mug in the sink, he disappears through the dining room. Joy brandishes her best smile for Malcolm. "Hey, hey." She sits on the couch. He moves over, practically leaving a ravine of space between them.

A vague memory from last night becomes clearer in her head—when Malcolm visited her room, he didn't lie on the bed with her. Right. He's starting to draw boundary lines between them. Enforcing the rules his partners—*Summer*—asked for that'll keep Joy at a physical distance. Accusations of emotional cheating are never far behind.

Needing to do something with her hands, Joy pulls out her phone. Scrolling will do.

"Don't."

Joy snaps, "So you just want to sit here in silence enjoying each other's silent company? Or are you going to talk to me?"

"About what?"

"Yesterday, maybe? Five minutes ago? Why you're being so weird?"

"How am I being weird?"

"Would you like a list? I could also take your picture." She gestures with her phone. "Your whole vibe is *I'm feeling weird energy.*"

He grimaces, partially turning away. "Conflicted. Not weird."

"Now we're getting somewhere. Conflicted about what?"

Malcolm shuts back down after that. He scowls through breakfast, grumbles his way through washing the dishes, and barely speaks. Not even Summer, trying to get his attention, can get him to break his vow of silence.

# Twenty-Four

Believe it or not, they all pile into Malcolm's Jeep right on schedule, automatically slotting themselves in their assigned seats.

Fox and Joy in the back. Malcolm and Summer in the front.

They're on the road, listening to Summer's playlist again, when Fox slides his hand across the seat to find Joy's. His palms are still callused but noticeably less rough. The heat from his skin grounds her, solidly bringing the present back into focus.

They haven't spoken since she tried and failed to comfort Malcolm after their walk. Realization zings through her like a current of electricity—he might be upset about her deciding to spend time with Malcolm instead of him. He doesn't look it, though.

Keeping her voice nearly silent, she mostly mouths, "Did she talk to you?" and nods toward Summer.

Fox shakes his head. He mouths back, "She seems fine? Why is he mad?"

"He won't tell me."

Fox nods, giving her hand a comforting squeeze. "Are you okay?"

When Malcolm and Caroline got engaged, she couldn't get out of bed for three days.

Now that he's dating Summer she feels . . . accepting. She accepts what happened. At the start of this trip, all she wanted was to tell Malcolm how she felt. And she did that. Several times over, in many different ways. Same as Jules in *My Best Friend's Wedding*, Joy didn't get the ending she wanted. But she still feels like a good person on the inside. A good person who loves her best friend and only wants to see him happy. She still feels like herself.

There's a dash of optimism and a sprinkle of hope in there too.

"I think so? Nothing hurts right now." Joy sighs. "I just want to have a good day today."

He grins. "I'm sure I can help with that."

Joy feels herself smiling—every part of her down to the tips of her toes, tingling with excitement. Her days with Fox were numbered from the beginning and now she's eagerly anticipating what number four will bring.

Malcolm finds a parking spot a few blocks away from the strip. Summer slips on her sunglasses. "I *love* being a tourist."

The shops are a mix of standard, cute, kitschy, and downright strange—everything housed in brick buildings. Almost all of them are two stories tall with balconies and shingles out front, their company names emblazoned in an array of fonts. It reminds Joy of a stereotypical Wild West setting. Especially when they get to the horses tied to posts and hooked to carriages for rides.

There are museums, jewelers, and saloons; places where you can take old-timey photos and get tattoos; coffee shops, bakeries, and an ice-cream parlor; and restaurants boasting their world-famous specialties with strange names like May's Bottom Butter Brew and Kitchen Sink Spaghetti. Street vendors sell even more food, like cinnamon churros, hot dogs, and roasted corn on the cob dusted with parmesan cheese, and fun items like bubble wands, wildlife stuffed animals, and attraction maps.

Within the first five minutes, Joy pulls Fox into a photo booth, swinging the curtain closed behind them. She demands for him to, "Smile, damn it!" after each flash, only to end up cackling at how he manages to be even stonier than usual just to spite her. For the last shot, she drapes herself over him, pressing a smiling kiss onto his cheek.

"For you." Joy hands Fox the completed photo strip. He takes it, carefully folds it in half along one of the white spaces, and tucks it into his wallet.

They split an oversize salty soft pretzel drenched in mustard and two different kinds of ice-cream sandwiches, and ditch Summer and Malcolm for an hour to go on a private carriage ride around the train depot. When it's over, Fox texts Summer—they join them in watching a performance of an Old West shoot-out.

Later, Fox buys Joy a deer stuffed animal in secret, presenting it right as she's in the middle of chugging a root beer float for a restaurant's sidewalk competition. She thanks him through the brain freeze and then blames him for making her get second place.

Summer says, "Press your tongue to the roof of your mouth. It'll make it pass faster."

Joy tries. "It's not working. Holy god. *Ow.*" She sucks in a breath, rubbing her forehead.

"Where should we go now? We have a lunch reservation soon, right, Malcolm?"

Malcolm nods, still not speaking.

Summer continues, "I've eaten way too much street food, so I want to walk some more to make room." She taps her stomach.

"We haven't gone that way yet." Fox points toward a side street with more shops. "Did you guys?"

Summer shakes her head, bouncing on her toes again. "Let's go, let's go."

"My feet are starting to hurt. I should've worn different shoes." Joy's platforms are disco chic and most definitely not made for walking. She's sure there's a blister making its miserable self at home right above her left heel.

Fox stops short, turning to her. "Do you want to hop on?"

"Hop? On?"

His rumbly laugh catches her off guard. "My back. I'll give you a ride. Come on."

"Oh, no. Fox, no. I can't do that."

"You can, actually." He stands with his back to her, lowering himself down to a crouch. "Come on. Just until your feet stop hurting."

"Oh my god, I can't believe I'm doing this." Carefully, she wraps her arms around his neck, mostly resting them over his shoulders. His arms loop under her legs to support them as he stands up. "Isitokayamitooheavyohmygod." She feels his rumbly laugh in his chest, vibrating against her torso.

"You're fine." There's barely any tension in the firm muscles in his arms and back, none on his face either. He walks at the same pace he has all day, barely hindered by carrying her.

"You didn't have to do this at all, but thank you."

Fox turns his head slightly to meet her gaze. His dark eyes are the warmest she's ever seen them. "It's your day. Whatever you want."

The romantic clichés are not messing around today. They're hitting her hard with the force of a superpowered wrecking ball. All she wants to do is stare into his eyes for as long as she can. It's so strange to go from consuming media about something for literal years to experiencing it up close and personal.

Joy has spent so long waiting for Malcolm with the purest form of tunnel vision, it honestly never occurred to her that yes, if she *tried*, there might just be someone else out there. Someone out there among the billions of people on the planet. What are the odds?

They cross the street and head straight for the first building, which looks like a souvenir shop. Joy slides off Fox's back and wanders through the store alone for a while. She ends up crossing paths with Summer, who has already filled her basket with shot glasses, playing cards, and postcards with the city's name scrawled across them.

"For game night," she explains. "Oh, Joy, you should come to our next one. It's on Wednesday."

"Maybe." Joy browses a turnstile with mini license-plate key chains, searching for Fox's name. "Board games aren't really my thing."

"We don't just play games. I just call it game night because that's how it started. Really, it's just a bunch of my friends hanging out weekly. You know, something to look forward to."

"Wait, it's every week?"

"Yep."

"Malcolm went every week?"

"Uh-huh." Summer moves on to the hats, trying one on.

Joy's not sure why that's so surprising. Maybe it's not because Malcolm was with her so often. Rather it's that he managed to keep it a secret. How did Joy not know? She doesn't keep close tabs on him like she's his FBI agent, but she has a general idea of his goings-on at any given time. And yet he invested so much time in Summer without her knowing.

Maybe she didn't want to see it because she only wanted to see herself. Her hope for herself overshadowed everything else. Selfish.

"Hey, Joy? About yesterday." Summer's gaze is fully trained on the hat display. "I want to apologize."

"I'm listening."

"I thought about what happened all day. I didn't work through what I wanted to say first, and it got all jumbled up and came out wrong. I'm still trying to figure out the right way to say what I want to say, but for now, I want to say I'm sorry. I didn't mean to make you upset."

"Thank you. That's really considerate. But, Summer, I haven't even thought about it at all. Honestly. I'm fine. It's not worth worrying about."

"Oh, okay. Cool."

"Since we're here," Joy begins. "Is Malcolm okay? Did something happen yesterday?"

"Um. Sort of." Summer *flinches* with discomfort, fidgeting and shrinking herself down by hunching her shoulders. "I'm going to, um, uh. I want to look at the shirts. I want to get some for my roommates." And just like that she flits away to the shirt wall, leaving Joy alone.

Neither of them wants to talk about it? Okay. Weird. More than weird. Possibly horrendously bad.

"I can see you thinking," Fox says, materializing out of nowhere. He's standing in front of her, next to the turnstile.

"Hallo."

"'Hallo'?" He grins. "Not 'hey, hey'?"

"Oh, that's only if I greet someone first."

"There are rules. I didn't know this. Hmm." Fox picks up a nameplate from the *J*'s and tucks it away in his hand. Joy pretends she didn't see it, smiling that they had the same idea.

"Something's not right with Summer and Malcolm."

"I noticed. There's also this." Fox pulls Joy into a hug. He dips his head, so his jaw touches her forehead, and holds her tightly inside a Fox cocoon. She sighs, *actually* sighs, from contentedness. She hugs him back, surprised by how relieved she suddenly feels. And how much she needs this. From him.

Joy lifts her head so she can read his expression. "Not that I'm complaining, but is there a reason why we're hugging in the middle of a novelty shop for tourists?"

"Yep."

"Are you going to tell me why?"

"Because"—he pauses, voice going low and extra rumbly—"I haven't hugged you in two hours." He exhales, gaze flicking to something behind Joy. "And I'm sure you can guess the other reason."

"Is he looking?" Joy sighs. "He's looking, isn't he?"

"You're right about what you said this morning. I was projecting. But I was also right." Fox's deep frown returns. "He doesn't want me anywhere near you."

"Joy. Can I talk to you for a second?" Suddenly, Malcolm is there, next to them.

"Ah, right now? I'm kind of—" She glances at Fox, who quirks an unhelpful eyebrow and winks. "Sure." It's almost painful when Fox lets her go. She wants to change her mind, and cling to him for a few more minutes while he rubs her back, but Malcolm's already walking away. So she follows him.

"What are you doing?" Malcolm asks as they stand in a corner filled with gag birthday gifts.

"Standing in a corner of questionable moral character with you."

"I'm talking about Fox." His gaze slides past and behind her. Over her shoulder, she sees Fox, still waiting by the turnstile for her to come back. "I know I asked you to keep him company, but don't you think you're taking it too far? Summer is . . . worried."

"Yes, I've heard the jumbled version of her worry." Joy stares him down. "You asked me to keep him company. Turns out, I like his company."

A lightbulb clicks on behind Malcolm's eyes—a giant 1,000-watt monster that leaves him blinking and stammering. "You like his company." His disbelieving monotone almost makes her change her answer.

"That's what I said."

"You and *him*?" Malcolm tries to say something else, but no sound comes out. He's struggling, truly *struggling* to find the words he wants to say next.

Joy isn't sure what's happening. The moment feels surreal and blurry, like she's not getting enough air, but her lungs are fine. Everything in working order and falling apart.

"But you don't like anyone." His voice is a ragged whisper, both certain and confused. "You just met him."

"You do realize I'm allowed to like people, right?"

Is that what's happening? Is she really telling Malcolm that she likes Fox? *Now?*

"Of course, you are." He says it like he believes it. "That's not . . . It just seems like the kind of thing you would've told me."

She shrugs. Her fingers are cold when she squeezes them into a fist. "Doesn't matter," she says quietly. "It's your weekend."

"We always focus on me. You can"—he pauses, swallowing hard—"you can talk to me about this. It's me."

"There's nothing to talk about."

Malcolm doesn't need to know the specifics. What she has with Fox is both real and temporary. When they leave here, their pretend relationship stays behind. That's what they agreed on.

"Sometimes when I try to talk to you, you shut me out, which I don't get because that's not how we work. That's not who we are. I just . . . I want you to be happy," Malcolm says, licking his lips. "That's what's most important. And if . . . I, uh, I need a second to think. I'll be right back."

Joy doesn't go after him. She isn't sure her legs will work even if she wants them to. Her mind is whirring at full capacity, wheezing like a laptop about to blue screen itself to death because she cannot process what just happened.

Did he . . . ? Was that . . . ?

And why . . . ? Why now . . . ? She finally met . . .

"Hey." Fox touches her back, face close to hers. "You look like you're not okay."

"I'm fine," she lies, grabbing him and holding on for dear life. "Everything is fine."

Something very old, and very hurt, begins to stutter back to life inside of Joy.

Malcolm announces that he's canceling the rest of the day. For as long as Joy's known him, he's *never* canceled plans before. *Ever.* He's more reliable than the post office and they boast *neither snow nor rain nor heat nor gloom of night* can stop them.

The car ride back to the cabin is dead silent. No one says anything, no music plays. Malcolm grips the wheel like he took some *Incredible Hulk* pills and he's trying to hold back his rage. When they arrive, everyone gets out of the car except for him. They watch as he puts the car in reverse, backs out of the driveway, and leaves with zero warning.

"Where is he going?" Summer asks.

Fox says, "Not to be that person, but do either of you have keys to get inside? Because I don't."

Summer gasps. "Oh no."

*Oh, Malcolm.* "I do. It's fine." Joy retrieves them from her purse. "I have the spare keys." Light pours in from the curtainless windows, but all the small interior lights are off. The noticeable hum of electricity is also missing.

"Is the power out?" Summer clicks a light switch repeatedly, but nothing happens. "I can't believe the ghosts are upset too right now."

Fox says, "I'll go down. I think Malcolm said the circuit breaker is in the basement."

"I'll go with you," Summer volunteers.

"I will not. It's probably racoons or worse messing around down there and that's simply not my ministry." Joy tries to smile, knowing it's not convincing whatsoever. "I think I want to head up and change into something a little more casual. I'll be back down in a little bit."

Joy changes, deciding to keep it comfortable in an oversize off-the-shoulder tee and a pair of leggings. She slips her clothes on with shaking hands—it seems they developed a slight traitorous tremor and haven't stopped shaking since she left the gift shop. Her heart has been positively trilling in her throat ever since then too. She can breathe, but she also can't. She can speak, but her thoughts are flying through time, ten years in the past.

She's clammy, an unwelcome shade of gray is popping through her makeup, and her eyes are wide and wary. Any sudden moves and she'll take off, bolting for safety even though she has no clue where that is.

*You just met him*, he said.

Her heart skips a beat from pain. Because Malcolm looked exactly like how she felt when he told her he proposed to Caroline. *Stricken. Defeated. Helpless.* She presses a damp towel to her cheeks and closes her eyes to focus on her breathing. She needs to push those thoughts away. That isn't real. It's her brain playing tricks on her, making her see things that aren't there. Malcolm was just surprised, that's all. Really, *really* surprised.

"Knock, knock."

"Summer. Hi."

"Hey, I was wondering if you'd maybe want to go for a walk with me? There's another cool trail I wanted to explore. I thought it'd be fun if we could go together again."

Well, Joy did it once. She can do it again. To be honest, she could use the distraction. "As long as it's not the demon trail by that wooden bench."

"Oh no." Summer shakes her head vehemently. "Even *I* won't go in that one. It really does look like a portal to hell."

# Twenty-Five

J oy changes her mind about the hike the second they walk out
the front door.

The empty driveway. The way he left without a word. How he's
not responding to her messages. She needs to be here when Malcolm comes back.

"Why don't we stay here? See this porch swing? It's a good
one. Sure, it could use some cushions, but the hard wood isn't
*so* bad."

Summer laughs. "This is fine. Way more peaceful."

Joy sets their pace on the porch swing—as silent as ever, it rocks
them back and forth with a steadiness worthy of a lazy afternoon.
The front yard, while obviously not as picturesque as the lake, has
its charms too: the flowers, the trees, the grass and gravel. It has
the same comforting quiet minus the overt water sounds. The
porch overhang blocks the sun, cooling down the area.

"I think I'm ready to tell you what happened now."

Joy sighs. "Yeah, I had a feeling."

Summer retrieves her phone out of her pocket and pulls up a *bulleted list*. When she sees Joy's face, she says, "Oh, I made this to make sure I say everything right to you."

"Efficient."

"I get that you and Malcolm are a package deal—I have to accept both of you, and I do—but I'm looking for someone who really, truly loves me with all his heart. Malcolm might someday, and I'm willing to walk that road with him to see if we could make it work. We could really be something great, you know? But that's not now. He has a lot of, um"—she pauses to check her list—"he's very invested in someone else."

"Saying 'someone else' makes me sound like the other woman, and I'm not nearly that notorious," Joy jokes. "I know you're talking about me. Please just use my name. It's okay."

"Sorry. Yeah. Okay." Summer turns to face Joy. "When Malcolm invited me on this trip, I had an idea. I invited Fox so I had a reason to ask Malcolm to invite you too, which was kind of dishonest, I guess. I'm sorry. I just wanted to see for myself instead of calling you up and starting shit, you know? You didn't deserve those things that Caroline said about you because they're not true. You didn't do any of that. I didn't want you to think I was like her before you even met me."

Joy briefly considers whether she should pretend to be surprised. Did it hurt to hear Summer confirm what she'd done? Not really. Diabolical mastermind, she was not. Fox knew something was off immediately and it only took Joy another day of observation to narrow down specifics. She appreciates the validation, though—Malcolm didn't have anything to do with Summer's plan, just as Joy said. He got roped in, same as Fox.

Summer consults her phone one more time, biting her lip. "I'm not crying. I'm not." Her breath hitches but it's like she says, she's not crying. "I really do want us to be friends, Joy, but I understand if you don't think you could ever like me. Because the thing is, it doesn't matter, to me, how you feel about Malcolm. I only care about his side. His feelings."

Joy slowly closes her eyes and covers her face with her hands. "That's fair," she says into her palms.

"At the festival, we talked for a really long time. He told me everything, I think, from the beginning when you first met. I think you two need each other in a way I won't ever understand, but that doesn't mean it's not real. It would be wrong of me to come between that."

*Oh.* Joy tries to keep her face neutral, open and listening, as opposed to mind-blowingly astonished. None of Malcolm's partners have ever said anything like that to her before.

Usually, Malcolm's heart-to-heart moments consisted of him telling them he's asexual and explaining why monogamy is so deeply important to him. He has to have a commitment in place, they have to be exclusive, or it's game over. He'll walk away because casual dating just doesn't work for him.

Joy should have known his heart-to-heart with Summer would be different. For one thing, Summer already knows Malcolm is ace. He even used some of his confession time to talk about Joy, all to try to make Summer understand.

And it *actually* worked.

"Thank you for saying that," Joy says quietly.

"I wouldn't have said it if I didn't mean it, you know? I don't agree at all with how Caroline handled everything, but I think I understand how she felt too. I *needed* to see you and Malcolm together with my own eyes and now that I have, I get it." Summer nods and sniffles. "I don't want to feel like I come second with Malcolm either. I don't know anyone who would feel okay with being second in their relationship. But I'm equally not okay asking him to choose between us."

"That's also fair."

"He said he wants to be with me. Not you."

"I know."

"And I believe him."

"As you should." The final mystery from the trip, finally revealed. "How did you answer?"

"I said yes"—she pauses—"with some stipulations."

Here it comes. Joy grips the bench seat with both hands, gaze trained on the ground. No matter what Summer says, she won't react. She'll keep her word, step aside, and accept it. More than anything, she wishes she could hear what's coming directly from Malcolm, but this is probably for the best.

It might be too hard for him. He might not be able to push Joy away while looking at her.

"Before I said yes, I made him promise that he'll always be honest with me and to always talk to me *first*. Any time he feels conflicted or unsure or wants to go to you? I want him to stop and think if it's something he can talk to me about instead. I want him to give me a fair chance to try to learn how to be who and what he needs in life. His actual partner. For real. Not some runner-up because he knows he has you too."

"Summer, that's—"

"Wait. Let me finish, because I realized something else." Summer exhales in a *whoosh*, completely emptying her lungs. "The more I thought about everything, I couldn't shake the feeling that I was still wrong. That maybe I wasn't being any different than Caroline had been. By making Malcolm promise that, I *was* asking him to choose. And then it hit me: it's not *really* about who comes first or second. It's about who Malcolm *chooses* to let in. If it's going to work between us, he has to be willing to let me in too. That's what I need from him, and I don't think he's ever done that before. Not with Caroline or anyone else besides you. He just thinks he has. I want to know the *real* Malcolm. Good and bad. All of him. Or nothing at all."

"Well." Joy leans forward, covering her trembling mouth with her hand. Her jaw and eyes ached from the force of not crying. "I think you might be the first person who decided to not make this into a competition for Malcolm. Me included."

Summer sits up a little straighter, a tentative smile appearing on her face. "Because it's not. Accepting Malcolm means accepting you too. As long as you respect me and my boundaries, I promise to always do the same."

Maybe she and Malcolm wouldn't have to let go. Maybe Summer is the one they've both been waiting for.

"When Malcolm first told me about you, he said it felt different and that you were special. I think he might have been onto something."

"Really?"

Joy nods. "This might not be as easy as we're hoping it will, optimism really will only take us so far, but I promise too. All I want is for Malcolm to be happy."

Summer frowns. "You should want to be happy too." She makes a show of inhaling and exhaling a few times as if to center herself. "It wasn't fair of me to say you're leading Fox on. Instead of talking about Fox like I wanted, I made it about you, when it's not. What I really wanted to say—no, what I wanted to ask was"— she pauses, hands clenched into determined fists—"please don't hurt him. When he finds someone he likes it's usually pretty serious. He likes you. A lot."

Joy links her hands together, placing them in her lap, and focuses on the trees across the road. She can't stop the way her thoughts spin around kissing and kissing and kissing and being carried upstairs. A connection lasting longer than a few hours. A feeling with the power to overshadow the despair and pain that comes hand in hand with loving Malcolm. "I like him too."

"No, Joy." Summer fidgets, uncomfortable and frustrated. "What I'm saying is that he *likes* you—as in he would want to *date* you. That kind of like. So if you're just flirting with him for fun, please don't. Please stop. Because it's real to him."

Joy lets that roll off her back. Ace people could date same as everyone else. Did she suddenly forget Malcolm is ace too? "All right, well, since we're laying everything out on the table, I should tell you, it's not entirely real. At least it didn't start that way." Joy explains Fox's proposal and why—to protect Summer.

"*Oh.* I think I'm going to hit him." Summer's surprise shifts to a frown. "But you like him now, right?"

"I do."

"Okay, because I'm sure about that part too. He really does like you. Please be gentle with Fox. No matter what you decide to do. Please, please don't hurt him."

Joy nods. "Trust me, Summer, there's nothing in this world I'd rather not do."

"Okay." Summer blows out a huff of air. "That wasn't so bad. I don't know why I was so scared to talk to you." She laughs. "I think I'm still going to go for a walk. Do you want to come?"

Joy glances at the empty driveway again. "No thanks. You have fun, though." She watches Summer trek down the road alone, her ponytail swinging in time to her stride.

That was . . . *way* too much emotional labor to endure without a drink to get her through it. Joy tries to clear her mind, focusing on the feeling of being blank, on the sounds surrounding her: the chirping, the wind, the faint creak of metal. Just Joy and nature with a side of technology. She pulls out her phone, takes a quick picture of herself to immortalize the moment she decided to commune with a porch swing, and opens Rule of Thirds. She'll have to post a picture to her main grid soon, lest the algorithm AI gods forsake her, making her engagement rate plummet. Her powershots, though, have been a hit.

Everyone wants to know who the grinning Silver Fox is.

She's replying to comments when she hears a scratching sound. Joy looks around for the source and doesn't find it, but then she hears it again, louder and more insistent this time. She places one foot on the ground to stop the swing from moving. Eyes wide and unblinking she scans the area again, slowly coming to a sitting position.

More scratching. And a crunching sound. Something rhythmically swishing through the grass. They're not footsteps—they're not heavy enough—but it sure as fuck isn't the wind.

It's an animal.

Joy's brain goes into hyperdrive—it's a bear or a raccoon or a fox or a coyote, because they don't fear people at all. They'll steal your food *and* eat your pets. It's scratching against the side of the house. It's digging, trying to find a way in. Not in the mood to play Mother Nature with anything on four legs that isn't a domesticated cat, Joy slides off the bench, careful not to make a sound. She lands in a crouch, backing away slowly toward the front door to go inside where it's safe.

One brown ear flicks into view through the railing. Joy freezes, unblinking. Another ear. And then a brown face with a black muzzle.

She gasps. It's a deer. A deer is staring at Joy and she's staring at it and it's staring at her. It's watching her with those wide dark eyes, just as frozen because it wasn't expecting to see her there either.

Joy gasps again—farther back there's another one! This deer doesn't notice the first one keeping an eye on Joy and calmly makes its way toward the wooded area across the gravel road. It stops to eat something on the ground, but she doesn't think it's grass.

They must have gone down to the lake for water.

The first deer's ears flick again, drawing Joy's eye. There are two small nubs on its forehead and a patch of white around its muzzle and down its neck. She's never seen a deer before. It's both bigger and smaller than she thought it'd be. It's hair also has a grayish tint to it, not a solid Bambi brown that her scared brain initially thought. Judging by the tiny nubs, it must be young too.

"Hey, hey," she whispers. "I'm just having some me time out here. You can go do your deer thing. I won't move until you go."

To prove it, she sits on the ground and patiently waits for it to leave.

But it doesn't. Not for a while.

Not until it hears the chime caused by a text from Malcolm:

Pack your bags. We're leaving. Tonight.

# Twenty-Six

M alcolm breezes into the house shortly after sending his text. He gathers his things, only sharing words and directions with Summer.

They're packed and out of the cabin fifty-seven minutes later. All the non-perishable leftover food and drinks are set out for pickup to go to a local food bank.

Joy takes her time saying goodbye to the lake and all her favorite spots in the cabin like the hammock, the kitchen, and the front porch. It's hard to believe that when she first arrived, she threw herself into the lake because she felt so suffocated by the situation she put herself in, and by Summer.

And now, as they're leaving, she's made her peace with Summer, facing an uncertain future with Malcolm, and saying goodbye to her fake boyfriend, who, according to Summer, has developed *real* feelings for her.

Oh lord, are those feelings mutual.

One last time, they all climb into Malcolm's Jeep. Summer navigates again, playlist of warbly whiny boys back in rotation. This time, Malcolm frequently glances upward to check on Joy through the mirror. Instead of sitting behind him, Joy takes up the middle seat to be closer to Fox.

Fox holds Joy's hand, and she rests her head on his shoulder. Every so often he presses a kiss to the top of her forehead. Malcolm's text had been so sudden, Joy didn't have time to process that going home also meant an early end to the deal with Fox. And now that she has there's this peculiar encroaching sadness growing inside of her with every minute that passes, every mile they travel.

The drive home always feels faster than the original trip. Joy's never understood why. She has a poor understanding of time to begin with and being sad only makes it worse. It doesn't slow down to give her more time with Fox. No, it seems to speed up to spite her—just rubbing it in that their brief engagement has been forcibly cut short. She wanted to experience, wanted to live those handful of remaining vacation hours with Fox.

What couldn't have possibly been two hours later, Malcolm pulls into his driveway and shuts the car off. Summer and Malcolm jump out, slamming the doors behind them.

Joy doesn't move, staying right where she is, counting every stolen second until Fox's lips brush against her forehead. "Are you resting?"

"No." She lifts her head and kisses him.

Joy wants to remember this moment.

Fox's thumb massaging small circles on the back of her hand. The subtle smell of roses and aloe. His stubble pleasantly rubbing her face. The rise and fall of his chest supported by his steady breathing. The rumble of his voice. His reluctant laughs and hard-won smiles.

She forces her brain to catalog it so she never forgets the five minutes when someone made her feel enough to eclipse Malcolm's constant presence in her mind.

"Okay." Eyes closed, Joy takes a deep breath.

He nudges her, kissing her cheek.

"Okay," she says again. "We should go."

They get out of the car and Joy heads for the trunk.

"Where are your keys?" Malcolm is standing with her suit-cases.

Startled that Malcolm's speaking to her now, she fishes them out of her purse and beeps her car without question. He doesn't wait, immediately loading them into the trunk for her.

Across the street, Fox loads his and Summer's suitcases into a blue car. She's waiting by the passenger side door and when she spots Joy watching her, she waves and yells, "Don't forget game night on Wednesday!"

"All set." Malcolm returns to Joy's side. "Text me when you get home so I know you made it safely."

"Did you want to talk at all? You—"

"No," he says firmly, already walking toward his house. "I really don't."

Joy's hands tighten around her purse strap as she watches him go. The ache in her heart continues to grow more insistent. What is he thinking? What is he feeling? He seems to be okay with Summer, so things can't be all bad.

In the gift shop, he specifically said she could talk to him about anything, that he hates it when she shuts him out, so why won't he talk to her now? Is he upset about Fox? Is he mad at her? Is there anything she can do that won't make things worse?

"You can get in," Fox says to Summer as he crosses the street. "I'll be right back."

Oh no. Not this too. Their time can't be up. It *can't* be.

At some point, her heart turned into a steel trap. She let Malcolm in and hardened herself to keep everyone else out. Because it was the safest thing to do.

A relationship with Malcolm was a known quantity.

But Fox. What if he changes his mind? What if he decides he can't love her? Can she trust *him* not to hurt her? The risk of heartbreak looms over her so large, it's overtaking everything else.

Joy waits for him to join her. She knows what she wishes she could say but that's not what comes out. "I've never broken up with anyone before." She frowns. "I don't think I like it."

He gives her a quizzical smile—the first one she's seen. "Is that what this is?"

"That's what you asked for, right? Until we go back home. Here we are. At the end. Home."

"Hmm."

That *hmm* cracks through her sadness, making Joy grin. "I can see you thinking."

"Because I am."

"About?" She tries not to sound hopeful. Fox hasn't mentioned being friends. To be fair, neither has she, but she has a feeling that's not what either of them really wants.

Fox opens his mouth, but then closes it, shaking his head. There's an uneasiness in his expression. "Sixty-five percent."

Joy lets out a breathy, anxious laugh. "Until the very end, huh?"

"I guess so." His jaw is tense, flexing. He has something he wants to say—Joy can practically feel it reaching toward her. But she can't read his mind. She wants, no she *needs* to hear him say it. Is she not worth the risk for him?

"Well. Thank you for volunteering to be my grumpy fake boyfriend." She can't bring herself to say goodbye. Because if she says it, then that makes it final.

Fox opens his arms, and she steps right in as if she's walking in the front door of her apartment—guard completely down and happy to be there. She holds him as tight as she can, face buried in her favorite hiding spot.

If Joy goes to Summer's game night, she'll see him again, but it won't be the same. She wants Fox like this, with hugs and kissing and long conversations about their lives with terrible, terrible jokes shared between them.

It's silly, but she feels like she's been cheated. Like something has been stolen from her and she'll never get it back. Never get another chance.

The drive home is filled with red lights and traffic—so much so that Joy decides to stop at a pet store to kill some time by buying Pepper some *please forgive Mommy* treats. About an hour later, she knocks on Mrs. Norman's door.

"Oh, Joy! Hi, baby, come here." Mrs. Norman gives her a tight hug complete with rocking back and forth. "You're back early; did you have a good trip? How was the weather? Was it nice? You know, we had nothing but a nasty muggy overcast here."

"It was really great," Joy says. "The cabin and lake were absolutely perfect. So beautiful."

Pepper starts meowing, squeaky as ever, from somewhere deep

inside the apartment, getting louder and more frantic as she gets closer.

"Oops, she done heard you," Mrs. Norman says with a laugh. She moves out of the doorway to give Pepper a clear path. "Here she comes."

"Hi, Pep," Joy croons. "Did you miss me?" She scoops Pepper up, holding her in the usual position—curled up and close to Joy's shoulder. "Thank you for watching her."

Pepper hides her face in Joy's braids, purring like she's entered a motorboat contest. She'll be like this for the rest of the day, only asking to be put down to use the litter box or eat, coming right back directly after and expecting to be picked up again like the princess she is.

"No problem. Let me go get all her stuff."

In her apartment, Joy tries to relax by doing nothing, but after days of constantly being around people, with an agenda full of activities, it's hard to slide back into sloth mode.

She takes a shower while Pepper sits dutifully on the toilet waiting for her to finish, unpacks under Pepper's direct supervision, makes something to eat while Pepper rubs against her legs, and then . . . crashes. She falls asleep with Pepper partially laying across her face to make sure Joy doesn't go *anywhere* else.

It's completely dark outside by the time Joy wakes up. She yawns—and gets a mouthful of cat hair. "Pepper! No sleeping near Mommy's face!" She rubs around her mouth and sits up. Not completely awake yet, she knows all she needs is a quick glass of water and she'll fall right back asleep. But instead of doing the smart, healthy thing, she checks her phone.

Grace sent a few video messages:

*What are you doing? Why haven't you called me? Don't make me worry about you, you know I hate that shit. I'm assuming you're not dead since the hospital hasn't called me to identify your body, which makes your lack of calling even worse. Why don't you love me?*

*Anyway, I expect to hear all about your Silver Fox. Every single detail down to the smallest thing. Did the pie idea work? I bet it did. He looks like someone who loves pie. Men love it when you cook for them. I know, I know you want Malcolm or whatever, but I'm just saying you should keep your options open. He seems into you.*

*Oh, and I have family gossip, like some good, good shit. Call me, love you.*

Grace would be asleep by now. Joy decides to wait and reply tomorrow. She gets out of bed and walks down the hall of her empty apartment. Pepper follows closely at her heels.

Happy to be home, she sits at her refinished dining table and eats a pint of her favorite ice cream.

But it's impossible not to think of everything all at once too.

How are things worse than when she left?

# Twenty-Seven

TUESDAY

Everyone knows the first day of work after a vacation makes the top ten list for worst workdays ever.

Joy arrives at Red Warren early to get the jump on the impending brain fog, the relentless dread of checking her email, and losing the will to do anything except spin in her office chair.

Surprisingly, everything adheres effortlessly to her usual routine. She begins the day with her work playlist, a brown sugar scented candle, a so-so cup of coffee, and a glazed donut.

"Oh, you're here today. I thought you'd be out." Megan peeks into her office from the hall about an hour in.

"I was supposed to be, but then I thought of the ever-growing throng of unread emails festering in my inbox and, well." Joy shrugs. "Capitalism won."

"Funny." Megan doesn't laugh but she does smile bright enough to make you think she means it. "Malcolm said the same thing. Oh, not the *exact* same thing. He said he got back from his trip early and decided to just come in."

"He's here?"

Megan nods. "I said good morning not even five minutes ago."

Ah, he must have got in recently. His car wasn't in the parking lot when she arrived.

"Oh, here he comes. We were just talking about you."

The hair on Joy's arm stands straight up. She knows she's gone full deer in the headlights, unsure what to expect from Malcolm. He hasn't called or messaged her, when normally she'd have an early morning slew of them by now. It hurt to see her inbox like that, completely devoid of any recent traces of him, the pain piercing her right in the chest.

Respecting his silence, his need for space seemed the better option than bothering him, but now he's standing in her doorway next to Megan, all smiles.

"Good morning, Joy."

*Good morning, Joy?* That's *all* he has to say to her? Doesn't he think that's a bit *brief*?

Joy, ever the professional, waves at him. Her voice can't be trusted to do any heavy lifting where he's concerned in front of mixed company.

"I'm off to my office," Megan says. "Joy, I'll see you at ten for our meeting?"

Joy nods at her.

Megan departs, leaving them alone. Malcolm doesn't seem any worse for wear. The hard, cold look has melted and he's back to his usual reserved boss self. His suit is a thrilling black and white houndstooth paired with a black shirt and mustard yellow tie.

"How early did you get here?" he asks.

*Oh, you're talking to me now?* "Seven."

"Did you sleep okay?"

*Of course, I didn't. Pepper's separation anxiety roared back to life,* someone *hasn't responded to any of my messages, and suddenly my apartment feels too quiet.* "Just fine."

Malcolm nods. "We should take advantage of our mostly cleared calendars today."

*Yes, that's exactly how I want to spend most of my workday: with you, in denial and pretending everything is fine between us.* "Sure. What did you have in mind?"

Joy and Malcolm slide back into their work dynamic with ease—catching up, scheduling meetings, and fulfilling orders. They even have lunch with a couple of the girls from finance to discuss the new changes they'll be implementing for payroll *and* have coffee with a prospective client.

Everything as seamless as ever, just as it's meant to be. Being at work feels normal. Their instincts and trust in each other slot back into place as if it had never been tested—their undisputable bond in action.

And that's where it ends.

Red Warren the office typically shuts down around six p.m., with the last of the employees filing out of the building by then. As soon as work is no longer between them, Malcolm shuts Joy out again.

He doesn't even walk her to her car, disappearing while she grabbed her purse from her office and clocked out for the day.

"I can't *believe* he's acting like that," Grace shouts through Joy's car speakers.

"I know."

"So he's just going to avoid you during non-work hours? Pretend like you don't exist?"

"Seems like it."

"Oh, that's fantastic. If that's how he wants it, he must have forgotten who the true queen of petty is."

Joy sighs.

*I'm trying to figure out how much I'm willing to let go to move forward. We can't stay like this. It's not working.*

Maybe this is what Malcolm decided he could handle—purely having a working relationship with Joy.

Not knowing for sure sits like a rock in the pit of her stomach, weighing her down. She doesn't feel much else apart from that. She knows the resigned numbness she feels is for the best. It's her body's way of protecting her from further harm because Malcolm feels tied to her DNA. His absence has the power to send her unraveling if she loses control over her emotions.

Grace continues, "For someone who claims to love you, he's incredibly selfish. And childish."

Joy understands. She sees where he's coming from, how this makes it easier for him. But Grace is right too. He *is* being incredibly selfish. The least he could do is respect Joy enough to tell her to her face that this is how he wants it to be. Instead, now she's stuck in limbo wondering what exactly the truth is.

"I'm not disagreeing with you, but I think it's more complicated than you're making it seem."

"It's not. You just feel that way because you're so used to taking up for him. He's grown. He doesn't need you to play devil's advocate," Grace says. "Anyway. When are you seeing Fox again?"

Joy's hands jerk on the wheel in surprise. A car next to her blows its horn at her for drifting into their lane. Jesus—she waves apologetically, mouthing, "Sorry!"

"What was that?" Grace asks.

"Nothing. Just someone honking their horn. I'm home," Joy lies. "I'll call you back after I'm settled."

"You better. I want a Silver Fox update."

Joy hangs up. "Well, you're not getting one." Her heart stutters as she panics, double-checking to make sure she did in fact hang up and didn't just say that out loud to her sister.

She made it almost the entire day without crumbling into a ball whenever she realized she missed Fox by following a very simple rule: she's only allowed to think about him for five controlled minutes every hour.

Grabbing donuts at the cute little bakery down the street from Red Warren reminded her of making his birthday cake and sharing apple pie.

Refilling her water bottle reminded her how Fox can't swim and she volunteered to rescue him, naked if need be.

Reviewing furniture samples for a possible Red Warren office redecoration reminded her how skilled he is at carpentry.

She took a break with Megan to watch some cute viral animal videos—one of them about a woman who played guitar for a sleepy brown cow who rested its head in her lap.

Dropping off mail in the blue postbox made her realize how truly committed she is to ensuring her own unhappiness because she didn't ask for his phone number.

Malcolm occupied the bulk of her immediate thoughts, but Fox was there too. All day.

When Joy actually arrives home, Pepper meets her at the door as always. She picks her cat up, saying, "At least you're happy to see me." Her evening routine proceeds as normal too (minus another call with Grace, who does not appreciate being ignored).

By the time Joy goes to bed, at a rebellious eleven p.m., she feels like she's waited long enough. Flipping through her photos, she watches the knock-knock joke videos they made together at Fable's.

Joy's chest feels too tight, breathing too shallow. She isn't going to cry, it doesn't feel like a sobbing kind of sadness. It's a creeping desolation—the kind that builds so slowly, you're used to it by the time you notice it.

They were always going to end this way. She knew it the whole time. She has no right to feel sad about something she had three and a half days to experience and prepare for.

Why did this feel so hard? Why couldn't she shoot him with finger guns, give him a wink and a smile, and walk away like she normally does when a connection ends?

Pepper meows loudly, trying to walk across Joy's face because she holds nothing but utter contempt for personal body space. "Look, this is Fox." She turns Pepper around to show her the phone.

All at once, Joy realizes she has truly fallen to a new low. She's showing her cat, who could not care less, videos of someone she's probably never going to see again because she has no way to contact him without going through Malcolm.

Except she does. *She does!*

Before Joy can think twice about it, she opens her Rule of Thirds DMs and sends him a message: *text me* with her phone number. There. Olive branch extended. If he wants to talk to her, he'll meet her halfway.

This romance shit is stressful *as hell*.

Joy sets her phone down in favor of picking Pepper up and letting her lay on her chest for scritches. Five minutes later, her phone rings and she doesn't recognize the number, but it's local.

"Hello?"

"Joy?"

That familiar rumble almost makes her astral project straight into her next life. Joy holds in a squeak, simultaneously cradling Pepper and kicking her feet into the air. She calms down quickly, sitting up and saying, "The instructions were to text me," with a huge grin on her face.

The line goes silent. Joy knows he's there. She keeps checking the screen and the call hasn't dropped. He's just not saying anything because he's *thinking*. Oh my god, this is gonna be hell. She can imagine it: ten-to-fifteen-minute-long pauses as he sorts through his thoughts with only a *hmm* as a clue she should wait. She needs to see him in person, to stare him into talking. Maybe she can convince him to stick to video calls or—

"But I wanted to hear your voice," he says. "Do you really want me to text you instead?"

Joy slides down farther into the bed, melting like a piece of ice in the sun, and pulls the blanket over her head. She doesn't want her empty room to see her face. "Absolutely not."

"Hmm."

"Oh no. *Oh no*," Joy says, beginning to giggle.

"What?"

"I think I can *hear* you thinking. You're thinking, aren't you?"

"Yeah." Fox sighs. "Damn it."

Joy bursts out laughing.

Fox waits until she's done and asks, "How was your day?"

"Not entirely miserable. Not great. You?"

"It's definitely better now."

She shoves her face into her pillow. When she's regained control she says, "Oh, that's good."

"Isn't this late for you? I would've expected you to be asleep by now."

"Oh, me and my old lady internal clock are definitely in bed. Sometimes it takes a while for me to drift off if I'm not dead tired. I usually watch a movie or something."

"No wonder you fell asleep during our Nic Cage marathon. We started it too late and you're used to going to sleep with a movie playing. Makes sense now. I thought you just didn't appreciate one of the greatest and most opportunistic actors of our time."

"It's probably also that."

Fox laughs. "What are you watching tonight?"

"Nothing yet. Do you want to watch something together? We can use the sync projector app."

"Uh, sure. Yeah. That's a great idea."

They choose a movie, something they both wanted to see, and spend the next two hours creating their own running commentary. It's not perfect. It doesn't magically feel like they're back in the cabin talking under the stars until she falls out, but it's close. Hours are passing, she doesn't notice them at all, and before she knows it, the movie is over and he's asking, "Are you resting?"

"Not even close." Joy feels wired, like she accidentally had a full cup of coffee right before bed. Pepper is out cold and kitty-snoring on her back.

"Are you coming to Summer's game night tomorrow? Or I guess it's tonight now."

"I haven't thought about it. Do you think it would be weird if I did? Because of all the stuff with Malcolm."

Fox pauses before answering, "Summer attracts really horrible people. They use her and treat her like a doormat because they know she won't fight back. She'll just take it and cry. I thought Malcolm was one of those people at first."

"Ahhh."

"Yeah. He was always talking about someone named Joy and it was pretty obvious how much he cared about her. I think Malcolm sold Summer on the idea of you without realizing it. He had her convinced you walked on water. The most supportive and faithful person to ever exist and you just have this big open heart that loves people just as they are. That's part of why she was so excited to meet you. She wants what you two have."

"With Malcolm?" Joy laughs to lighten the mood. "There's a *Single White Female* joke in here somewhere but with colorblind casting where race suddenly doesn't matter."

"With you, Joy. She really wants to be friends with you too."

"I know." She sighs. "Summer's not so bad, but I just don't know. I don't even know if Malcolm wants me around him if we're not at work. And if I start taking the steps to heal on my own, part of that will probably involve separating from him *anyway* because I'm scared I don't know how to live without him. She's dating him, and if she and I are friends, I'll most likely see him before I'm ready."

"Which defeats the entire purpose," Fox says. "Hmm."

"I'll have to think about it."

"If you decide to go, I'll be there." He pauses again. "Also, my shop is opening next week."

"I remember."

"Would you want to see it before then? Everything's set up already. Maybe Friday evening if you're free."

"I would love to. That's so exciting." Joy bites her lip, wondering if she should go for it, telling herself she should, and nearly succumbing to doubt. She squeezes her eyes shut, bracing for impact. "And maybe after we could get dinner?"

"Yeah. That'd be nice," he says. "Whatever you want."

# Twenty-Eight

## WEDNESDAY

Grace has been calling non-stop all day. To be fair, Joy sent her updates by text to help her sister's twin spider-sense relax, but she didn't want to talk to her yet. If she did, Grace might influence her, convince her to do something before she's ready.

Everything with Fox feels so delicate, like it could snap and fade away at any moment. One wrong move and Joy's back to square one. She picks up her phone, planning to silence the ringer, when she sees a text from Fox.

FOX: Has work been okay?

JOY: I think so. But I don't know if I'm strong enough to handle this.

JOY: I'm thinking of putting in my too weak notice.

Her phone rings approximately six seconds after she hit send.

"Hey, hey," she answers, wondering if her text made him laugh.

There's a slight static noise in the background. "Joy."

"Where are you?"

"Driving to a worksite."

"Is your window rolled down?"

"Yeah." The noise stops. "I didn't expect you to answer so soon."

"Phone in my hand. Thumbs got eager."

"Are you okay?"

"Yeah. Yeah, I'm fine."

"Hmm."

Even after talking for hours last night, not seeing him feels too heavy. She leans back in her chair and closes her eyes, trying to tap into the memories she has of him. How entertaining it was to be near him while he processed. How she busied herself around him like a moon orbiting a planet when he took too long. Did she have an effect on him too? Would he ever tell her?

Joy says, "My text was just a joke. I'm fine. Really. Everything is normal at work."

In his quiet, fear grips her like a vise almost immediately. Was that the wrong thing to say? During their talks, the silences never felt like this—punctuated and prolonged. Each word working just as hard as the pauses.

Finally, he says, "Have you decided about tonight?"

"Still spinning my brain hamster wheels about it," she jokes, but her heart isn't in it.

"Hmm."

It wasn't like this before, was it? Searing, agonizing, like cauterizing a wound. No spontaneous moments. Try too hard and this tenuous lifeline between them would collapse.

"Joy?" Malcolm knocks on her door. "You busy?"

"Oh, hold on one second." She ducks her head and says to Fox, "I gotta get back to work. If I don't see you tonight, are we still on for Friday?"

"Of course. Whatever you want."

Joy hangs up, filled with that strange longing again. But she turns to Malcolm, smiling anyway, and says, "What's up?"

Much to Joy's surprise, after work Malcolm *asks* her if she wants to go to Summer's house. They're standing by her car in the parking lot. She's holding on to her purse strap for dear life with both hands. "Do you think that's a good idea?"

Malcolm shrugs. "She asked me to remind you."

"Do *you* want me to go? Because, Malcolm, I—"

"Joy." He holds up a hand to stop her. "It's not about me. Summer really wants you to be there."

"Sorry to be the one to break this to you, but it's absolutely about you too. Tell me what you need from me." Joy can't help it. The offer flows out of her as natural as water running downstream. Is it always going to be this way for her? Continually self-sacrificing to make sure he's happy?

Malcolm exhales, looks to the left and back to her. "I don't know yet."

Joy shakes her head in disbelief. Grace is right. Fox is right. They really don't communicate anymore. She's never been afraid to talk to Malcolm about anything, and here she is, so terrified about what he'll say to her, she's shaking. But she has to know. They can't stay in limbo like this forever.

"Can you at least talk to me, then? I don't understand what's going on with you at all right now."

"Not yet. I'm still trying to figure out how to do this." Malcolm can barely look at her, but she sees the tension in his stance: fist balled in his pockets, jaw set, determined to not stand too close to her. "In the meantime, like I said, Summer would love it if you came."

*Fox*, she thinks. *Fox said he'll be there too.* The thought of seeing him fills her with electric anticipation. A welcome relief.

"Okay," Joy says, unlocking her car. "I'll follow you there."

Summer lives in a suburban neighborhood, flush with the kind of houses that all look similar enough for non-residents to easily get lost. She parks behind Malcolm after he stops in front of a gray house trimmed with white, two stories high, with an abundance of windows. Summer mentioned having roommates. Between three or more people, a house that size in a neighborhood that screamed *Model Houses! Visit today!* could definitely be affordable.

Malcolm walks next to her up the stone path leading to the front door. He rings the bell, and she presses the pleats in her skirt to make sure they look neat. After talking to Fox last night, Joy woke up feeling giddier than she's felt in years. That giddiness translated to a plaid mini skirt and matching jacket à la *Clueless*.

Someone with long black hair, a chubby, ruddy face, wearing the cutest daffodil dress Joy has ever seen, opens the door. They greet Malcolm like an old friend with an accusatory, "You're late."

"Never." He grins as he moves inside and then turns back. "Sally, this is Joy. Joy, this is Sally."

"Joy?" Sally blinks.

Someone else in the house says, "JOY? SHE'S ACTUALLY HERE?" loud enough to make Joy's eyes widen. Straight to the back there's a kitchen, and someone wearing a full-blown pirate costume marches to the door with a perplexed expression on their face. "HOLY SHIT, SHE'S REAL."

Having had enough of being gawked at, Joy says, "Is there a reason why you thought I wasn't?"

The pirate has on a bright red wig and an eye patch. Her sun-kissed skin looks radiantly natural, like she was born with it instead of it coming from a tanning bed. "He talks about you so much but never brought you around. I figured you were some sort of delusional imaginary best friend. Bring it in, come on!"

The pirate traps Joy in a bear hug before she can get away. She practically lifts her over the threshold, all but dragging her into the house. Slightly unnerved, Joy tries to cover it up by asking, "And Summer didn't vouch for my existence?"

The pirate laughs, letting her go. "Oh, she did. I just figured she was pretending to believe the delusion to make him feel better."

Malcolm says, "Joy, this is Rebekah. She routinely enjoys being loud and wrong."

"Hello, Joy." Fiona's blue hair is just as vibrant as it is in her pictures. She saunters out of the darkened hallway directly on the left, hands behind her back. "I've heard so much about you."

Feeling wary and on guard, Joy says, "Good things, I hope."

"No, not really." Fiona doesn't have the grump gene like Fox does but her entire vibe feels divinely menacing. As if she'll either make your dreams or worst nightmares come true. And you won't know which one it is until it's too late.

"Ah."

"Just kidding." Fiona unleashes a dimple punctuated grin identical to Fox's. She grabs Joy's arm, pulling her forward and into the dark hallway. "Come on. I want you to sit with me."

"Um, is Fox here?"

"No, my brother heard you were coming and decided to stay home." Fiona glances at her and laughs. "Just kidding. Relax."

Joy narrows her eyes. "You do that a lot, don't you?"

"Oh yes. And it's only going to get worse." She laughs. "Fox had to work overtime. He said he'll drop by."

The room they end up in is decently sized with an adjacent kitchen. There are two couches and a recliner that has seen better days, band posters cover the walls, and a glass coffee table in the center is filled with cups and bottles of alcohol. The TV is on but it's not playing something Joy recognizes.

"Joy!" Summer hops to her feet and runs over. "Hug okay?"

"Well, Rebekah beat you to it, so sure."

Summer wastes no time, enveloping Joy too. "I'm so glad you came. Do you—"

"Nope, she's sitting with me." Fiona says, guiding Joy to the couch once Summer lets go. She picks up a blue cup that matches her hair. "So. You and my brother, huh?"

Joy almost snorts. She certainly didn't waste any time either. "Not exactly."

"Hmm."

*Dear god, not her too.*

Fiona continues, "Calling him grumpy was genius. It got under his skin like that." She snaps her fingers.

"He told you about that?"

"Oh, he told me *everything*." She takes a sip of her drink, one wickedly perfect eyebrow up. "We're very close. But even if we weren't, Summer also told me everything."

"I see." Joy recognizes that look. Fiona is giving her a hard time on purpose, but not because she has a kink for watching people squirm. She's testing Joy.

"Here's the thing about my brother: he's dense as hell. You're going to have to make the first move, darling."

"'Dense' is . . . definitely not a word I'd use for him."

"Give it time. Trust me. I've known him longer. You like him, right? If you want anything to happen with that, you're going to have to take charge."

Joy's phone vibrates in her pocket. It's a text from Fox:

Running late. I should be there soon.

Anything Fiona tells you is a lie. Don't trust her.

She laughs, sliding her phone back into her pocket. Deciding to go with the flow, she asks Fiona, "Take charge how exactly? What do you think I should do?"

"I'm *so* glad you asked that. How secure are you in your femininity?"

"*What?*" Joy laughs around the word.

"You're going to have to woo him, darling. I'm talking flowers, dinner, presents, the works. He's a total homebody nerd with an incredible sweet tooth—think books, movies, and making him fancy desserts. It's the only way to get through to that thick brain of his. Besides, he deserves it."

"Hmm," Joy says with a snicker. "Well, if he told you everything, then you should know about Spa Day."

"Spa Day?" Fiona eyes her, clearly sensing a trap. "He didn't mention anything about that."

Joy grins. "I bet he didn't."

Just as Summer said, game night doesn't involve games, even though there's a large stack of board games in the corner. They all sit around the glass coffee table, talking and drinking. That's it.

Malcolm sits with Summer on the floor. His arm is wrapped around her waist and she's leaning into him, completely relaxed and happy. Joy doesn't feel much of anything seeing them like that. She's not numb—that absolutely has a contradictory feeling. It's more like the absence of angst hasn't left anything behind. It's a blank slate waiting to be filled with whatever Joy wants it to be.

*Happy*, she thinks. *I want to feel happy when I look at them together.*

Everyone takes turns telling stories about their lives, like that game Summer taught them to play on the trip. Joy chooses to listen rather than participate, with Fiona helpfully filling in background details for context every so often. After about an hour, she asks where the bathroom is. Joy doesn't feel entirely unwelcome but there's an unmistakable undercurrent of anticipatory vibes floating around the room—and she's certain it's centered on her. It's like they're all waiting for something to happen, for Joy to do something specific.

Instead of heading back into the main room, Joy stops by the kitchen to get a drink. She's mid-pour when a familiar rumble greets the room at large.

Fox doesn't see her as he walks in and takes off his jacket, passive grumpy frown in place even as he says hello to his friends. She shrinks back against the counter, using a red cup to hide the bottom half of her face.

*Oh no. Oh no. Oh no.*

Joy doesn't want Fox to look at her like that. She doesn't want him to look at her like he's bored and would rather be anywhere else. It took her being clever and honest and watching him to earn his smiles. And cake—he loved her cake so much he smiled.

Now that they're not in the cabin, things will be different. She can feel it. He's had time to think about it and change his mind about her.

She won't be able to handle it because it's Fox.

*Fox.*

And then he sees her. His smile is slow and deliberate. The rest of the room melts away as he approaches her, arms raised for her hug. She practically leaps into them, burying her face into his neck, holding him as tight as she can.

Fox smells different—it's sawdust, dirt, and sweat. He touches her face, fingers tracing her jaw, before he wraps his arms around her again and whispers, "Hey, hey."

Joy laughs, pulling back to look at him. "Hallo."

Summer had the right idea. It isn't about who comes first or second in someone's heart. Joy *wants* Fox—independent of Malcolm and not at all as a consolation prize.

Joy's desire for Fox stand on its own as what could be. As what she hopes will be. She forgot how terrifying and exhilarating this realization feels. That once again, there's a *more* to *want*. To decide to not run away from it, to not wait, to not hide. She's choosing Fox. And hoping with all her heart he'll choose her too.

"*Ooh shit*, Summer wasn't kidding." Fiona stands to their left with a huge kid-in-a-candy-store smile on her face. "Don't mind me. I'm just standing here—continue. Please." She places her elbows on the counter, cradling her face in her hands, looking back and forth between them. Behind her, almost every face mirrors Fiona's, but not Malcolm's—he's focusing on the table, jaw set—and Summer's—she's focusing on Malcolm.

Suddenly, Summer lifts her gaze and meets Joy's. There's no hurt or upset. Just that same patient understanding she had while they sat together on the cabin's porch.

Fox clears his throat, arms falling to his sides, and Joy takes a step back from him.

Fiona says, "I can't *wait* to tell Mom."

"Tell Mom what, exactly?" Fox rumbles.

"Don't you grump at me."

Fox glances at Joy. "Do you see what you started?"

She laughs. "Well, maybe you shouldn't have told her *everything.*"

# Twenty-Nine

J oy doesn't stay at Summer's house past eight p.m. It's a work
night after all.

Fox walks her to her car with promises to call her later and confirming their plans for her to visit his workshop. Once she's at home,
she does a speed-run through her nighttime routine, hoping to already be in bed by the time Fox calls her for their next movie date.

Well, he didn't call it that. Joy decided some creative, hopeful
liberties were in order.

Someone knocks on her door as she's pouring Sleepytime tea
into her favorite giraffe mug. She checks the peephole first—her
breath catches in her throat, and she quickly unlocks the door to
open it. "Malcolm. Hi. What are you doing here?"

He's standing in her hallway, rubbing his forehead, anxiety
levels clearly on the rise. "Can I come in?"

"Of course. Yeah."

Joy steps to the side, and he barely enters her apartment. He stops near the couch, not sitting or moving beyond it. She knows this stance—whatever it is he has to say is important enough to stress him out like he's about to give a big presentation at work. Once he's in the thick of it, he's smooth as butter, working the attendees until they're putty in the palm of his hand. But before? It's DEFCON 2. Joy always has to talk him down and gas him up.

"Malcolm," Joy says, using her patented best friend calming voice. "Is everything okay?"

"Do you remember how we met?" Malcolm doesn't wait for an answer, instead telling the entire story by himself, but when he gets to the part where Joy asked for his number, it suddenly changes. "I waited all day for you to text me. Checking my phone and getting my hopes up that maybe you wanted to hang out. That day passed. And then another. And then it was a week later. I still couldn't stop thinking about you."

Joy's frown feels intensely epic. She's positive, absolutely sure he's never told her that last part before.

He continues, "I couldn't get you and the way you smiled at me out of my head. I figured you just forgot about me. I didn't see you anywhere on campus. A friend of mine said they saw someone who looked like you around his dorm. I went there every day hoping to see you. But you disappeared. I started beating myself up because I found my dream girl and she got away. You didn't tell me your name, so I started calling you Cinderella."

When Malcolm resumes the story with the ending Joy knows, her heart must be going for a new bpm world record because she's breathless and weak, like she's been running for several miles. Or years.

"After we went to lunch, I knew I was going to fall in love with you. And then I did."

"I need to sit down," Joy says quietly as she collapses on the couch. For five full seconds, she forgets how to exist. Her heart skipped a beat so hard, it shut everything else down—brain, lungs, senses, everything gone and offline.

"Joy." Malcolm hesitates. He takes a step toward her, pauses, then tries again and ends up sitting next to her. "I'm not changing my mind. I *want* to be with Summer," he says firmly. Not a single hint of indecision anywhere.

"Good." Her nerves hit the overdrive button, rattling back to life like an old muffler.

"But I need to know something. I won't be able to let it go until I do."

"Good," she echoes, still incapable of using other words.

Malcolm touches her arm but strangely she can't feel it. She stares at him like she's never seen this version of him before. An imposter Malcolm who fell in love with her.

"Joy?"

"When?" Her voice sounds wrong, aching and too high. "When did that happen? Please."

Malcolm nods and answers, "When I kissed you at the bar. Afterward, I didn't want to pressure you. I waited for you to come to me. I thought that would be best. You didn't pull any punches back then—if you wanted me, you would have made that known. I thought you just weren't interested in me. And then, when there was never anyone else, and you said you weren't interested in dating, I figured that was that. I tried to move on."

"Oh. I see." She sucks her bottom lip into her mouth, biting down on it enough to hurt.

"But then this weekend when I saw you with Fox"—he pauses

to breathe, in and out—"it was like everything came rushing back. Suddenly, it changed from you not being interested in anyone to you not being interested in *me*."

"Well." Joy interlaces her fingers, holding her hands up to her face like she's praying. "You weren't completely wrong. I really wasn't interested in anyone else. Up until *very* recently, I only wanted you."

It's Malcolm's turn to be stunned into disbelief. "For how long?"

"This whole time. Since before the bar."

"Okay. Cool. All right." He sits back against the sofa. "Okay. I really wasn't expecting you to say that."

Joy sits up, taking a deep breath and closing her eyes. She tries to center herself, to focus on what she knows she needs to say next and ignore the small nagging voice in her heart demanding she do the opposite. It has to be this way. It's time. She reclines against the back of the couch angling her head toward him. "Does knowing how I feel make you want to change your mind now?"

Malcolm's answer is immediate. "No. Summer and I are—it's good. Really good."

"Then it doesn't matter." Joy shakes her head. "You wanted to know and now you do."

"But this whole time? Really? Why didn't you say anything before?"

"Because I thought the same thing. You didn't want me." Joy laughs despite the situation. "In the souvenir shop, you told me I could talk to you. Is that offer still open?"

"Always."

Joy collects every scrap of bravery she has within her and says, "I think you're making the right choice. I think—I hope—

Summer is the right choice. Because it's not me. I know that now. I've held on to you for so long, *so, so long*, because I truly believed you were all I was ever meant to have. No one would ever love me or understand me the way that you do.

"I don't think I'm particularly hard to love." There's a wet warmth building behind her eyes, an ache burning through her throat and jaw. "But sometimes I feel like no one will ever want me. Not forever. No one will ever see me beyond how they can use me. No one will ever want me because of the way I am. I'm weird and needy and dark-skinned and asexual. I guess I convinced myself that if it wasn't you, it would never be anyone."

"That's not true, Joy."

"Yeah, well, it feels like it is." Joy wipes her nose with her sleeve. "I think I knew, deep down, that it wasn't ever going to work between us. We don't even want the same things out of life. I just—I just couldn't let you go. And I think you knew how alone and unlovable I felt. That's why you stayed with me. Because that's who you are."

"Actually, I stayed because I felt that way too. I just kept dating while you didn't." He scoff-laughs. "How are we perfect and all wrong for each other at the same time?"

"I don't know," Joy admits, and Grace's words come back to her. "I don't want to live without you, but I think I have to for a while."

"I don't." Malcolm looks stricken. "Being apart won't solve anything."

"Then what should we do? I realized how selfish and needy I can be when it comes to you. I don't trust myself to change overnight." She laughs lightly. "I'm very fragile and tired, and old habits die hard. I'm not talking about romance or dating or anything like that. You're still one of the most important people in my life, period. I don't want to accidentally do anything to hurt you or Summer."

"Then let's face it. Try harder to be better. Honestly, I think twenty-year-old me is always going to be waiting for you. My dream girl. My Cinderella. But I'm not twenty anymore."

Malcolm takes her hand. This could have been much harder. They could've shouted and cried and poured their bleeding hearts out, but that's never been them. Minus a ten-year-long miscommunication mishap, they've always been like this. Back and forth. Open and honest.

Until they lost themselves.

Malcolm continues, "Who you are now is much better than that frozen, idealized image I've held on to for too long. You're my best friend. And business partner. And general light of my life. Now that everything's out in the open, we owe it to each other to be who we know we are."

# Thirty

**FRIDAY**

The weather report said it'd be curiously chilly for a summer night.

After tearing her closet apart because she simply has *nothing* to wear, Joy calls Grace for help. They settle on a red bodycon dress with a plunging neckline and a black double-breasted swing coat. Her jewelry is limited to earrings—medium-sized diamond clusters—and star hairpins pulling her braids back on the left side.

Standing on the sidewalk, Joy shivers a little, bouncing up and down in her black wedge heels while waiting for Fox to answer the door. The glass windows are covered with newspaper on the inside, but the front door already has its window sticker: Fox's company logo with *MonahanWoodland* in a classic script.

Fox finally opens the door, wearing a gray button-down shirt, black vest, and dark pants. Joy's so surprised at the sight of him, she laughs in appreciation. "Hey, hey and *wow*. Look at you." He dressed up for her. She's sure of it.

"Hi," he rumbles, and invites her in. "I'm sorry, I didn't mean to make you wait. I was in the back." He closes the door, locking it and leaving the key there.

The front area is one large open space with items displayed in thematic sections—tables together by size, chairs in sets or singles, cabinets, drawers, mirrors, and artistic wood carvings and sculptures.

Joy bends at the waist to inspect a wood carving of a sea turtle coasting on some waves. "Did you make all this?"

"A good portion of it. I've contracted with a couple of local woodworkers to sell their stuff here too."

"This is incredible, Fox." She looks at him, awestruck. "You should be really proud of yourself."

"Hmm." But he's smiling. "Let me give you the tour. This is the showroom, I guess. I don't have a better name for it. There'll be someone out here during business hours."

"You have staff?"

"I have a sister and volunteers, for now."

"Gotcha." Joy laughs.

Fox guides her to the left into a room about half the size of the showroom packed with tables, equipment, and a projector screen. "This is the classroom. I'm going to teach here every other Saturday. Nothing major—a couple of rotating items for fun. You know how you can go take a pottery class? Same idea. They'll get to make something small to take home with them at the end of class."

"If you're trying to impress me, it's working."

They leave the classroom, proceeding back the way they came and straight past the showroom. "This is the storage room, for overflow, duplicates, returns, that kind of thing. I was thinking about making it into a small break room at some point."

It's much smaller than the other two rooms, with all kinds of items haphazardly strewn about. Fox leads her to the back of the shop, where there's a door propped open. "And this is the private back area."

Joy stops in the doorway, eyes wide and feeling mighty suspicious. Three circular wooden tables with two chairs each are spread out under a canopy. Everything is covered in white string lights and what has to be hundreds of mini multicolored flowers—wound around the tent poles, hanging from the ceiling like wisteria, and sprinkled all over the ground.

She narrows her eyes. "What's all this? This is very un-Fox-like."

"That's the point." Fox is standing in the middle of the canopy. "I'm not very romantic. I don't . . . This isn't . . ." He huffs in frustration. "Speeches and talking about my feelings aren't really my style. But very, very quickly you changed a lot for me, Joy. I know you love Malcolm." He pauses, rubbing his palms along the sides of his pants. "So I'm here to plead my case."

"Your case?"

"For why I think you should be with me."

Joy's hand shoots out, gripping the back of the nearest chair. She covers her mouth with her free hand to make sure she doesn't *embarrass* herself because she's absolutely on the brink of losing it. This is so close to Alleged Romantic Bucket List item number three she might burst into tears.

"Umm." Fox wipes his forehead with the back of his hand. "I'm a little nervous. Bear with me, please. Summer recommended I write everything down first." He pulls out a piece of paper from a dark blue journal sitting on the table next to him.

Joy is going to faint. She's going to keel over from too much stimulation. Pulling out the chair she's already holding, she carefully sits down and places her hands in her lap.

"Joy," he reads, "the first time I saw you, I thought you were having a panic attack in your car—"

A manic giggle shoots out of Joy before she can stop it. "Sorry," she whispers, covering her mouth again. The interruption seems to do the trick. He seems less tense now, like he suddenly remembered that she's Joy, Queen of Laughing at Her Own Jokes. Absolute seriousness need not apply to this moment.

He continues, "I thought about helping you, but then you pulled it together and walked into Malcolm's house. You know what happens after that. I don't know a lot of people because I choose not to. I like to keep to myself. I like being alone. If I don't have something to say, I don't." He pauses to inhale, shoulders moving as he does it. "I live in my head because it feels better there. Faster. I don't have to wait for people to catch up to me when I'm already ten steps ahead. Hopefully, that makes sense." He turns the page over. "Joy, when you walk into a room, it's like I forget how to think. I can't look at anything or anyone else. You're so warm and so funny and so beautiful.

"I realized your mind races just as fast as mine does, except you're loud about it. You don't hide it. You're not ashamed or frustrated by it. You embrace it. I love the way you dress, the way you laugh, the way you stare at me, your humor, your heart, your selflessness, how hard you try even when you know you might fail. I love spending my mornings with you. I like being alone with you. Everything about you is devastatingly wonderful and so unexpected. I even love the things I don't like about you because they mean you're not perfect. And if you're not perfect, it means you're real and not a dream. I think I see the difference now.

"I don't care that you love Malcolm or that you will always love him. If the situation were reversed, I would never expect you to love only me. But I've seen how big your heart is, Joy. I can only hope there might be room in it for me too someday."

Fox folds the paper and places it back into the notebook. "That's it." He stands tall, with his hands folded in front of him.

"Funny story," Joy says, throat tight from struggling not to cry. "This strange thing happens to my knees sometimes where they disappear. I would get up, but I'll probably just fall on account of not having knees, so if you could just come over here. Please."

Fox's face folds in confusion but he does as she asks, bringing the second chair around the table and sitting in front of her.

"I had—" Joy stops to catch her breath because that's gone too. "I had no idea you felt that way about *me*." Her voice cracks and so does the rest of her. She's crying and trying to talk and it's not working.

"Joy, please don't cry." He wipes her tears with his thumbs while she tries to stop hyperventilating.

She launches herself at him—arms around his neck and holding on for dear life. She finds enough control to wail, *"How could you do this to me?"*

"I'm sorry," he says, as he holds her. "I thought you'd like it."

"Of course I like it!"

Sometimes she can be a little weird around strangers." Joy unlocks her door. "It's best to let her come to you." As expected, Pepper flies to the front door, squeak-meowing for Joy to pick her up.

Fox places the take-out boxes on the counter.

"Pep, this is Fox. Remember in the video Mommy showed you?"

"You showed your cat a video of me?"

"Shut up. Nobody asked for your judgment. Here, hold her."
Joy smiles as Pepper passes between them with no complaints.
"I'll get some plates."

After setting up the coffee table with their food, Joy runs to
the bedroom to change into comfy pajamas and grab some blankets and pillows. They sit together on the couch, watching the
next Nicolas Cage film on their list while they eat. A fabulously
low-key evening that suits them both perfectly. Joy sits in Fox's
lap, her back to his front, and he wraps them up in a blanket.

When the credits begin to roll, Joy is full of food, dizzy with
happiness, and her old lady timer is about to start screeching. She
yawns, then says, "If someone told me how this past week would
play out in advance, I probably would've laughed myself to death."

"So I'm a joke to you?"

"Now isn't the time for wordplay, don't do that," she whispers
quickly, and he laughs. "Everything's changing so fast. I want to
be okay with it, but I'm high-key kind of scared. I need to tell you
something."

Fox tightens the blankets around them, pulling her closer. "Go
for it."

Joy says, "I was fourteen when I realized I was asexual. I didn't
know that word existed yet. I just knew I was different. I remember the exact moment it happened, down to the smallest detail."

At school, in the cafeteria, where everything smelled over-
cooked and well on its way to being slightly burnt. Filled with the
kind of loudness that echoed until it became a cacophony of voices,
shouts, and the scraping plastic utensils against metal. There was
no privacy, not even an illusion of it, as Joy sat at a round table
with her sister and three friends.

Clustered together, as close as the table would allow, heads bent toward one another almost as if in prayer. Words like "gentle" and "nice" but also "painful" and "intense" floated out of Kelly's mouth and around their circle. Joy, already feeling confused and not understanding, watched everyone carefully—their faces frozen in rapt fascination, and even a little jealousy. She had wondered, *Do I look like that?* Then she saw the same looks on Grace's face: awe and wonder and scandal. And then she thought, *Oh shit. I'm* supposed to *look like that.* Joy copied Grace's expression as best she could before anyone could notice.

At home, Joy asked Grace about it because her sister wouldn't look at her weird for asking obvious questions.

Their fourteen-year-old consensus: Joy hadn't met the right guy yet.

Their twenty-year-old consensus: there would never be the right guy. Or girl. Or person of any gender.

"I started researching by reading romance novels before I moved on to forums and wikis. There were no two ways about it: I *was* different. Then college happened. I met Malcolm and he was like me. We fit together like we were tailor-made for each other, and it was enough. I didn't need anyone else. Being with Malcolm was easy. That's part of the reason I stayed by him for so long—it was easy and he understood me."

"There's nothing wrong with that, Joy."

"There is, though." She tilts her head back to look at him. "I've been scared for a very long time. I know who I am and I accept myself, all of me. But all this time, deep down, I truly believed no one else would. If I took a chance on anyone else, it was pretty much guaranteed I'd get hurt, because I was different. I still am and always will be."

"Hmm."

"I don't know what comes next. I don't know if it'll be good or bad. I don't know if I'll get to keep being as happy as I am right now. But I do know that every time I think about you, I want to see you. I want to talk to you. I want to hear your grumpy *hmm*s and smooth out that little forehead wrinkle with a kiss."

Fox kisses her temple. "Joy."

"Wait, wait." She sniffles, wiping her tears. "I never learned how to be in a relationship with someone because I didn't want to. And I'm *scared* because I want to try. I want to try so bad it almost hurts. I want to find out, and I want to find out with you."

Fox smiles in a way that Joy has never seen before. It's his best one yet—his biggest, his brightest, his supernova.

And it's only for Joy.

# Acknowledgments

I never thought I'd write a book like this again.

I promised myself I wouldn't because it's too painful, both while writing and post-publication.

But then, I got an idea and after a few false starts I found Joy. I guess it's true what they say about promises after all.

I'd like to thank my agent, Carrie Pestritto; my editor, Kristine Swartz; the cover designer, Rita Frangie; Alex Cabal for illustrating such a wonderful cover; and the entire pub team at Berkley. I guess it's true what they say about dreams too.

A special thank-you to Anna S. for keeping me on the up and up, and for reading my rough drafts with unparalleled speed. Same to my usual suspects—Mom, Sarah, SHINee, Issa Bebe, Jevon—and all my friends/family who let me steal their names (Nikkiee, Allie, Megan, and the Normans).

And thank *you* for reading.

See you in the next one,

Claire <3

# The Romantic Agenda

CLAIRE KANN

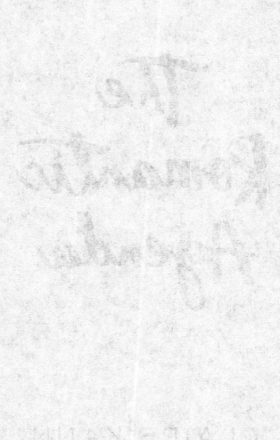

# DISCUSSION QUESTIONS

1. The story begins with Joy's best friend, Malcolm, asking her to join him on a trip. Do you think it was fair for Malcolm to invite her? What would you have said in Joy's position?

2. How does Malcolm and Joy's first interaction in college shape the rest of their friendship? Do you have any friends that helped you discover a crucial part of yourself?

3. Joy identifies as asexual. What did you know about asexuality before reading *The Romantic Agenda*? What did you learn from the book?

4. If someone were to plan a weekend full of your favorite things, like Malcolm did for Summer, what would the agenda be?

5. Joy, Fox, Malcolm, and Summer all have different ideas of what it means to be in love. Discuss how they all define romance. How does it compare to your definition?

6. Do you think Fox or Malcolm is a better match for Joy? Why?

7. Summer is in a difficult position throughout most of the book. If you were in her shoes, how would you have handled the events of the trip?

8. Joy is forced to work against multiple identity-based stereotypes throughout the book. How did these impact her choices? Have stereotypes impacted your life as well?

9. Where do you see Joy and Fox's relationship in a year? What about Joy and Summer?

*Photo by Anrah Designs*

**Claire Kann** is the author of several young adult novels and is an award-winning online storyteller. In her other life she works for a nonprofit you may have heard of where she daydreams like she's paid to do it. She loves cats and is obsessed with horror media (which makes the whole *being known for writing contemporary love stories* a little weird, to be honest).

CONNECT ONLINE

ClaireKann.com